D0168119

A Disgrace to the Profession

by

Charles Newton & Gretchen Kauffman

Linda !
You've never
been a disgrace
to any profession.
thanks for your
interest.

Gretchen
Kauffman
8/24/2002

Myers House
Des Moines, Iowa

This special first edition is intended to seed the
market in preparation for release through a major
publisher. Please send reviews of the book to the
contact numbers listed on the back of this page.

Published by
Myers House
P.O. Box 23068
Des Moines, IA 50325-6468
myershousemail@aol.com

Cover design and inside layout by Mindy Myers Photography
and Design, www.mindymyers.com.

Manufactured in the United States of America.

To order additional copies or receive information on special
discounts for bulk purchases, please contact
myershousemail@aol.com.

This special first edition is intended to seed the market in
preparation for release through a major publisher. Please send
reviews of the book to myershousemail@aol.com, fax 515-278-
2245, or write to Myers House at the address listed above.

Your support will help us get this story out to a wider audience.

ISBN 0-9721900-0-7

This book is dedicated to Joyce Renquist,
the first person who believed in us.

A Disgrace to the Profession

one

Karen caught an unflattering glimpse in the back door—dark glasses sliding down her sweaty nose, a tube of Coppertone's all-day protection peeking from the bra of her two-piece swimsuit, a lawnchair hanging from her shoulder, the distorted reflection of her leg resting on the cement stoop. This image, disheveled and disorganized, mirrored her feelings about this day. And all that remained of it now was the ritual sunbath performed at this precise time every year.

She dragged the chair into the backyard near her garden scorched by a late-August drought. Green plants turned brown on the edges. Dry cornstalks rustled. Eggplants, peppers, and tomatoes were pint-sized. Hard, cracked soil burned the bottoms of her feet as her tour around the plot confirmed her suspicions: The crop was lost. Soaking rains would regenerate the rich Iowa soil, but Karen knew it would take more than rain to regenerate her.

Grasshoppers clattered away as her feet crunched

the parched grass. No one had mowed in the neighborhood for weeks. She unfolded the chair and fell onto it with a rebellious thud. A jet silently spread a white contrail overhead while the kids next door in a plastic pool tried to out-shout each other. Summer had been so relaxing in June, but now time galloped toward that fierce red "X" on her calendar. The muscles of her neck tensed. For days Karen had forced Martha Y. Bancroft to the rear of her mind, but the stubborn old biddy refused to go away.

How did a graduate of the University of Iowa, summa cum laude no less, descend into this funk? Her attitude had deteriorated the very moment back-to-school ads hit the newspapers. Karen's ready smile evaporated, and her mother accused her, rightfully so, of being curt.

Karen Merchant taught English at Martha Y. Bancroft Senior High. She didn't want to go back.

The consequences of scratching her name on a new contract five months ago had now come home to roost. She'd tried to cram everything into those last days—cleaning closets, lunching with friends who didn't work, shopping for groceries during the day, reading non-stop until she fell asleep at night. But none of her dodges would stop the inevitable. Tomorrow she'd go back to exactly the same thing. Each year was a reprise of the one before it; the names changed, the song never did.

Her body swiveled on the chair like a piece of meat on a spit, back exposed to the hot sun, then her belly. Tardy bells, fire drill bells, the babble of teenage voices, the metallic clang of locker doors rang in her ears. Her nose wrinkled as she remembered the odors—institutional food (warm milk, onions, french fries), perfume (Obsession had been big last year), aftershave dowsed on faces untouched by razors, the pungent stench of those who weaseled out of PE showers. Forms—piles of forms. Hand them out, fill them out, press hard. Names—hundreds of new names. And one name, crazy and exasperating. Aneyh, Robert D., Bancroft's principal. She'd forgotten how to spell it over the summer, but never how to pronounce it. "On ya," accent on the first syllable. "Is Aneyh on ya?" was the teachers' favorite bit of alliteration. That name, that man, stood out as the most pervasive irritant of all.

Karen bolted upright, her mind twisted, the name Aneyh still on her lips. She filled her hands with sunscreen and massaged her legs, first the good one, then the other. Touching that leg, cold even under the hot sun, always gave her a jolt. Gooseflesh slithered down the thigh toward her knee. She plucked at the swimsuit drawn tightly into her crotch and closed her eyes against the glare.

Acrid smells of dusty earth and distant sounds of a lazy afternoon wrapped her in semiconsciousness where thoughts jumbled together. The heat. School bells. The hollow clunk of a car door across the street. A young male voice yelling, "Where's Eddie?"

Where's Karen?

The boys had always wanted her. She was one of three girls among 20 boys in a high school physics lab. The four boys on her team picked her brains for creative assignments, allowed her to record data, write reports, make graphs. She knew they were using her. But that didn't matter; being close to bright, cute young men did. Hormones raged. She would have done anything for them. But not one ever asked her out.

Hidden in a carrel one day, compiling data for an experiment, she had heard them talk about an after-game dance.

"You going?"

"No date."

"You don't need a date. Pick something up at the game."

"With my luck I'd end up with a fatso or Karen the gimp."

She collapsed, each cackling laugh a rivet fastening her to her chair. Her sex appeal had been dismissed with one word. Gimp.

A siren in the distance brought her back to reality. There were problems in the world more urgent than hers. Self-pity fixed nothing. Karen struggled to her feet, folded the lawn chair, and trudged to the back door tracing web marks on her stomach with her fingers. Tomorrow she started her seventeenth year as a public school teacher. Where had the summer gone?

Karen cradled the phone under her arm on the way to the bathroom. She and her mother had papered the walls of this cramped space several years ago without a single argument. Pale yellow accented by small red flowers created a cheerful atmosphere where she enjoyed leisurely soaks in the tub.

Karen jerked her toes from the water and

answered the phone jangling in her hand.

"Hi, Karen. Just checking in. Ready for tomorrow?"

"Mother, hold on. Let me get in the tub."

Mrs. Merchant called a couple of times a week. This was the annual keep-your-chin-up call. Karen dreaded sermons on attitude adjustment, especially about her job. She'd considered leaving teaching for several years, a move her mother vigorously opposed. Since the death of her husband when Karen was sixteen, Grace Merchant had taken the role of matriarch seriously.

She sank into the scented suds.

"OK, Mother."

"Aren't you excited about tomorrow?"

"Mother, don't do this to me."

"Now, Honey Bunny."

"You said you wouldn't call me that any more."

"All right."

"I saw Meg Smith this afternoon."

"Who?"

"A former student. Her daughter's going to be in my English class."

"How exciting."

"Remind me to quit before her granddaughter shows up."

"Why do you say things like that?" Grace asked in her nasal twang. "You're such a good teacher. Everyone says so."

"Sure."

"That's true. Everyone does. Your father would be proud of you."

"You know what being a good teacher means, Mother?" Karen changed phone hands. "You're always on, eight hours a day. No let up. Kids swarming in and out every fifty-five minutes. No coffee breaks, no smoking breaks..."

"You don't smoke!"

"I know that, Mother. But we don't even have time to go to the bathroom. All good teachers should have bladder infections."

"They're wearing long skirts again."

"Yes, Mother. I've noticed."

"Do you have one for tomorrow?"

"A new one."

"That's wonderful. And you'll look so nice. That's all, Karen. You call me tomorrow night. Everything will be fine."

Karen shifted in the water and stared at the long red dress hanging from the bathroom door. "Long" was a code word that Grace Merchant used to allude to her daughter's flaw, a generic yet powerful word defining a bond between them so strong and touching that the word "long" sometimes made Karen misty-eyed.

At the age of three, Karen had contracted paralytic polio. She didn't remember much, only pieces. Days and days of staring up from her bed at Porky Pig's mailbox on the mural decorating her hospital room. Her mother's enveloping arms when the quarantine officer burned her childhood toys. Grace had a body, but to Karen in those days, she was a voice always in her ear urging, a presence that encouraged and cajoled. "Just one more, Honey Bunny. Lift one more marble with your toes. Push that sandbag harder." Grace Merchant had stamina. She grafted that determination into Karen's nervous system. "You can do it. Chase that nasty bug away. You'll be perfect again. I love you, Honey Bunny. You can do it."

Her mother persevered. Years of physical therapy and two transplant surgeries restored Karen's mobility, but left her with feet of different sizes, a withered right leg, and a limp that became noticeable when she tired. Years of exercise had made her lean and trim.

Karen lifted her legs from the bubbles and examined them. No one could miss the truth, even when camouflaged by a long dress. Words couldn't make that go away.

She climbed from the tub, wrapped herself in a towel, and cleaned steam from the bathroom mirror. Dark wet hair flowed to her shoulders, and brown eyes or hazel, they seemed to change with the light, an angular neck, and a narrow nose gave her face a certain elegance. Karen smiled at her reflection, revealing straight white teeth and a dimple under each cheekbone. She put down her comb and dialed.

"Hi, Mother. Thanks for the boost. I'll call you tomorrow night."

two

On the first day of school, Karen always entered Bancroft from the front. That added an extra block from the parking lot, but she didn't care. A cobbled hodgepodge of boxy brick wings of various sizes and styles greeted teachers from the rear; but the front, the original building, presented a classic edifice of American educational tradition, a strong, two-story brick fortress capped with twin crenellated battlements. "The Truth Shall Make Ye Free" was chiseled over the massive triple doors. Considering the state of public education, she sometimes felt "Abandon Hope All Ye Who Enter Here" might be more appropriate.

Familiar routines took over. Sixteen years of conditioning steered her toward the office, an air-conditioned oasis in a desert of hot, suffocating classrooms. A summer's accumulation of junk mail and keys waited in pigeon holes with teachers' names stuck at the top. In the pile of litter she saw the envelope—white, legal sized, the system's largesse to

14

all teachers. The contents were the same every year: five paper clips, three rubber bands, a roll of generic Scotch tape that never stuck, a red pencil, two lead pencils, and a 3" by 5" scratch pad. On her first day at Bancroft, she thought the envelope was a joke, couldn't believe someone earned a wage for counting this stuff out. Now she bought her own supplies.

Karen and the secretaries exchanged hellos and stories about the summer vacation before she ascended the stairs to her two-toned blue classroom. Sealed tighter than a mausoleum over summer, the room reeked with the smell of chalk, dusty carpet, musty books. Air. The room needed air. Karen, half-mesmerized as Venetian blinds gently slapped the window casements, stared at the empty student chairs. Who would fill them? What motivation would the new students bring? How many hours would she sacrifice pouring over the wordy outcroppings of their minds?

After only twenty minutes back, Karen felt as if she had never left.

Click. "Teachers, it is now 8:15." The patronizing voice of Hattie Reins, Aneyh's personal secretary, oozed from the PA. "Your faculty meeting will begin at 8:30 in the little theater. That is all."

Karen fingered the PA.

Robert D. Aneyh had called an early session. In every other building throughout the system, a new school year kicked off with a faculty meeting at 9:00, a policy reinforced by personal letters from the district to each teacher. Aneyh sometimes disdained this guideline in an effort to cow his staff and enhance his authority. Every other year or so he or his secretary grabbed the PA mike, announced an 8:30 meeting, and scolded those teachers arriving "late." His faculty learned the hard way. On the first day of school, veteran staff were in the building before 8:30.

Casually dressed teachers emerged from rooms up and down the long hall, some slamming doors, some shaking their heads. The hot dead air of the windowless corridor wilted their short sleeved shirts and blouses as they moved toward the little theater grumbling about the early meeting. Karen fell in behind.

"Aneyh's got to show all these new teachers who's driving the car."

"I'll bet you lunch he says 'We've got to keep the lid on' within the first three minutes. Any takers?"

"Hell no, that's a slam dunk."

"Hey, one day down. Only 194 to go. How 'bout that!"

"Allen Garbon's in my first hour tenth grade class for the third straight year."

"Why'd he come back?"

"So his old lady could get her ADC check. He'll be gone by November."

"Elaine, you're going the wrong way. He's called the meeting early again."

"What'd you do this summer, Tim?"

"Clerked at Quik-Trip. How else could I stay in this profession?"

"Anyone see my desk chair? How could it just walk away?"

"Aneyh told Nelson he'd better have a winning wrestling season or he's history."

"Ha! He can't do that."

"Hell he can't. Aneyh's the biggest ass-kissing game player in this system. He can do anything he wants."

Hal Delaney, one of three vice principals, stood outside the little theater door. He was a Bancroft fixture, as solid as the twin towers standing astride the school's entrance. Teachers trusted Hal Delaney. He had character; he refused to play the games that others played or kiss the behinds that others kissed to push themselves up the career ladder. Teachers wanted him at their sides when a conflict with a student got out of hand. Long before Robert Aneyh appeared at Bancroft, Hal Delaney provided a quiet leadership that Aneyh would never achieve.

"Here's one face I'm glad to see." Karen clasped Delaney's hand. "How come you're hanging around out here, Hal? Don't you want to go in?"

Delaney grinned broadly and leaned close to her. He was slight and wiry with wavy hair combed straight back. His strong jaw, expressive eyes staring from beneath arched brows, and a forehead delicately furrowed gave him the appearance of a man who knew what he was about.

"I'm connecting faces with names. Twenty-four new ones. Are you ready, Karen?"

"Sure, Hal."

He squeezed her shoulder and turned to greet a newcomer.

17

Bancroft was becoming a four-year high school; a freshman class of 650 would be joining 600 sophomores who were also entering high school for the first time. And along with them came twenty-four new teachers, mostly from the schools these students were leaving. Administrative estimates set this year's student population at 2,600 while the number of faculty members swelled to 150.

Karen stood inside the little theater looking for her friend David who taught English across the hall. Many new faces were sprinkled among the old. David sat hunched in a back row chair, his red head buried in a computer magazine.

"So how was your summer?" Karen asked.

"Too short," he snorted without looking up.

"How are you?"

"I'm back in this dump. How the hell do you think I am."

"I almost forgot what you were like." She eased into a chair beside him. "You won't believe this. There were times this summer when I actually missed your bitching. Have you met any of the new teachers?"

"No. I'll see 'em soon enough."

She knew two of them. Lydia Fletcher taught at Bancroft ten years ago. She had taken a maternity leave which ended in a miscarriage and had been assigned to a junior high school for years. Lydia would have the room next to Karen's. The other, Mr. Dan Tennant, had been Karen's ninth-grade science teacher. Now she'd have to call him Dan.

Faculty members trickled in tanned and rested,

and precisely at 8:29 Robert D. Aneyh made his appearance. He ascended three steps to a small stage in front of the first curving row of chairs, pulled a few papers from his coat pocket, and placed them on the podium like a preacher unfolding his text.

"Has he put on his glasses yet?" asked David without looking up from his magazine.

As if David had been a prompter, Aneyh's glasses appeared from the other pocket and were attached to his ears one bow at a time. Conversation and laughter stopped. The atmosphere suddenly changed as if an unseen hand had turned a knob. The principal stood quietly in the stale, humid air and scanned the faculty. Dressed in a suit and tie, he seemed to be making a sartorial statement.

Born Roman Dmitriovitch Aneyhalov, he broke with his ancestors by anglicizing his Slavic name which he viewed as an impediment to his career. He was short and powerfully built, with a huge head hunched into a thick neck. His flat, wide face with a broad nose and small, penetrating grey eyes seemed perpetually constricted, not only by the tie that girded his neck, but also by the realization that he had to wear it every day.

He opened his mouth, christening the new school year.

"I want to welcome you all back to Bancroft," he began. "It's going to be another fine year. As you know, we'll be serving 1,250 new students this year, and we need to rise to the challenge." His eyes danced over the faculty. Frozen smiles emerged on a few faces.

"Here at Bancroft," he continued, "we have always prepared for and met our challenges. No one here expects you to work miracles, but if we keep the lid on..."

Karen didn't listen. She knew his bromides by heart and sat, chin in hands, looking at the faculty. Old. They were getting old, many approaching retirement. Who would replace these hoary veterans? A career in education wasn't even on the radar screen for her college-bound students. They made fun of teaching. They knew the system; they'd been through it.

Aneyh droned. She drifted.

"Why did you become a teacher, Miss Merchant?" The question had dropped in out of the blue while the class waited for a pep assembly.

"Seemed like the thing to do." Karen smiled and spread her arms toward them. "And look what I got."

"Teachers don't make much money," another student said.

"Money isn't everything," Karen countered.

"Uh huh. Give me the big bucks."

Another interrupted him. "You know those TV ads, the ones trying to talk you into becoming a teacher? They're phony. They tell you you'll have power as a teacher. Teachers don't have any power. One of those goons in Mr. Lichty's class called him, well, a rectum." Laughter rose and then tailed off. "Mr. Lichty sent him to the office, and the kid was back in class the next day. Some power."

"They don't mean that kind of power, Brett," said the girl next to him.

"You can't have one without the other."

"I wouldn't take foul-mouthed crap off the jerks in this building for a million dollars."

"I'd be afraid to teach Mr. Lichty's classes."

"Are you ever scared, Miss Merchant?"

"No," Karen laughed. "I've got a reputation. Kids are afraid I'll hit them with my broom."

The assembly bell cleared the room. One student lingered. "You know, Miss Merchant," he said, "you couldn't touch us with a broom or anything else, even if we had it coming. Mr. Aneyh would go crazy, TV would be everywhere, and you would lose your job."

"John, your insight amazes me," Karen had said, smiling.

Meanwhile, back at the podium Aneyh talked football. "Come on down, Coach," he said.

Bancroft's football coach, Rick Cook, a distillation of Vince Lombardi and Bozo the Clown, vaulted to the stage. Every year Aneyh had him preview the season. And like every other year, Cook hoped Bancroft would get to the state play-offs. His speeches transported one to the locker room with the smell of sweat and liniment.

"Win one for the Gipper," she whispered to David.

He shrugged his shoulders.

Aneyh took the podium again. "Joining us this year are a number of fine teachers, all transfers from the junior highs. They'll be working with the new class, the ninth graders, for the most part. Each and every one of them will be a welcome addition to Bancroft High School."

The staff squirmed as he read the new list of teachers. Karen would get to know a few of them, but not many men. Habit separated the sexes at Bancroft. Although changing times had stripped the signs "Men" and "Women" from the doors, everyone knew Aneyh wanted separate but equal lounges. He avoided drinking coffee or telling sappy jokes in the presence of women and promoted the feeling that any male who entered the upstairs women's lounge needed a shot of testosterone. A woman who wandered into the first floor men's lounge was silently harassed with something resembling a public shunning.

"Let's give a Bancroft welcome to Nicholas Staal from Crescent Junior High. Nick will be teaching in the ninth grade World History program." Aneyh peered over his glasses. "Nick Staal?"

Bob Melville, a balding man, thin as grass, struggled to his feet. His fingers drummed the chair back in front of him. "I knew Nick Staal at Crescent years ago, Mr. Aneyh. I told him the meeting would start at nine o'clock. It's my fault he's late."

"I see." Silence dug into the room. "Well. Next is Dan Tennant from Caldwell. He'll be teaching General Science and a section of physics."

Karen watched Tennant rise and wave to the group. Once his student, now she was his colleague, his peer. She felt melancholy.

Aneyh reached the end of the list. "And from Green Valley comes Marsha Zellerman in the Business Department." At that moment, every eye in the room not closed turned to the door in the far left corner framing a tall, muscular man wearing tan slacks and a white polo shirt.

"Excuse me," he said in a deep voice. His eyes cast about for a seat. "I'm Nicholas Staal. I guess I'm late."

Karen felt a twinge of compassion. Staal squeezed through the crowded aisle, stepped over feet, dodged the knees of those refusing to sit in front. They had endured dozens of Aneyh's embarrassing harangues, but this, after all, called for discretion; there were twenty-four new faculty members present. The staff hoped he would show mercy, some common sense.

"Here it comes," said David. "All these new teachers are about to learn what a son of a bitch their new principal is."

"You'll find, Mr. Staal, that we run a tight ship here at Bancroft." Aneyh's words were deliberate and hectoring. "Don't get the idea you can amble in any time you please. And you had better learn that." The mini-lecture exploded from his mouth in a spray of spittle.

Nicholas Staal seemed unaffected. "Well, sir," he smiled, "I guess I'll just have to stay after school."

Spontaneous laughter took over the room.

"Look at Aneyh," squealed David. "He's speechless. He looks like he's been whacked between the eyes with a two by four. He'll crucify that poor bastard."

Karen sighed. No one got in the last word with Aneyh.

Nicholas Staal sat quietly, unaware of the feelings unleashed by his offhand retort.

The faculty left the meeting with elevated spirits. In ten years, they had never seen anyone strip away Aneyh's principal's persona.

three

Karen shoved a shoulder into David whose short, choppy steps slapped the floor of the front corridor. "Slow down! We have twenty minutes before the next meeting."

"Maybe this guy could cross swords with Aneyh," David said plowing ahead. "'I guess I'll just have to stay after school.' Beautiful. What did you say his name was? Maybe he can help us."

"Nicholas Staal." Karen stopped at the giant staircase leading to the second floor. "Fight your own battles, David. A little backbone would improve your image."

"Who gives a rat's ass about image. Anyway, I've tried that. You can't fight fair with a megalomaniac like Aneyh."

During the principal's first year at Bancroft, David raised Aneyh's ire at a faculty meeting and soon learned the true relationship between the lord of a manor and a serf. Within a week Aneyh saddled him with additional extracurricular assignments: sponsor of the eight-member Bancroft Future Teachers, chairman of the Hospitality Committee, and host of the North Central States spring FTA convention. Aneyh had him by the throat, and David knew it. He hatched dozens of Walter Mitty-like plans for revenge which never left the drawing board.

"So? What do you think this new guy can do?"

"I don't know, but I think he's got guts. Look." David nodded down the corridor.

Nicholas Staal came toward them with a cigarette in his hand. "Is there any place you can smoke in this building?" he asked.

"Not in the hall," David said. "Try the first floor lounge."

"Yes, of course. I guess I forgot where I was." Nicholas Staal stared at Karen for several moments and smiled. "Where's the lounge?"

"Wait a minute," David said. "I need to take a piss. I'll show you how to get there."

Karen climbed the stairs alone. Her chest heaved with a spasm of excitement. A woman would need to be blind or hormonally challenged not to notice his looks. Standing beside him in the hall, she had to look straight up; he had to be 6'4". The white polo shirt couldn't hide the definition of developed pectoral muscles and biceps. From the rear, broad shoulders cut away to a narrow waist and slim hips. Strands of grey glistened in a full head of dark brown hair. Categorizing all grey-headed men as distinguished bugged her. But not in this case. The word fit. She could still feel those eyes! So soft and icy blue she wondered how he could possibly see through them.

She'd have to ignore his good looks. Handsome men never gave her a second glance if they had looked closely the first time. Prince Charming might be out there, but not in search of her.

Since college Karen's infrequent dates, two uptight widowers with children trolling for mommies and several men with whom she had absolutely nothing in common, had resulted in only one significant liaison. Dean Dawson taught Advanced Placement English at McGovern Senior High. He had spotted Karen at a curriculum meeting and swept her away with constant chatter about Elizabethan England and contemporary authors. Slight and balding with an affable smile, Dawson appeared at a point in Karen's life when she put a high premium on a date's intellect. Dean Dawson was an intellectual, but in time his discourses became stuffy. Karen suspected he picked an obscure subject like John Dryden's panegyric poetry, boned up on it, and then paraded knowledge like it came from the top of his head. At times she simply tuned him out. The relationship fell apart when Dawson corrected people's grammar at the movies or in restaurants one too many times. She dated him to get away from school, not to be constantly reminded of it.

Karen heard them before she opened the upstairs lounge door. A dozen women, some standing, packed the cluttered space which hummed with laughter and animated conversation.

"Lordy, did you ever see such eyes!"

"He could steal Joanne Woodward from under Paul's nose."

"Did anyone get a look at his feet?"

They all hooted.

"His remark to Aneyh was perfect."

"Perfect! How 'bout his butt!"

"I hear he's a bachelor. Wouldn't you like to introduce him to connubial bliss!"

"Introduce. Mon dieu," said Michelle Valder, a very Frenchy French teacher. "He's probably had more connubial bliss than the rest of us put together."

"No. He's been married." Alice Cain, who didn't object to the epithet "queen sized," completely filled one of the chairs at the table. "I heard he divorced his wife. Maybe she got fat and sloppy."

"Maybe he's gay.

"No, not that one."

"I'll bet he gets around."

"Do you know him, Alice?"

"Do you mean in the Biblical sense?"

"My God, get serious, Alice."

"So how old is he?"

"I'm guessing in his late thirties," Alice volunteered.

Darlene McGimpsey, Bancroft's grande dame at sixty years old, positively cackled, and when Darlene cackled, people listened. "I'd love to rob the cradle if I could find a hunk like him under the covers," she said, fanning her face with one hand. "I'd teach him a thing or two."

Karen smiled. Darlene probably could. She was a

living advertisement for life-begins-after-forty. She climbed, swam, fished, boated, hiked. An outsider would never suspect that Darlene's retirement was only two years away.

Static on the speaker above the door ended the conversation. All eyes turned toward it in unison. "Teachers are reminded that the vice principals' grade-level meetings are at eleven o'clock." It was now 10:55. "Teachers with no homerooms should choose a meeting to attend. Please bring your policies and procedures manual from last year. Attendance will be taken."

Women scurried away in search of their manuals. As the room cleared, Karen glanced at the deserted lounge from the doorway—cast-off furniture, cigarette scarred table, and a small door leading directly toward the toilet, a sterile cubicle equipped with stool, sink, and Kotex dispenser. No wonder men avoided this place.

David hustled through the hall. "Where the hell did I put my manual. Haven't seen the damn thing since last year."

"Did you get a line on the new man?" Karen asked.

"Forget him. He can't help us."

"Us? You mean he can't help you."

"Listen, Karen, he's more at home with those coaches than jock itch. They took right to him. He played baseball or something in a semi-pro league."

David ducked into his room. Karen followed.

"He murders the king's English. He said 'It don't

matter' when I told him there was only one smoking room."

Karen watched David tear his desk apart. He was short and slim with red hair artistically combed over a rapidly emerging forehead. A pleasant face with boyish features belied his bad moods, which, over the years, had become more frequent. David's most noticeable trait was his motor mouth constantly in gear.

David looked up from the mess he was making of his desk. "This will kill you. He lives on a farm."

"So?"

"He'll track shit all over this building."

"Oh, come on."

"He's a hick, Karen. Aneyh'll tear him apart unless it's shooting free throws or maybe a hog calling contest."

"Aneyh didn't do very well in the faculty meeting."

"That's my point. Aneyh's going to get even."

"You think everybody who spends time in that men's lounge is a jock or a hick." She didn't mean to defend Nicholas Staal, but hated David's making judgments for her. "Learn how to get along, David. He'll be teaching right up the hall."

"That's nice. We can talk about plowing furrows. I'll bet the plow he uses on furrows is hanging right between his legs."

"That's really sleazy. But then, you always go too far. You'll never find your manual," she yelled over her shoulder on the way out. "I have an extra one in my room. Don't ask. You don't deserve it."

Nicholas Staal had created a stir. Karen wondered other than catching Aneyh off guard and his good looks what he had to commend him. Could he be as worldly as the women thought or as dumb as David suspected?

None of this mattered. She didn't even care.

four

An asphalt expanse at the rear of the building etched in yellow grid marks had spaces for 162 cars. Early risers glommed on to the spaces in front; stragglers got stuck at the end, a block from Bancroft's back door. Karen could log the times she missed out on the coveted first spot on the fingers of one hand, but on Monday of the third week, she parked in space number two beside a mangy, dull red pickup truck. Rust ate away at the fender wells, and large splotches of paint were missing. Some workman had nabbed her space!

She puzzled over the truck's Adair County license plate. Des Moines School service vehicles were registered in Polk County and parked in the service drive. She walked to the rear of the pickup and glanced at a roll of barbed wire, two coils of rope, a half dozen fence posts, a bale of hay, equipment that only a farmer would claim. Her watch said 6:30. What was Nicholas Staal doing here this early!

Since day one Staal had been invisible, hiding out

for all she knew. He never surfaced for hall duty between classes, dropped out of sight immediately after school, and up to this point, escaped the plethora of teacher-based committees organized by Robert D. Aneyh. Teachers hated these millstones dangling from their necks, and Karen felt resentment, at least of the perception, that Nicholas Staal avoided what the rest of them had to endure.

Ahead in the hall, a custodian's backside labored behind a wide mop. He stopped abruptly, muttered something she couldn't hear except for the expletive, removed a putty knife from his hip pocket, and scraped at a purple gum glob glued to the tile floor.

"Morning, Bill," Karen said, passing by.

"I'm sorry, Miss Merchant." A sheepish grin showed irregular teeth. "I didn't know anyone was in the hall."

"Relax, Bill. Didn't hear a word."

"Well, some of these little devils should be spanked. Throwing gum and candy wrappers and pop cans wherever they please." He dabbed at his head with a handkerchief. "No respect for public property. No respect."

"I know," Karen said over her shoulder.

"Oh, Miss Merchant. Wait!" Bill leaned on the mop handle. "There's a surprise for you in the upstairs lounge. My wife picked a bunch of asters last night. You've got a nice bouquet right in the middle of the table."

"You're great, Bill, and thank your wife for me."

There was more than asters in the upstairs

lounge. A man sat in her chair. "What are you doing here?" she asked with an edge in her voice.

Nicholas Staal sat at the table smoking, a newspaper spread before him. His eyes held her for an awkward moment before he answered, "I work here, remember?"

"Yes. But don't you know? Men don't come in here."

"Really? Would you like me to leave?" He got to his feet, glanced at his cigarette. "I'll finish this and clear out."

"No, I didn't mean that," she said, fidgeting. "I'm just surprised."

Nick slipped back into the chair. He wore a blue blazer, light blue oxford shirt, maroon tie, and grey slacks with snappy seams. How could anyone so sartorially appealing crawl out of that filthy truck?

He stared at her curiously as Karen stood stiffly by the table. "What's wrong with the downstairs lounge?" she asked.

"The downstairs lounge is downstairs. This is a hundred feet from my room."

"Well, I just hope the conversations in here aren't too tame for you."

"Oh, what do you talk about?"

"Women's things," she said too quickly. "We talk about women's things."

Nick smiled. "Would you believe women's things have always interested me?"

A rush of blood replaced the smile draining from Karen's face. David's assessment of this guy screamed at her. What he'd just said, to a perfect stranger no less, was coarse. Karen had always been afflicted with fear of this kind of banter and had no desire to exchange double entendres with this interloper. Silent concentration on her work would keep him quiet.

Karen sagged into a chair opposite Nick, carefully drawing her right leg under her skirt. She pulled an aster from the vase and held it to her nose.

"I'm Nicholas Staal."

"I know." She didn't look at him.

"You probably have a name, too."

"Merchant." The word slid from the corner of her mouth.

"Merchant Marine?"

"Karen Merchant."

"Really?" he said. "My grandmother's name was Karen."

"That's nice."

Karen's unresponsiveness sent him back to the newspaper.

Finally, a soft tap on the door shattered the silence.

"Come in," Nick said.

She wondered who'd put him in charge.

A muffled voice came from the other side. "George Moore out here."

"Open the door," Karen said. "He won't come in here."

Nick pushed the door open. A mousy little man, a frown frozen on his gray face, peeked around the corner. Reading glasses teetered on the end of his nose.

"Come on in, George. We've been integrated. Nick Staal's in here."

"I can see that. I don't need to. Why don't you tack this sign on the board for me, Karen." He pushed it through the door.

Nick took the cardboard sign. "You trying to sell something?"

"No," he said emphatically. "This sign advertises a wine-tasting benefit for the American Cancer Society. My wife's chief organizer. This helps smokers like you who get lung cancer."

"Please come in for a while, George."

"No, Karen, I've got two more of these to put up."

"Next Friday. Capitol Square. All domestic wines," Nick read. "Good. None of that French stuff."

"You're a wine drinker?" Karen blurted. "I would have expected beer and beef jerky." She immediately wanted to cut off her tongue.

"This is a good cause, George," Nick said. "I've had some experience with this. I may drop by."

George closed the door.

"Is he real?" Nick asked.

"George just puts in his time."

"Why?"

"Putting up that sign is the most important thing he'll do all year. Aneyh's turned him into a pencil-pushing clerk along with the five other counselors. He does busy work—shuffles papers, student schedules, mindless surveys. Stuff like that. Aneyh's made the job demeaning. And George knows that."

"Oh." Nick tacked up the sign.

"You're not interested, are you."

"In what?"

"What I just told you."

"Give me a break. I'm just putting up his sign."

"Yes, of course."

Nick returned to his seat. "What's with the beer and beef jerky crack?"

"A poor attempt at humor." Karen shifted uncomfortably. "I am sorry. I don't even know you."

"Would you like to know me?

She didn't know what he meant. "Oh, I guess I'll just see you here. That's enough, isn't it?"

He shrugged and rested his arms on the table. "Nice outfit. I like what you wear."

"What do you mean?"

"That long red dress you wore Friday. Wasn't that the same one you wore the first day?"

"I guess so." Her stomach tightened. She hadn't seen him since the opening day, but he was right about Friday. The red dress. How could he know the precise day? Why would he even notice? Amazing. This guy was after something. Maybe he got up with the chickens to con her into checking his papers or selling football tickets for him. Sweet talk! She'd been down that road before. Let him stroke some other woman's ego.

She ignored his next three questions.

Except for the graphite scratch on student papers and the occasional expulsion of smoke from Staal's lungs, the room fell silent. Nick studied the sports pages as clouds of cigarette smoke drifted lazily near the ceiling. Karen glanced at him, sniffed the air disdainfully, and allowed her eyes to fall on the ashtray. But his eyes fell on her face, lowered to her blouse, and shifted to her face again.

She really didn't think Staal's stare was prurient, but she felt as naked as Lois Lane being measured for a bra and pants. He seemed to be searching, plumbing for something she didn't understand. What she did understand was the need to escape this appraisal.

Karen got up and walked quickly toward the bathroom door.

"I checked out your can." Nick paused. "Not a very big one, is it?"

Something snapped. She whirled to face him. Blood slammed at her temples as his feeble pun about her rear end resonated. "My God, you are a farmer, aren't you!"

"What?" He seemed surprised. "How do you mean that? It sounded pejorative to me. I'm a teacher just like you are."

Karen hyperventilated. "Oh, no. No, you're not. You're not at all like I am."

The rattled Karen gathered her things, fled the formerly all-female lounge, and stomped toward her room mouthing "pejorative." How would he know a word like that? He must have read it on a feedsack!

She dropped her bookbag next to her desk and slid into a student chair in the back of the room. A good looking, slick dressing farmer with limited intelligence had just provoked her into an adolescent tantrum. Tears blurred her vision, but fleeting images focused. An expression of loathing crept over her face.

Why should Nicholas Staal remind her of him? Her slender fingers touched her hair expecting to find it wet, plastered against her neck and forehead the way it had been six years ago in Charleston harbor.

Hundreds of teachers had converged on that southern city for a three-day meeting of the National Council of Teachers of English. During her tour of Fort Sumter, Lloyd Fraser, who according to his nametag taught at nearby Isle of Palms, had latched on to Karen. He was very good at what made her leery, small talk and double entendre. She ignored him, evaded him, and made an unsuccessful attempt to escape by lolling around in the restroom for 15 minutes. But he waited just outside the door, a Coke for him in one hand and one for her in the other. His eyes, amused and dancing, revealed that he knew what she was up to, that dumping him would require more cunning than simply hiding in the ladies' john.

As they scampered around the Fort's breastworks, Fraser showered her with a torrent of minutia about his life and times, pausing occasionally for compliments on her appearance and intelligence delivered with such boyish glee that Karen felt like a doll in a toy store being admired by a harmless juvenile.

A rain squall pelted the ferry on the return trip. In drenched blue jeans and her Bancroft sweatshirt, Karen stumbled down the gangplank on rubbery legs.

"You're limping," Lloyd Fraser said.

Karen's internal warning system sounded. "I'm soaked, that's all."

Fraser pushed up the sleeves of a black Fair Isle sweater. A scoop of blond hair banged on a tanned forehead as he walked beside her. "I live two blocks from here. Come on over. I'll dry your clothes and give you some tea."

Dry her clothes? No, she couldn't—he'd see her leg. "I really should get back to the hotel," Karen said, dodging a group of tourists heading for the next run to Sumter. "My plane leaves early tomorrow. I need to pack."

"You're holed up at the Omni?"

"Yes."

"That's what I thought you said. You can't go back there."

"What?"

"The Omni's a classy joint with a sophisticated clientele. You'll raise every eyebrow in the lobby if you go in there soaked to the skin." He stopped in front of her and put his hands on her shoulders. His demeanor suddenly changed. No toy store boy here, but a man whose brown eyes spoke of something serious. "Look, you had a good time with me out there," he said, pointing over the water.

"I guess so."

"Come on, then. I'll take care of you."

"Take care of me?" Karen said incredulously. "Now what's that supposed to mean? You walk up to me, a perfect stranger, start a conversation, and you expect me to go to your apartment. I don't even know you, Mr. Fraser."

"Hey, call me Lloyd." A lash rolled over his eye in

a languid wink. "And how can you say we don't know each other? We're teachers. That means trust. What are you afraid of?"

Waves crashed against the breakwater behind the Old Custom House. The sun chased roiling clouds toward the horizon. In the distance, a ship's doleful horn muted the chattering tourists boarding the ferry. Karen shielded her eyes and looked into a face that just missed being handsome.

What was she afraid of?

Could there be any doubt of what he wanted? She knew exactly—a quick lay and good-bye. What drove her crazy was a surge of interest in a guy she'd tried to shake for the last two hours. Karen had entered her few relationships with high expectations, but her hopes always foundered on her perception of some man's perception of her leg. She had never felt that she was on an even playing field. This time might be different. This was Charleston, South Carolina. Lloyd Fraser would never see her again. Would there ever be another chance like this, so surgical and uncluttered, so far removed from the banality of her usual routine? Wasn't she entitled to a taste of life?

Karen felt she inhabited one of those diabolical niches in time when common sense and caution struggled against a libido strangely aroused.

During a tense few moments while Karen stared at reflections in a puddle near their feet, Lloyd pulled her against his wet sweater. "What do you say, baby? Should we go get dry?"

Any doubt fluttered away on quivering lips. "Yes."

Her voice sounded like someone else's. "I think I want to."

Fraser stopped at a bookstore, unlocked a side door, and led her up a narrow staircase. At the top he unlocked another door. They entered a small studio loft overwhelmed by two building-block and board bookcases and a daybed covered with pillows. He flipped a switch and watched for Karen's reaction as synthesized music, something like she'd heard on "Music from the Hearts of Space," flowed from speakers nestled among the books. Karen smiled inanely as he grabbed a match from the mantel of a fake fireplace and lit a gas log.

"Well, now." He rubbed his hands together. "Isn't this romantic?"

She didn't answer.

Fraser pointed toward the bathroom. "There's a robe in there. Throw your clothes out. I'll toss 'em in the dryer."

Karen nodded. She took off her waterlogged shoes and entered the small bathroom painted a surgical white. She peeled out of her wet clothes, glanced in the mirror, and reached for the robe hanging from a hook on the door. Lloyd was tall; the robe reached her ankles. She sponged at her wet hair with a towel and stepped back into the loft, her soaked garments wrapped inside the Bancroft sweatshirt.

"Your dryer?"

"Next door." He took the bundle. "I'll be right back."

Karen stood before the fake fireplace watching the gas jet. A 1963 Royal Command Performance Beatles' poster hung above the mantel, the same one she'd kept since high school, and a charcoal Albert Einstein grinned at her from amidst a grouping of framed certificates—three diplomas and his permanent professional teaching license. She stepped back, gazing at the father of relativity, and shivered at the sound of footsteps coming up the hall. How would he proceed? Awkwardness, ineptitude, or an ill-timed comment or gesture from her would betray her inexperience. This seduction was going to be up to him.

Fraser locked the door behind him and joined her at the fireplace. They sat with their backs against the daybed. He shed his rain-scented sweater and pulled her face against his bare chest. Karen knew she had little choice now; she was committed.

"Are you comfortable?" he asked.

"Yes."

"Glad you came?"

"I think so."

"You think so? I'll bet you've had a lot of experience."

"What?"

"With men."

"That's not very nice." She intended to pull away, but her face seemed glued to his chest. "Maybe I should get my clothes and leave."

"Don't be so touchy. I didn't mean what you're thinking."

"What did you mean?"

"You're a good looking woman. I just thought

you probably had every man you ever wanted."

"Wrong." Karen felt the need to be precise, even tell him the reason for her apprehension. "I've had very little experience," she said slowly, "and in case you haven't noticed, I'm extremely uneasy about this."

"You needn't be."

"Well, I am. You should know..."

"Hush." Fraser touched her lips, then kissed her eyes and the bridge of her nose. He rubbed her breasts through the terry cloth robe, which fell off her shoulders. "Beautiful." Fraser stared in the flickering light. "Absolutely beautiful." He pushed gently until she lay on her back. He massaged her hips and stomach; his lips whispered and kissed. His hands brushed the insides of her thighs and gripped her calves. Abruptly, the rhythmic squeezing stopped.

"Wait!" The word bounced around like an echo in a well. Fraser pushed himself to his knees. "Wait!" he said again angrily. "Are you some kind of freak?"

The feel of her withered leg, the sight of it under the flickering light of the gas log produced in him a revulsion even more powerful than his ardor of moments ago. Lloyd Fraser struggled to his feet and stood above her looking as if he'd been used. He jerked up his pants, walked to the fireplace, and glowered at Karen, who was frantically pulling the robe around her.

"You little bitch. You hid this from me. Get the hell out of here," he had snarled through clenched teeth. "I don't do mercy fucks."

Karen was sucked into a black hole that day. She

had no memory of reclaiming her clothes, of how she escaped the loft, or of the flight home. But the crushing memory of that one cruel declaration always lurked close to the surface. And now, Nicholas Staal had stared her back to Lloyd Fraser, from whose snarling lips she had heard the truth: men didn't want her.

Karen considered her study a safe haven from the world, a small niche of stability carved out in the corner of her modest home. The atmosphere mirrored her persona: floor to ceiling bookshelves, a desk cluttered with mementos, posters and photographs, boxes of teaching materials, all a contemplative extension of the classroom—a place to tie off loose ends and hatch plans for tomorrow.

Not tonight. Perched on a chair, still wearing her school clothes, she fiddled with a stack of unmarked student compositions, poked at them, replaced the top paper with the bottom one. Suddenly she bolted from the chair and faced the wall behind her.

"Go ahead. Say it. You think I made a fool of myself."

Always on guard, Martha Y. Bancroft—captured forever in an unflattering sepia tint, severe in a high lace collar, her hair drawn into a tight bun—regarded Karen from the wall. Karen's mother had discovered the photograph in a pile of junk at a garage sale.

Miss Bancroft had been the first Iowa woman principal of a coed high school, a noteworthy accomplishment, made more so since a city school bore her name. Karen loved that picture, a portrayal of the consummate spinster schoolmarm. She'd seen pictures like this on Old Maid cards. She sometimes used the photograph as a sounding board because Martha always listened.

Karen turned her back on the picture and paced away. She ran her fingers across the spines of several books, slapped at the pile of compositions, stumbled over magazines stacked on the floor, and stood again before the picture like a fly that had found a place to light.

"Do you think you could have done better? He'd charm the pins right out of your hair." She stepped backwards. "What bothers me about him? Is that what you want to know? Everything. Especially his blue eyes. I'm out of sync. I don't even know how to talk to him. So you tell me. What about those piercing looks? That's not just casual eye contact. Is he interested in me? Or is he making fun of me? God."

Karen sat in the desk chair. "There's something magical about him. But I can't let myself be interested. I'm not attractive. Men don't want me. He's just like the others. This is about my leg. I know that look. I've felt that look all my life."

The attack on the first student theme sputtered in a matter of moments. She stared beyond the window. The oak leaves looked shiny and slick under the streetlight. "That farmer will not drive me out. I've more right to the lounge than he does. Seventeen years' more right. Don't worry about me, Martha. I can handle him."

News of the second-floor lounge integration swept through the school like a rumor of early dismissal. By Friday morning, the denizens of the upstairs lounge were Nicholas Staal and as many women as could fit into the room's pitiful array of chairs. Karen noticed women who had never been in the lounge before. They brought cookies and leftover cake. Nick was the centerpiece, lacing conversations with rural anecdotes. They giggled and cooed. She knew damn well some of them didn't know one end of a cow from the other; but they knew how to look at him with bovine eyes. She decided that Nick seemed entirely comfortable surrounded by this herd—any bull would.

On Sunday night before the fourth week, Karen pored over an Iowa map. An Adair County license placed him two counties over and one down. She worked a ruler along the legend at the bottom and measured out about forty miles. Staal had told McGimpsey that he lived south of Stuart and left home at 5:15. She thought he must get up in the middle of the night if he did his chores or whatever farmers do. Forty miles, some through downtown traffic, made about an hour's drive. He must be showing up at about 6:15. She wondered why the police hadn't picked him up or condemned his truck.

The phone rang.

"Hello."

"So how's it going, Honey Bunny? Are you busy?" Grace Merchant twanged in Karen's ear.

"Kind of." Karen played with the ruler.

"Lots of papers?"

"Homework's done. I'm looking at a map."

"Planning a trip?"

"No. I'm checking to see where a man lives."

"A man?" Grace's voice brightened. "So tell me about him."

"Mother, you're grilling. It's not what you think. I just want to know where he lives. That's all. I don't even like him."

"Well, I'm not prying..."

"Good. Because there's nothing to know."

"But a little social life wouldn't hurt you, Karen."

"My social life's just fine. Mother, I have to take my bath."

Monday morning at 6:00 Karen eased into a deserted lot and parked in space number one. Not one person appeared on her way upstairs. She flipped the light switch on a silent lounge. No cackling women. Her things thudded onto the table, and her eyes fell on George Moore's wine-tasting sign. "Nick Staal tryed them all" was handwritten on the bottom. Karen got closer. Big loops on the capitals, t's, and l's. She hadn't seen his handwriting, but who else would have written this? He had the ego to write that. "Tryed." Nicholas Staal couldn't spell. One small bungled word. No big deal. But if he were dumb, then the other things David thought about him were probably true, too.

Here was a farmer, who couldn't spell,

masquerading as a teacher. Probably mixed his tenses, too. If he weren't such an ass, she could help him.

At 6:20 Nicholas Staal entered the lounge, an unlit cigarette in his mouth. Without taking his eyes from Karen, he fumbled in his coat for a lighter.

"Good morning," he said smiling. "What are you doing here?"

Her own words! He was mocking her.

"Hello," she mumbled.

"Where have you been?"

"Don't start," Karen said.

He shrugged and sat across from her with an open newspaper, but his eyes peered over the top. The staring didn't matter this time. She had the goods to make him look bad.

"Did you write that?"

"Write what?" He looked around.

She pointed at the sign.

"Why?" he asked.

"Did you?"

"Why do you want to know?"

"Never mind." She smugly acknowledged to herself that this guy was not bright enough to know he'd misspelled a word.

Nicholas Staal folded his paper and placed it on the table. "You assume I wrote that because I slop up beer and eat beef jerky."

Karen shrugged.

"Winston Churchill was a lousy speller, Karen, but he wrote some of the best prose in the English language. I'll bet he didn't even know how to spell 'tried.'"

Overwhelmed by the possibility that she might have miscalculated Nicholas Staal's intelligence, Karen positively gaped.

He leaned as close to her as the small table would allow. "You don't like me, do you?"

"No, I don't."

"Why?"

"Because you stare at me."

"I didn't realize I was staring. I should tell you something. There's a reason..."

"Of course there's a reason," she exploded. "I know what you're looking at. You're rude. No one else in this building does that to me."

"What are you talking about?"

Karen rose.

"Look, let me explain something," Nick said.

Darlene McGimpsey and Michelle Valder stormed into the lounge. Karen felt rescued. She didn't want to hear any more from him. This guy was a bastard. She didn't need his pity. She didn't want his interest.

five

BETWEEN FIRST AND SECOND PERIODS
Principal Aneyh made standing in the hall between classes a martial duty. During these frantic four minutes 2,600 students scurried to new locations. A faculty meeting rarely ended without a sentry announcement: "Teachers will be in the halls. I want you out there, people. Be visible." Form letters dispatched from his office jogged the memory of any soldier not walking his or her post: "You were not outside your door after ____ period on ____ (date). Continued negligence of this important detail will not be tolerated."

Lydia Fletcher mingled with teachers and students in the hall patting shoulders and broadcasting gratuitous comments. Karen found unbelievable the fact that Lydia had been away from Bancroft for ten years. Nothing about her had changed. Today she wore red high-heeled shoes (with matching purse), watch-plaid kilt, red belt, and a black silk blouse. Stones on her fingers and ears glittered under the fluorescent light. Standing beside her in a long grey dress with a black belt crunched around her narrow waist, Karen once again felt like a schoolmarm in the presence of a cruise director at the captain's table.

David, who paid scant attention to anyone's wardrobe, poked a pad of hall passes into the pocket of his plain brown suit. "Right here," he said, "you have the whole problem with this damn school."

"What?" Lydia asked.

"You know what our job is out here?"

"Sure."

"Well?"

"Keep the kids moving so they won't be tardy," Lydia answered.

"What do you do when they are tardy?"

"What is this, an inquisition?" Lydia fiddled with an earring. "I give them a second chance. Then I make up my mind."

"What do you do?" David arched an eyebrow at Karen.

"You have the floor."

David smirked. "We don't have a policy, do we? We're under marching orders to stamp out tardiness, and we have no policy. You know why?"

"Why?" Lydia asked coldly.

"Punish kids for being late and you have a hassle with them or their parents. Aneyh wants no part of that. He makes every teacher devise his own punishment. Get in over your head and he zaps the rug from under you. Hell, he'll even take the parents' side. Anything to cover his ass."

Passing period ended. Karen returned to her room. Even though she hated his pompous performances, David had put his finger on a common problem in schools everywhere. Leadership rarely fought for strong and effective behavioral standards any more. Those in charge had been pushed into the corner by the crazies out there. Rules for conduct were lost in murky language that enabled boards and administrators to wiggle out when the crunch came. A threat from a wild-eyed parent with a lawsuit on his mind had forced public schools to abandon their standards. For seventeen years she had watched the slide. Activist groups of every persuasion exacted their pound of flesh until policy decisions were predicated on fear—fear of lawsuits, fear of ethnic groups, fear of the press, fear of shadows.

"Miss Merchant, are we going to do anything today?"

Karen looked up from her desk into the troubled eyes of a diminutive blonde girl. "Sure, Joyce, we do something every day. I was daydreaming."

"Can I ask you something first, outside?"

Karen grabbed her gradebook and headed toward the hall.

"Something wrong, Joyce?"

"You know I work in the office in the afternoon?"

"Yes, you put that on your information sheet."

"Well, I was just wondering about Mr. Staal."

Karen wondered about him, too. After her rage toward Nicholas Staal had worn off, Karen's feelings about him seemed to slide into a bewildering ambivalence. She defended him against David's attacks and then wondered why she hadn't joined in instead. One thing was certain and troubling: she thought about him a lot.

"Go on, Joyce."

"Well, is Mr. Aneyh mad at him or something?"

"Why?"

"The other day Mr. Aneyh told Mrs. Reins to turn on the PA and listen to what went on in Mr. Staal's room. He told her to write down anything she heard that was questionable or subversive. Can he do that, Miss Merchant?"

"Mr. Aneyh can do anything he wants." Karen stopped short. She hadn't realized the depth of Aneyh's ire. Nicholas Staal must have really bruised the principal's ego. This student had observed a covert declaration of war. Spying on teachers was despicable. Karen glanced toward Staal's room. Even he didn't deserve that.

"I mean, he has lots of different ways of evaluating staff, Joyce. Maybe this is a new one." The hypocrisy of that answer stuck in her throat as she turned toward the waiting class.

BETWEEN SECOND AND THIRD PERIODS

"David's so bitter," Lydia said. "Why doesn't he just quit?"

"He's a good teacher, Lydia. I get a lot of his students in twelfth grade. They're well-prepared." Karen picked up a gum wrapper. "He's married with two kids and has fifteen years in the pension system. He can't afford to give that up."

"But he's so vitriolic. I'd worry about a coronary."

"Are you kidding! He thrives on chewing at the system. His histrionics get old, but half the fun of these passing periods is listening to him bitch." Karen looked up. "Speak of the devil!"

"See those two?" David asked, joining them.

"What two?"

"Mr. and Ms. Hormone over there by that locker." He nodded toward a tall, pretty girl wearing frayed bluejeans full of holes, a T-shirt with a picture of Kurt Cobain draped across her bosom, and her moussed blonde hair pulled back in a pony tail. At her side with his hand squeezing rhythmically in her hip pocket stood a boy wearing a black T-shirt, jeans, motorcycle boots, a chain anchoring a wallet to his skinny behind. Bancroft students labelled his ilk "gearheads." "I've got five bucks says she'll be pregnant before the year's over."

The gearhead embraced the girl passionately before she disappeared into the classroom.

"Why don't you stop them?" Lydia asked.

"Give her your civics lesson, Karen."

"Never mind," Karen said.

"I will. Karen took a couple to the office last year, caught them dry-humping by the fire extinguisher over there. She should have turned the extinguisher on 'em. Would have gotten better results. Aneyh yelled at the culprits, sent them back to class, and formed a committee of kids, teachers, and parents to study the problem. Guess which lucky person got to chair it?"

"Karen!?"

"Yup. There's a lesson for you, Lydia. Don't bring a problem to his attention."

"What'd you decide, Karen?"

"Nothing. Aneyh filibustered every strong proposal."

"Aneyh's afraid if he takes a stand, the ACLU will get into it," David said. "After all, we can't abridge these kids' constitutional right to suck each other's tongues in public."

Karen rolled her eyes.

"Why don't you talk to Mr. Aneyh, David, if it bothers you?" asked Lydia.

"Talk to him! Have you been listening? Find me a career educator with guts and I'll show you a guy in every board member's gunsight."

"David, tell Lydia about Aneyh's announcement last year."

"Well, the language got so foul in the halls even Aneyh couldn't stand it. He got on the PA and made a hard-hitting policy statement. Honest to God, I'm quoting verbatim. 'Bad language in the halls,' he said, 'will result in a one-day suspension unless it's a slip of the tongue.' Can you believe that shit! When you nailed a student for swearing, he looked at you with pubescent innocence and said, 'Oops. Excuse me. Slip of the tongue.'"

Class bell.

David followed Lydia down the hall. "You want that bet, Fletcher? Five bucks says she's pregnant before school's out."

"You're on, buddy."

BETWEEN THIRD AND FOURTH PERIODS

"How many weeks have there been?" David wondered.

"Week Five," Karen said. "Lost track already?"

"Five, huh?" David nodded toward Nicholas Staal's room. "Why do you suppose Glamour Puss never does hall duty? And why hasn't Aneyh nailed him about it? Every bulletin has an announcement. How could he miss—hey, maybe Staal can't read."

"I don't know what he is," Karen said, "but I don't think he's dumb."

"How would you know?"

"Because of a couple of things he said to me."

"He probably only knows a couple of things." David got serious. "Be careful, Karen. Don't get caught in that lounge alone with that two-bit Lothario."

"Oh, please."

"You don't go in there anymore. What'd he do to you?"

"You've asked me that five times," Karen said curtly. "Just drop it."

"I'm in there every morning. He isn't hitting on anybody." Lydia fluffed her hair with both hands. "I sort of wish he would."

David shrugged his shoulders.

"Why, mercy me!" Lydia patted his shoulder. "You're jealous."

"Yeah, right."

"Then why don't you go in there? Nick's broken the ice, and he talks about something other than teaching."

"Like what?"

"He raises livestock out in Adair County."

"Good! Maybe you'll learn how to de-nut pigs."

"You are afraid to go in there, aren't you, Davey boy? Afraid Mr. Aneyh will find you out and fill up your classes with bums."

Another bell.

"That's stupid, Lydia. The gong just squelched your stupidity."

"Bye, Davey," Lydia said. "See you after school."

AFTER SCHOOL

Alice Cain lumbered down the hall. She wore sensible shoes and voluminous skirts that billowed around her like flowing water when she walked. Her thigh-like upper arms and smiling moon face presented a familiar outline, identifiable from Bancroft's longest halls.

Alice, the only woman in the social science department, taught economics, was the department's chair, and served as the building representative for the Des Moines Unified Teachers Organization, DUTO.

David leaned against a locker, his head buried in a magazine. "Alice is in the area. I can hear her pantyhose rubbing together."

"Don't be mean, David," Karen said waving at Alice.

"Hey, Alice, pull up a couple chairs and sit down."

"That's an old one, David." Alice planted herself in front of them. "I don't have time for jokes. You all need to hear this."

"What?" David folded his magazine.

"Do you know Chad Bergen?"

"No."

"Special ed kid. He's a mess. Always trying to get out of class. He asked the librarian for a pass to the john early in first period. She let him go. The minute he got back he started hounding her to go again."

"So?"

"She wouldn't let him go. And right there in front of God, the librarians, and fifty kids, he let everything hang out and peed all over the floor."

"God."

"Oh, no."

"You've got to be kidding."

"Marcie's furious."

"Who?" Lydia asked.

"Marcie Reynolds, one of the librarians. Hal Delaney sent the little pisser home. But his mother brought him right back and raised so much hell Mr. Aneyh let him back in."

"Quit calling that bastard 'Mr.,'" David said. "Anyway, you can't keep a special ed kid out of school. He's worth too much money. Remember what happened at McGovern High last year? A special ed kid broke into the gym in the middle of the night and sawed up forty thousand bucks' worth of bleachers with a chainsaw. He was eighteen, convicted in criminal court, and they didn't get rid of him! You can't screw around with federal programs."

"Anyway," Alice shifted her weight, "when Aneyh started blaming Marcie, she began talking sort of wild. You know, Karen, how red her face gets when she's flustered."

Karen nodded.

"So Aneyh told her not to worry, that he's forming a committee to solve the problem. Guess who's chairperson?"

"Oh, Alice," Karen gasped, "please say I'm not."

"You're not. Guess again."

"Listen, Big Mama," David marched up to her. "Who the hell is it?"

"Nicholas Staal."

"Well, well," David said with a chuckle. "By the time Aneyh finishes with him, he'll be broke for riding. How'd you know all this stuff?"

"Nick told me. He eats lunch in his room. Aneyh stomped in there over the noon hour and chewed him out about hall duty. He'd ignored five of those little notices. Aneyh handed Nick a paper with the committee members and told him he'd damn well better show up for that."

"Who else is on the committee, Alice?" Lydia asked.

"Nick, Bob Melville, Coach Cook, and George Moore."

"That's only four." David said. "He always has five. Who's the other one?"

Alice nodded at Karen, whose shoulders went limp. She withdrew from the group without comment and sank into the desk chair in her room across the hall from where they'd been standing.

David peered through the door. "Look at her. Pathetic. Karen'll waste hours dinking around with this."

"At least," Alice agreed, moving away from Karen's door.

"And the final insult for her has to be working with Nicholas Staal," David said. "Oh, well, I'm not on the damn thing. That's all that counts."

"Why doesn't Mr. Aneyh handle this himself?" Lydia asked.

"Look, honey, principals don't take a stand anymore," Alice said. "They talk fluff from both sides of their mouths. And then, of course, Aneyh has site-based management. Didn't you have that at Melcher?"

"Sure," Lydia said. "How does it work here?"

"Beautifully, on paper. Students, parents, teachers, and administrators sit in a circle expressing feelings, posturing, exploring possibilities, with Robert D. Aneyh pulling strings, tickling egos, stroking the members until he gets what he wants. If the committee decision doesn't work, he blames the committee. Site-based management is sort of like the flies capturing the fly paper."

David smacked the magazine against his hand. "Crap! Only five weeks gone. Kids peeing on the floor, these stupid committees, and Homecoming next week. I just want this year over."

Alice cleared her throat and drew air into her ample bosom. "Shall I sing, David?"

six

Karen's black canvas bag, packed with books and papers, slammed into her back as the large figure of Dan Tennant suddenly loomed before her in the doorway.

"Karen," he said, "I got here too late. You're leaving."

"Yes, this has been a long day."

He patted her bookbag. "A long night, too. I've wanted to stop by ever since school started." He looked around the room. "So this is your domain."

"This is the place," she said inanely.

"You're a good teacher, Karen."

"What?"

"Don't look so surprised. I've kept track of you."

Tennant ambled past the student chairs toward the rear of the room. He had gained thirty pounds since Karen was his student, but his tall, rawboned frame gracefully accommodated the added burden. Steel-rimmed glasses, grey hair, and a moustache now gave him a professorial aura. As his student over twenty-five years ago, she had recognized that this man was a fine teacher. Standing before him here, she felt fourteen again.

Imagine, he'd kept track of her! But then, she did that, too, with many of her former students. She jotted notes, clipped articles about their accomplishments, and tucked them away in a notebook labelled "Merchant's Alumni Association."

Tennant leafed through several books on top of the shelves in the back. The room had thirty-two student desks—pink plastic chairs with formica writing arms—arranged informally in a horseshoe. Over time the room had taken on the personality of her teaching style. On one side stood an old oak desk piled high with papers; a neat row of books stretched across the front, held in place by two massive iron bookends which also looked like books. Six rickety chairs and a scarred cast-off library table occupied the opening of the horseshoe where she conducted mini seminars while other students wrote. Old-fashioned slate blackboards spanned the front and back of the room, and a wall of windows covered by Venetian blinds, faded and bent by years of service, looked in on the place where she had spent seventeen years of her life.

He glanced at a makeshift bulletin board, a piece of burlap drawn tightly over a section of slate, and fiddled with a paper pinned to the burlap by a blue ribbon.

"That's Annette's Chaucer paper, Mr. Tennant."

"Come on, stop that. I'm Dan." He nudged her.

"You don't expect me to call you Miss Merchant, do you?"

"No, of course not."

"You gave her a B-. Why the blue ribbon?"

"I told the kids I'd display the first paper that had perfect mechanics. You know, spelling, grammar, and punctuation. Annette got twenty-five style points out of twenty-five, the only one out of all of my classes so far. She doesn't write as well as some, but we're working on that. She was absolutely thrilled to have her paper up there." Karen ran her fingers across the ribbon. "This is just an extra touch."

"Where'd you get these?" Tennant nodded at a pair of wooden masks, one smiling and one scowling.

"A gift." She unhooked the masks and handed them to him. "Three years ago six boys got dumped into Senior English when Woodworking III was canceled."

"This is really fine work."

"I know." She stroked the smoothly sanded faces. "Those guys fought me every step of the way. They didn't like homework, and their written work was a disaster."

Dan Tennant peered at Karen from behind the smiling mask. "Did they flunk?"

"No. They learned the difference between comedy and tragedy. You can see that." She returned the masks to their hooks. "They loved to talk. And they had opinions on everything. Their analysis of character motivation came right from the streets. Pretty insightful, too." Karen laughed. "Can you believe it! We became good friends. Three of them are carpenters in Des Moines, two left for California, one I lost track of."

"Were the masks one of your assignments?"

Karen followed Dan to the front of the room. "No. Tom Cleary, the one who fought me the most, dropped in after school just before Christmas last year. He claimed the room needed a little class. He'd worked on the masks for two months. I just love them!"

"The masks or the boys?"

"Both."

Tennant squeezed into a student desk, his long legs spilling out in front. In a complete reversal of roles, she looked down at him.

"I want to ask you something," he said.

"Sure."

"I'm new here. What's with Aneyh, anyway? The faculty doesn't seem to like him."

Karen leaned against her desk. "He's a tyrant. We don't like that."

"So why doesn't anyone fight back?"

"Why bother. He has too many friends downtown."

"That guy Staal got under his skin at the first faculty meeting."

"Yes, but he won't have the guts to try again. Believe me, Aneyh will take care of him. I've seen this principal humble teachers many times."

Karen sat down in the student desk next to Tennant. She felt at ease talking with him about

Bancroft. He seemed like an old friend who had appeared from the past. "I'll tell you what bothers me most," she said. "Aneyh stormed in here ten years ago claiming Bancroft was the best kept secret in Iowa. He was going to put us on the map, make us the best school in the state. 'Second to none,' he said. But all he really thinks about is image and how things look on the surface. He doesn't care about academics. Not once in ten years has he ever been in this classroom. I've seen him lurking in the hall, and he's popped his head in the door once or twice to hand me something. But he's never been interested enough to find out what goes on in this room or in any other class."

"So you people just put up with him?"

"Well, I'm here to teach. No matter what else he does, so far he hasn't meddled with what I teach or how I teach. As long as I have that, I guess I can put up with the rest."

"Is that all that bothers you?"

"He's committee-crazy. I'm on five. Last week he put me on another one. A committee on unauthorized urinating in the building."

"Yes, I heard about that one."

"Tonight's the only night this week I don't have a meeting. I spend too much time promoting that man's vision of the school's image." She nodded at the bookbag lying by the door. "I have to do all my preparation at home."

Tennant unwound himself from the desk and walked toward the door. "I'd better get out of here then and let you get started."

"Oh, no, that's not what I meant."

"You know something?" He leaned against the door jamb. "Back when you were in school, teachers sat around in the lounge and talked about teaching. All I ever hear now is bitching. I never thought I'd be counting the years I have left."

"I know. Sometimes I'd like to get out myself. I can't imagine doing this for twenty-three more years."

"You're thinking of quitting?"

"I have. But when I discuss that with my mother I get no support, only guilt."

"This system ought to be doing everything it can to hold on to people like you. But they won't. I don't envy you your twenty-three years, Karen." He stepped toward her. "Let's do this again. You remind me of the good old days. Does that make me sound like an old fogy?"

"You can't be an old fogy," she said quickly. "That would make me a semi-fogy! Come back, Mr. Tennant."

"OK, Miss Merchant," he said, smiling over his shoulder.

Karen sat at her desk and listened to his footsteps grow faint. Her eyes focused on the bulletin board, then the whole room. She wanted to be a good teacher. This man, for whom she had enormous respect, said she was.

seven

Band members fidgeted and blew spit from valves. Pompons swirled around half clad cheerleaders who exhorted the faithful into a spiritual frenzy. A stampede of teenage feet rhythmically stomped wooden bleachers to usher in the Monday morning first hour rip-roaring "Pin the Panthers to the Wall" kick-off assembly. White plumed toilet paper rolls launched from the bleacher tops spiraled to the floor. Hal Delaney chased a half dozen boys who darted along the sidelines squirting black and gold body paint into the crowd. As he herded the culprits toward an exit, Hal told the animated young director of the pep band to get the show on the road. Brassy sounds of "Bancroft Pride" slammed into every crevice of the building, overpowering a spontaneous student chant of "South High Sucks, South High Sucks."

"One down, two to go," Karen yelled to Alice and Lydia. They sat on the bleachers four rows up from the gymnasium floor.

"I wish it were three down," Alice yelled back.

Lydia sat between them. "Three? Did I miss something?"

Alice rolled onto the other half of her rear end on the hard board seat. "Read this week's calendar."

"What? I can't hear you."

"I said, did–you–read–this–week's–calendar?"

"Hey, I only do one day at a time. Yoo-hoo. Hi, Megan." Lydia popped up like a cork from deep water and waved at the cheerleaders.

Alice stuck three fingers in Lydia's face. "We have three assemblies this week."

"You're kidding! How 'bout the assembly that crowns the King and Queen?"

"Oh, yes, we still have that," Alice said, "but this is the new and improved Homecoming. Aneyh calls this week Backing Bancroft. We call it the week that wasn't."

"Homecoming only happens once a year, Alice. Kids need a little fun."

Alice barked at a clutch of students behind her chucking pennies onto the gym floor. "Yeah, right," she mumbled. "A little fun."

The last shrill trumpet blast faded away. Coach Rick Cook and Bancroft's football captains jogged to the center floor mike. Cook, with a rugged physique and chiseled face, looked fit enough to be one of the captains. The coach grabbed the mike. "Students." Electronic feedback stopped him. He adjusted the mike. "Students," he began again, "here's three hardnosed football players. Bancroft High, greet the Hogs–Chris Lumbard, Jeff Pantillo, and Darrell Gage."

The student body morphed into a herd of swine. Cries of "oink, oink" turned the gymnasium into a sty. The captains, clad in gold t-shirts with "B.H.S. HOG" lettered in black on the front, each took a turn at the microphone explaining why Bancroft would beat South High.

"What's this HOG stuff?" Lydia asked.

"Male bonding," Karen told her.

"You mean boar bonding," Alice said.

"Any player," Karen said, "who makes five tackles, or maybe ten, earns the title HOG and gets a t-shirt. The players think the shirt's a big deal. Maybe so."

Lydia generated a few oinks of her own, which brought up the whites of Alice's eyes.

The captains walked along the edge of the gym floor, fists clenched overhead. The logo on the backs of their HOG shirts screeched at the crowd, "LIQUOR UP FRONT, POKER IN THE REAR."

"See that!" Alice stood with her hands on her hips. "That's pornographic. Any parent who lets a kid out of the house with that shirt on ought to be locked up."

Lydia tugged at Alice's skirt. "Sit down; it's only a shirt."

"Only a shirt! I thought you were a feminist, Lydia."

"I am."

"Doesn't that shirt offend you? What do you do, pick and choose your own outrages?"

"I don't want to talk about shirts," Lydia said coldly.

"Well, then don't ask me what the BTIC shirts stand for when they show up this winter."

"OK, what do they stand for?" Lydia asked.

Alice stared into space.

"Come on." Lydia pulled Alice's arm. "Don't be like that."

"Best Team in the Conference," Alice said. "That's what the kids say they mean."

"So? That's it?" Lydia said, smiling.

"That's it."

"What's BTIC mean, Karen?" Lydia asked.

Karen cupped her hands over Lydia's ear. "Big Ten Inch Club," she whispered.

"Oh, my!"

"Right," Alice said. "Put the whole club together—lay 'em end to end—you wouldn't have ten inches."

The oinks and hog calls subsided. Robert Aneyh stood on the gym floor. He lowered the mike. "Welcome," he said stridently. "Welcome, everyone, to Back Bancroft High School Week. Is this the best high school in the city?" The crowd roared YES. He went on like a modern Dr. Pangloss. "Is this the best high school in the state?" The crowd roared YES again. "Is this the best high school in the nation?" The crowd rose as one, chanting "Bancroft, Bancroft, Bancroft, Bancroft..."

"This is about over." Karen got to her feet. "I've heard this same speech for ten years. If he says anything new, let me know."

"Right," Alice said. "I'll fill you in later."

Karen left the gym and walked slowly through the empty, poster-decorated halls toward her room. "The week that wasn't, the week that wasn't" rang in her ears as the noise faded behind her. A week of "oink, oink, oink" and hundreds of students, each one with a pass signed by Robert D. Aneyh, going in and out of classes like shoppers through a revolving door.

Homecoming Week's craziness had bothered her for ten years. Monday—the first hour kick-off assembly. Tuesday—Hat Day. Who could explain what crazy hats had to do with Homecoming? Wednesday—Dress Down Day. A precursor of Halloween, weird outfits, inside out and backwards. Thursday—Coronation of the Homecoming King and Queen. Finally, Friday—Game Day, also known as Color Day, featuring another pep assembly. Everywhere a sea of black and gold.

Homecoming Week and all other extracurricular activities fit perfectly into Robert D. Aneyh's philosophy of marketing the school. He worshipped at the altar of public relations. The positive image of his school became his focus. No matter that the image was a facade papering over the cracks. He knew where the glory lay, what excited patrons. Like a cunning military commander, he concentrated his efforts on those sectors where he could win victories, notoriety, and, perhaps, advancement to the ivory tower downtown. He had refashioned Bancroft into a theater for the performing arts. He lionized coaches, music directors, debate and drama instructors, anyone who had a hand in putting students on display. He was just a good old boy, a cheerleader in a gray flannel suit, a ready smile on his face for a winning team, but little room in his mind for academics. To him they were just a bunch of classes on a master schedule.

She caught an image reflected in the glass of a classroom door, but Karen didn't see herself. The face of her principal stared back like Marley's ghost, eerily mocking her dark thoughts about the week that lay ahead. Her mind sought refuge from the principal's ghoulish image in a world where a pep bus packed with screaming fans sped to a history meet. A huge oval stadium rippled with the wave, started in praise of advanced calculus. Rave reviews lauded a performance of Chemistry II. But in the real world, she knew the only headlines for academic classes read "Scores Drop."

"Look at that belly button," David commented. A young girl in short shorts, skimpy halter top, sandals, and two plastic leis slithered by, followed by two boys who wore their mothers' housecoats. Their heads bobbed as her hips rolled in front of them. David straightened his tie in an effort to disassociate himself with the weird Dress Down Day costumes parading through the upper hall. "I don't think I can stand this, Karen. Let's go eat."

"Some of these outfits are really cute," said Lydia, who wore a striped blouse, flowered skirt, and knee socks that didn't match. "We voted for the craziest outfit in every class."

"Why didn't you slip into something more educational?" David asked.

"Well, we wrote about Homecoming in our journals."

David's eyes rolled.

They turned into the lunchroom where Karen's nostrils flared at the odor of spaghetti and canned green beans. She had observed that on this day every year the bizarre costumes produced a decibel level in the cafeteria approaching critical mass. Eating lunch here on Dress Down Day was a painful experience. Just as she pictured Nicholas Staal eating a sack lunch in his quiet room, David nudged her ribs. He nodded toward the serving door. Nicholas Staal stood twenty feet in front of them dressed in a soft grey suit, grey shirt, and black tie.

Lydia stood on her tiptoes. "He must have forgotten his lunch."

"His hogs ate it," David said. "With all the oinking around here today, he ought to have on his Osh Kosh B'Goshes."

"Wouldn't make any difference," Lydia cooed. "He'd look good in anything."

Next to the vegetable server stood a well-dressed woman scribbling notes on a clipboard. The deference paid her by the serving ladies in white dresses and hair nets attested to her importance. As Nicholas Staal speared a melon piece from the server, the lady with the clipboard leaned forward and extended her hand.

"Are you the principal here?" she asked.

Nick placed his fork on the tray and shook her

hand warmly. "Of course not. I have an important job. I'm a teacher."

"Oh, I'm sorry."

"You needn't be. May I ask you a question?"

"Why, yes."

"Why would you think I was the principal?"

A red tinge appeared at the clipboard lady's temples. She glanced down the serving line. "Well, I—you're so dressed up."

"You mean, you think teachers never dress up?"

"Well, of course," she said, obviously flustered. "But it's just that..."

Nick saw David, Lydia, and Karen and smiled. He suddenly wheeled around and pointed beyond them. "There, madam," he said to the clipboard lady, "there's your man." He placed his tray on the counter. "That's how a principal dresses."

Karen looked behind her. Aneyh stood there with a tray in his hand. He wore a HOG shirt, farmer overalls with one bib strap undone, and an Asgrow seed cap. Suppressed giggling surged along the lunch line as the woman walked toward him. The urban farmer muttered under his breath; sweat beaded on his red brow. Students turned away or clamped hands over their mouths, teachers feigned dignity, and David unconsciously tapped his tray with his spoon in undisguised admiration for Nick. The lunch line gained momentum, fueled by those who wanted to escape the principal's glazed eyes. Karen, her tray loaded with spaghetti and green beans, heard Aneyh jawboning the clipboard lady about Dress Down Day, why he looked this way, and how he normally wore a suit and tie.

"Can you believe that?" Lydia placed her tray on the teachers' table near the swinging doors of the main cafeteria entrance. They called themselves the Second Lunch Bunch. "Mr. Aneyh couldn't defend himself."

"You hit the old nail's head, Lydia," David said. He took the chair beside her. "That farmer flat dab gets under his skin. I hate to admit this, but there are those rare moments when I could almost like Nicholas Staal. That farmer's got balls."

"Oh, yes," said Lydia.

"Well, sober puss," David said as Karen put her tray down. "How'd you keep from laughing?"

"I bit a pound and a half of flesh from the inside of my cheek."

"Look at Staal sitting over there all by himself." David jerked his head over her shoulder. "He doesn't want to get acquainted. You never see him anywhere. Eats lunch in his room out of a God–damned sack." David twisted his fork in a mound of spaghetti. "He's arrogant, thinks he's too good for us."

"You don't even know him, David. I see him in the upstairs lounge every morning." Lydia stood and waved her arms. "Yoo hoo, Nick, come and join us."

"That all right with you, Karen?" David asked.

"Of course. Yes. Why not. This is a free country."

"Just askin'."

Nicholas Staal threaded his way through the student tables. He placed his tray across from Karen.

"Well, big guy," David said breezily, "what do you think of Dress Down Day?"

"I'll get over it." Nick unfolded his napkin.

"If anyone can find one redeeming thing about this whole week, I'd like to hear about it," David said.

"I like football," Nick said.

"Did you play?"

"Yes."

David gave Karen an I-told-you-so kick under the table.

"Well, anyway, Nick," said Lydia, "Mr. Aneyh thinks Homecoming breaks the monotony of classes. I do, too. This is a time for people to get together, relive memories. Listen to this. I think it's neat. He told me about a couple who'd been divorced for three years who came back to Bancroft's Homecoming last year. They got caught up in the nostalgia. Everything happened for them. Memories of high school rekindled the flame, and they were married Christmas Eve. Isn't that romantic?"

"Oh, yes." David spit out a prune pit.

"Why don't you invite your ex-wife back, Nick? Something like that might happen to you."

David stared at her. "Mind your own business, Lydia."

"Well, I'm not prying or anything. I just thought this was a nice story with a happy ending."

"Where does your ex-wife live?" Karen asked.

The anguished look that flowed from Nick's eyes washed Karen in a wave of guilt. She had struck a nerve by probing an area beyond good taste. And yet, a curiosity so intense, so powerful, so out of control drove her to ask again, "Does she live in Des Moines?"

The buzzer announced an end to second lunch.

"Saved by the bell, Nick." David turned to the women. "I can't believe you two." He grabbed his tray and headed for the conveyor belt.

On Friday, Color Day, an incident occurred between second and third periods. Jeremy King, a second-year senior, prowled the upper halls squirting girls with black and gold body paint. One frightened girl ran downstairs and barged into Hal Delaney's office.

"Mr. Delaney," she screamed. "Upstairs. Jeremy King's attacking girls!"

Delaney charged from his office and up the stairs fully expecting to intercede in a rape in progress. He knew Jeremy King, a huge kid, 6'3", 250, capable of manhandling any Bancroft student.

At the top of the staircase, facing a row of hall lockers, King busily smeared black body paint on the back of a girl's neck. His huge form covered the screaming girl, now pushed against the lockers.

"OK, Jeremy, that's enough." Hal put his hand on the boy's shoulder.

King brushed Delaney's arm away. "I never hurt nobody."

The oafish-looking boy found no supporters among his peers.

"He's awful, Mr. Delaney."

"Look at this paint on my clothes."

"The big jerk!"

"I have to go home to change. He ruined my blouse."

"We need to go downstairs and talk this through, Jeremy," Delaney said calmly.

"Hey, where's your school spirit, Delaney?"

"Not in that tube of paint."

"You teachers ruin everything. This crap washes off. They're just whinin' babies."

"Come on, Jeremy. Don't make this difficult."

"Just fuck off, Delaney. I'm not goin' no place with you."

"Jeremy, you don't have any choice now. Girls, clear a path for us." Delaney grasped King's arm and steered him toward the stairs.

"Get your rotten hands off me!" King shoved Delaney, who toppled backward onto the descending stairs, still clutching the arm of his assailant. Students screamed as the two bodies tumbled end over end down the stairs, coming to rest outside the main office door in a pile of tangled limbs.

King rained insults on Hal Delaney, who appeared to be beyond hearing. Aroused by the racket outside his door, Robert Aneyh stormed from his office. He glanced at the unconscious vice principal lying on his back in front of the trophy case. "Go get the nurse," he screamed at a girl huddled against a locker. "Tell her to bring oxygen and a stretcher. Don't just stand there! Go!"

The powerfully built principal jerked King to his feet. "What's the meaning of this?" he bellowed.

"That bastard pushed me down the stairs." The boy looked down at Hal. "Why the hell is everybody always pickin' on me?"

A chorus of denials came from the ever-growing crowd of students gathered around the vice principal.

"That's not true, Mr. Aneyh. King pushed Mr. Delaney."

"Jeremy tried to kill him."

"It's all King's fault."

"He started everything."

"Shit, they don't know nothin'," screamed King.

Hal slowly regained consciousness. His eyes focused on his white shirt, darkened by black paint. He licked blood from his lips and made an attempt to roll to his side. The nurse arrived in time to resist his efforts to push himself up. She wiped blood from his nose and convinced the principal that Hal should not be moved.

"Go back to class," Aneyh roared at the kids. "Everything's fine. Nothing happened here. Go back to class!"

Students moved slowly through the hall. They peered over their shoulders to view a preposterous tableau: Hal on the floor holding his shoulder, his smashed glasses dangling from one ear, while Jeremy King pled his case, his arm held fast in Aneyh's grip.

eight

Alice Cain collared Frank Nolden, American history teacher and Bancroft's girls' basketball coach, at the cafeteria door. Nolden, a tall, stoop-shouldered man, had breathed life into an unimpressive girls' program. The team had gone to the state tournament three years in a row, which meant prestige and publicity for Bancroft. That put Nolden on Aneyh's A-list.

"You have to come with me, Frank." Alice had him by the arm. "We have an appointment with Aneyh."

"We?"

"I do. I'm representing DUTO. I need someone solid behind me."

"Is this about Hal Delaney?"

"What else? I just found out that Aneyh recommended a week's suspension for King. He can't get away with that." Alice moved between Frank and the door. "Come on. He likes you."

"He likes anyone who gets positive press." Frank adjusted his tie. "This is my lunch period."

"I know that. But this is the only time Aneyh has. Look, if I can fast for this cause, so can you."

"I don't want to get involved in this, Alice."

"Involved! My God, Frank, you're a teacher, aren't you? Hal has a fractured collarbone."

"Jesus," Frank sighed. "I didn't know that." He bit his lip and looked down the hall. "All right. Let's go."

They waited on a wooden bench outside the principal's office. Hattie Reins, her puffy face screwed into a look of importance, sat in front of Aneyh's closed door like Cerberus guarding the gates of Hell, ready to snap off the head of anyone who accidentally strayed into this realm. Between suspicious glances at Frank and Alice, she dropped her hennaed head and filed her nails with an assortment of emery boards lying on her desk top.

"The taxpayers are really getting their money's worth out of her," Alice whispered.

"Check out those claws," Frank said. "Suppose those emery boards are industrial strength?"

"What's he doing in there, anyway? This appointment was for ten minutes ago."

"Nothing," Frank said. "He knows you're here and what you're here for. He'll keep you waiting until a few minutes before class starts. You won't have much time to say anything."

Alice's eyes narrowed, and she slumped wearily. "I'm telling you, Frank, that man has cloven feet."

As Hattie blew on her nails, a red light flashed on her phone. "Yes. I'll send them in. Yes, them. Mr. Nolden is with her." Hattie replaced the phone, gathered the emery boards, and dropped them in her purse. "He'll see you now."

They stood at attention in front of Aneyh's desk. He swiveled in his chair. "Now, what can I do for you two?"

"Well," began Alice.

"Oh, by the way, Coach, how's the team look for this year? Rick Cook told me a wringer moved into our district from Omaha. 6'2"? That should put a grin on your face."

"Mr. Aneyh," Alice's shoe tapped on the floor, "we're not here to discuss basketball."

"I know what you're here for. I've already settled the matter."

"A week's suspension settles the matter?"

"Not just that. I've counseled Jeremy King and his mother. Believe me, this boy's filled with remorse. He intends to come back here after a week and put his nose right to the old grindstone. Look, Alice," he said patronizingly, "this, of course, was an unfortunate incident. Tempers got out of hand. Everyone needs to cool off. We don't need any more negative publicity."

"You call this an unfortunate incident," Alice said. "The teachers call it a mugging. King's dossier would fill a shopping cart. I've seen the thing–thievery, harassment, mayhem."

"Now, now, Alice. Take it easy. This will all blow over."

They could read Aneyh's thought process by the set of his jaw, which he thrust in Nolden's direction.

"What do you think about all of this, Frank?"

"Doesn't put a grin on my face," Frank said. "Hal has a broken collarbone. Don't you think that's worth more than a week's suspension?"

"Definitely." Alice answered for him. "I'm the building representative for DUTO."

"Yes, yes, I know."

"You should also know that teachers won't settle for anything short of expulsion. If you won't help us, we're going right to the superintendent."

"Now, you listen to me." The principal's face reddened. "I'll tell you why I'm sitting in this chair and you two are in the classroom. You don't know a damn thing about the pressures of this job or how to maintain the school's good image. I do. I feel sorry for Hal. But I'll be hanged if I'm going to let this stupid incident be splattered all over the media for the next month." Aneyh smiled at Nolden. "Now, Coach, you stick with basketball, and Mrs. Cain, I suggest you stick to your knitting."

Alice, enraged by Aneyh's attitude, loomed in front of his desk like a towering volcano on the verge of eruption.

"Don't, Alice," Nolden whispered. "Not now. Let's get out of here."

She stomped through the outer office and didn't slacken her pace until they reached the pay phone in the hall.

"Now what?" Frank asked.

"I'm going to call the executive secretary when my heart stops pounding. Did you hear that sexist slob?" she growled through clenched teeth. " 'Stick to your knitting, Mrs. Cain!'"

"He's an SOB. You can't let him get under your skin."

"He expects me to give up. I can't do that." Alice searched her purse for phone money. "You know what's crazy about this? If the situation were reversed, Hal would go to the wall for me no matter what it cost him. And I'll tell you, Frank, I'm going to the wall for him."

Alice Cain knew how to throw her weight around. With the help of DUTO's executive secretary, other secondary administrators in the district, and over Aneyh's heated objections, she persuaded the superintendent to recommend to the Board of Education the expulsion of Jeremy King from the Des Moines Public Schools.

nine

A long skirt whipped at her calves. Karen stormed past David, tossed a crumpled paper in his direction, and jammed a key into her classroom lock.

"Jeez! School hasn't even started yet and you're in a snit." David stood in his doorway across the hall. "What's the matter with you?"

"Read it."

He scooped up the paper and read aloud, "'Ms. Merchant: Re: Request to attend seminar at Grand View Monday p.m. Because we're saving substitute time, please inform the office which teachers will be covering your classes. Hattie Reins.'"

"Well," David said, "isn't that nice. He expects you to collar three teachers and dump your classes on them."

"Exactly."

"Hey, don't look at me."

"Who's asking."

"They've got money to blow on consultants. Then they nickel and dime on something like this."

86

David returned Karen's note. "Did you ever see the offices downtown they built for all of those jerks?"

"Oh, shut up, David. You're preaching to the choir."

"Hey, where are you going?"

"The office."

"Hattie, I need to see Mr. Aneyh."

"I'll see if he's available."

Hattie's practiced officiousness nauseated her. The secretary sat outside the principal's open door but chose to dial his office phone. "Ms. Merchant would like to see you."

"Ms. Merchant," Karen groaned under her breath.

Aneyh waved her in.

"This isn't fair, Mr. Aneyh." The crumpled note fluttered onto the principal's desk. "The downtown office approved this activity. I don't round up teachers and take away their planning periods. That's not my job."

"Now, now, Karen. We have only so many substitute hours to give. Teachers can't be running off to everything."

"Really. What if I were gone all day? How would you handle that?"

"Now, Karen," he said in his best avuncular tone, "you wouldn't do that. You're not a sick-leave abuser." Aneyh plucked a notebook from a shelf behind him and leafed through the pages. "Let me just check once more." His finger moved down a page with notations.

"Now, let's see. Six coaches at the University of Iowa basketball preview, two teachers on special leave, and you know more will be sick tomorrow." He closed the book. "I really am sorry, but I just can't get any more subs. I depend on people like you, Karen." His eye twitched with a mechanical wink. "Now, let's not discuss this any more. You need to find three people to cover your classes."

"I won't be going, Mr. Aneyh. Please tear up my request."

Before he could say another word, she left, went straight to a phone, and informed Grand View's Education office she couldn't participate due to negative administrative intervention.

The following morning another note peeked from her mailbox. "Ms. Merchant," it read, "Mr. Aneyh has used his influence downtown to procure a sub for you this p.m." Karen marvelled at the principal's arrogant revisionism. Her ploy had worked. She'd bet anything that Grand View had called someone downtown who probably got on Aneyh's case. She wanted to go but felt uneasy about what had to be done to get there. Nothing was simple and straightforward anymore.

Karen saw Margaret Watkins from Crescent Middle School standing at a table on the stage. Wilbert Armstrong from South High, the other panel member, chatted with two young women sitting in front row seats of the Grand View auditorium. Karen knew the two teachers professionally: grey-headed Margaret—studious, efficient, cheerful; Wilbert—computer-literate, young, affable.

Margaret waved. "Wilbert's down there with the students. Guess he can't wait to get started."

"He's a Grand View grad, probably knows them." Karen hung her purse on a chair at the end of the short table. "Wilbert can sit in the middle."

"How have you been? New year under control?"

"Oh, Margaret, we have twelve hundred new students."

"I know. How do you like the ninth graders we sent you?"

"I don't have any, but you can't miss 'em. They're walking hormones!"

Margaret laughed as she cleaned the glasses hanging from a silver chain around her neck. Karen had an uneasy feeling that Margaret cleaned them to get a better look at her, and she'd had enough of that lately. Margaret had been staring at her ever since Karen set foot on the stage. She self-consciously smoothed her dark hair.

"By the way," Margaret said, "how is Nick Staal getting along?"

"All right, I guess. He keeps pretty much to himself."

"He hasn't ruffled any feathers?"

Karen hesitated. "He's integrated the lounge and is late for everything, if that's what you mean."

"At Crescent we called him the itinerant iconoclast. Did you know he's been in seven different buildings counting Bancroft? Principals just keep moving him along."

"No, I didn't. He must be a lousy teacher."

"Are you kidding? Nick's an outstanding teacher. But he held our principal's feet to the fire. Tried to keep him honest."

"Harry Lonsdale?"

"Right. The man got so paranoid he'd do an about face to avoid Nick in the hall. He pulled every string he could get his hands on to get Nick banished to Bancroft."

"What's Nick's problem?"

"The problem is principals, Karen. They feel threatened by Nick."

"I guess I've seen that already."

"Oh, Karen, Nick's got guts. He says what he thinks about what goes on in this system. The same things I think but would never say. The truth drives administrators up the wall. And Nicholas Staal always gets at the truth, with a great deal of class, too. I don't know," Margaret sighed. "Maybe he's calmed down since he got back from his leave. My heart certainly went out to him. I lost my husband, Karen. I know what he's going through."

Karen clasped a hand over her mouth. "What are you talking about, Margaret?"

"Don't you know?" Margaret moved closer. "He was gone all last year to take care of his wife. She died of cancer."

Karen choked. No one at Bancroft had ever told her that. She had sat there with the lunch bunch and badgered him about his ex-wife. The memory of Nick Staal's face in the lunchroom that day, clouded with pain, numbed her.

"Karen?"

"I'm sorry, Margaret. I was thinking about something."

"Do you know why I asked you about him?"

"No."

"I noticed the moment you walked in here. The uncanny resemblance. You look so much like her—his wife, I mean—coloring, hairstyle. Your eyes could be hers. And your mannerisms, especially when you hold your head back and look down when you're listening. It's really sort of spooky." Margaret pulled her glasses up and peered at Karen again. "Well, tell Nick we miss him. He was our leader."

"Sure," she said distractedly, "I'll tell him."

"Get up here, Wilbert," Margaret called. "Here comes the moderator."

Twenty-three prospective English teachers had gathered in front of the stage. "Hello and welcome. I'm Sandra Leibler, director of today's program. We are lucky to have three veteran English teach..."

The voice drifted away. *Maybe he was trying to tell me I look like his wife. I thought he was divorced. Alice said so.*

"Ms. Merchant."

"What?" Sandra Leibler was looking at her. "I'm sorry. Will you repeat the question."

A young man in the second row grinned. "I want to know what annoys you most about teaching English."

"Being expected to spell on command," Karen said quickly. The audience chuckled. "I know. It's funny. But I'm serious. Students think you're Noah Webster incarnate and can spell better than his dictionary. Haven't you been in a social situation where someone discovers you're going to be an English teacher? I'll bet I can tell you what he said. 'Oops! Pardon my grammar. English wasn't my best subject.' People expect you'll pounce on their mistakes."

The next question, directed to Wilbert Armstrong, dealt with computers. *Maybe it wasn't my leg. I'll bet he's a nice man, but I didn't give him a chance. How can I go back into that lounge now? He'll think I'm one of those women.*

"Ms. Merchant."

Karen had lost the thread again. "I'm sorry. I didn't hear the question."

"How heavy is your work load?"

Karen had walked into her first classroom ignorant of the huge amount of time required to read student work. A one-paragraph assignment from her five classes meant kissing an entire evening good-bye. "Well," she answered, "you have to give up your private life. You can curl up each night with a stack of papers and just let the world pass you by." Glib, she knew, but her mind wouldn't stay on the discussion even while answering a question.

She got through the seminar, sleepwalking most of the way.

Died of cancer. Karen buckled her seatbelt for the trip across town. *A year off to be with his dying wife. He must have really loved her. I wonder if they had any children.* She had been watching Nicholas Staal on those rare occasions when he stopped to eat with the lunch bunch. His conversation was intelligent, clever. He certainly didn't stare any more.

Karen had told Darlene McGimpsey everything—about his allusion to her rear end, about the staring. Darlene, old enough to be her mother, was a source of maternal guidance. Grace Merchant always listened, but since Grace viewed the world through a filter of optimism, Karen counted on Darlene for realistic opinions. "Good lord, child," McGimpsey had said, "if he paid any attention to you, you're the only one around here. Quit your wishful thinking. All the femmes fatales in the lounge have struck out. He doesn't go in there to see them, Karen. He smokes and reads the paper. I wish he would notice my butt. Except he'd probably tell me it looked like one of the barns out there on his farm."

Tires whirred against freeway concrete, traffic teased her vision, but Karen's mind was frozen on something frightening. She was attracted to Nicholas Staal and had been all along.

She left the freeway and turned south. Everything came into focus. She had found a reason to reject him before he could reject her. *He wouldn't want me, but that was no reason for being unfair to him. I accused him of looking at me. But maybe he was looking for her. Who is he, anyway? What does he really see when he looks at me? Oh, what difference does it make?*

A shrill horn goaded her through the intersection.

Karen arrived at Castle Drive, her street, which ran irregularly for half a mile along a bluff above the Raccoon River. Most of the homes in her neighborhood were modest ranches. Hers, one of the smallest, reminded her of a wooden house on Baltic Avenue.

She shielded her eyes from the late afternoon sun and turned into her driveway which ended just beyond the sidewalk. Karen wandered along the side of the house to the backyard patio. It was a warm mid-October afternoon. Slanting rays of sunlight streamed through the red and gold leaves. Occasionally one released its grip and fluttered aimlessly to the ground. A wedge of geese, dark specks against the blue sky, drifted south.

Sitting on her lawn chair, summer's last relic, Karen pulled her knees up and clasped her arms around them. A euphoric rush of validation swept through her. Someone as handsome as Nicholas Staal had married a woman who looked like her. He had slept with her. She pictured an old red pickup chugging along a country lane toward a cool grove of trees. He sat at the wheel, and a woman who looked like her, a woman who was her, sat beside him.

Karen jumped to her feet. A scenario involving her and this man was crazy. "I can't think like this," she said out loud. "I just can't. Tomorrow I'll apologize and end this once and for all."

ten

The lounge doorknob felt cold in her hand. *Go right in, say I'm sorry, and leave. Be firm, but tactful. This is stupid! If he doesn't take this the right way, I'll look even more like a fool. Coward! What did I just say? Go right in . . .*

"Hi, Karen. Ready for another day?" Nick greeted her as if she had never left. He glanced over his paper and ground out a cigarette in the ashtray.

"I'm dreading BAG tonight." She stood by the side of the table.

"What's that?"

"The committee you're chairman of."

"Oh, that. The case of the library piddler. What in the hell does BAG mean?"

"Behavior Amelioration Group."

"I don't like acronyms. I didn't know they called it that." He sounded interested, sincere. Maybe this wouldn't be so bad.

"I've been on dozens of Aneyh's committees. You can figure on giving up fifteen hours." Karen watched him, waiting for the opportune moment.

"I suppose," he said. "Well, I'll be there."

She trembled with indecision as he disappeared behind the newspaper.

"Nick, I need to tell you something. Will you listen?"

"Of course." He placed the paper on his lap, leaned back, and clasped his hands behind his head.

"I found out you weren't divorced. I asked you about your ex-wife in the cafeteria, when in fact she was... I don't know how to say this. I feel guilty. I don't like to hurt people's feelings." She managed to look straight at him. "I am sorry."

"Karen, don't." Nick shifted to the front of his chair. He looked at her sympathetically. "You didn't know. You have nothing to feel sorry about."

"That scene in the lounge has bothered me, too. I accused you of staring at my leg. You tried to explain something, and I jumped on you like a shrew. Don't tell me that was nothing because it has been to me."

Nick got to his feet and pulled two chairs back from the table. "Sit down, Karen, please."

She sat, placed her things on the table, and stared at him. Nick leaned toward her, his arms resting on the table. She picked up the pleasant aroma of aftershave, felt his breath on her face, and looked into those blue eyes.

"I have been watching you. I admit that. Sometimes you limp." He paused. "I thought you might have sprained your ankle. I also noticed that every time you came in here, you sat on your right leg." Nick pointed his newspaper toward her. "You're doing it now. At first I thought that might be an idiosyncrasy, something you may have picked up at the kindergarten pasting table. But about the fourth week of school, I followed you up the main staircase. You didn't know I was behind you. I saw your right leg and knew that you had had polio."

She listened uneasily, without comment.

He leaned closer. "Karen, this is very important to me. You've got to believe I wasn't staring at your misfortune. That would be crude. Whatever you may think of me, I would never embarrass you or anyone else that way."

"I do believe you." The words hurt her throat as she fought off tears. "What were you going to tell me in the lounge that morning?"

"Staring is your word, Karen, not mine. You see, there's more to this than you know."

A racket outside the door announced someone's approach.

Nick's fingers brushed across the top of her hand. "Some other time," he said quietly.

Darlene McGimpsey burst through the door like an entire vice squad. "Well, look who's back," she roared. "Get lonely without us, Karen?"

Karen picked up her things. At any other time, she would be glad to see Darlene, but this noisy intrusion on a very private moment seemed like meddling.

Darlene picked a chocolate from a box someone had left on the table. "These are delicious. Say," she said, licking her fingers and shooting a sly glance at Karen, "am I interrupting something here?"

"No, of course not." Karen stopped at the door. "See you at BAG tonight, Nick, and thanks."

eleven

Aneyh had had some crazy committees, but teachers believed this one, designed to soothe their angst over the library urinator, set a benchmark for zaniness. He had a certain facility for coining short, catchy acronyms for his committees, sometimes jockeying words around on a sheet of paper for hours. He dubbed this gathering "BAG"–Behavior Amelioration Group–and asked the five members to invent a building policy to prevent, not punish, breaches of acceptable behavior.

At least one committee met before or after school every day, often both. Teachers fought back in small ways. They gave Aneyh's latest committee an acronym of their own. VOID. Victory Over Indiscriminate Dribblers.

Karen plodded toward BAG's first after-school meeting like a prisoner sentenced to the dungeon, agonizing over the approaching hassle with Educationese. Members of Aneyh's committees were put there for a purpose. She was there, officially, to represent the department chairs. But he needed her to write up the final report correctly. George Moore was there to represent the counselors, but also because Aneyh had already emasculated him. He'd be no threat. Bob Melville, afraid of his own shadow, would go along with anything. Rick Cook, Aneyh's jock buddy, was a muscular rubber stamp. Nick Staal's appointment meant punishment; Aneyh hadn't forgotten the opening day meeting or the fiasco in the cafeteria. He had a built-in whipping boy in Nick, and he intended to use the crop.

"Good afternoon, Miss Merchant." Aneyh smiled sweetly. He stood in front of the men seated at one end of a library study table. "I was just telling these gentlemen about Chad Bergen's background. He's in our learning disabilities program, you know. His mother is single and on welfare, a disadvantaged family if I've ever seen one. He hasn't had the benefits that other children have. We need to be more aware of these social problems in our population. This is a good time to set a policy so that homeroom teachers can work with their students to prevent behavior like his in the future." Aneyh's face screwed into that grin which preceded a cliche. "An ounce of prevention is worth more than a pound of punishment, don't you think?"

She wondered why he'd asked. He already knew the answer.

"I'd like Bancroft to develop a paradigm"–Aneyh had recently discovered this word and worked it to death–"for the other schools. We could be leaders in this area of behavior amelioration, maybe present our plan at the next district in-service. You people could make quite a mark for Bancroft with that presentation."

"God, how can I stand this," Karen muttered silently as Nick Staal entered the library and dropped comfortably into one of the study table chairs.

"You're late for everything, aren't you, Mr. Staal?"

"Sorry. Two students came in for help."

"These committees," Aneyh shot back, "and any after-school meetings for that matter take precedence. Don't you understand that?"

"I'm beginning to catch on."

"Let's get started then," Aneyh said impatiently. "I'll turn this over to you, Mr. Staal, since you're the chair. This is your committee. Do whatever you think will enable us to make a decision on how we're going to help boys like this and others. I've been telling these people, Mr. Staal, before you graced us with your presence"—each time he said "Staal," the name dripped with sarcasm—"that this is a disadvantaged boy. He probably didn't even know what he was doing. We need to help people like this fit into society, don't we?"

His rhetorical sop did not hang for long. Although Aneyh looked at no one in particular, he got a quick answer from the chairman.

"Mr. Aneyh, in the civilized world, potty training is over at the age of four. What have we got here? A seventeen-year-old boy comes into this library and urinates on the floor. It's not because he's disadvantaged. It's an act of defiance. That that boy never received any punishment is an insult to the librarians. It's an insult to the rest of the student body, the five teachers at this table, and, above all, it's an insult to you, Mr. Aneyh, because you're in charge of this institution. Hell, he knew exactly what he was doing. If he weren't disadvantaged and had some money, he'd bet the whole wad that he could pee on the floor and get away unscathed. He doesn't need a wet nurse. He needs to be told what he can and cannot do around here."

Karen looked quickly at Aneyh's narrowing eyes, his hands squeezing into fists. Steam seemed to seep from his ears. "Go, Nick," she whispered. "Go, go. My God, this is really happening." She'd had fantasies about somebody waging battle with Aneyh like this. And here, right in front of her, Nicholas Staal, of all people, had delivered a broadside into the principal's flank.

Aneyh spoke slowly and deliberately. "I don't like the direction this is going, Staal." His pitch elevated with each word, and his eyes flashed with anger. "Didn't you hear what I just said?"

"Mr. Aneyh, you just said this is my committee. I'm in charge here."

George Moore, eyes popping as his glasses slipped toward the end of his nose, mouth agape with amazement, stared at Nicholas Staal. Bob Melville sent Nick looks that clearly indicated "stop now, you fool." Rick Cook shuffled uncomfortably in his chair and studied his Reeboks.

"We don't need to waste everybody's time," Nick said, ignoring the tension around the table. "I wrote up a motion last night. Let me read it. We can vote this up or down. 'Any student urinating and/or defecating in unauthorized places will be recommended for expulsion or transfer to another school.' There." He smiled. "Simple, concise, effective. If we agree, we'll turn this motion over to our principal for immediate action."

Karen could see the typewritten page with a line on the bottom for the committee chairman's signature.

"I don't like that at all," Aneyh yelled. "We take care of our own problems here. We don't send them elsewhere. Did you hear me? We don't send them elsewhere. This committee wouldn't like that. This committee wouldn't agree with that at all."

"Well, Mr. Aneyh, let's dispense with that uncertainty and see what they think. Raise your right hand if you're in favor."

Karen now understood something. Nick Staal had Aneyh's number. They had opposed each other twice, and on both occasions Aneyh had seemed disoriented. Nick had the whammy on Aneyh. He had stolen the initiative, and the principal didn't know how to stop him.

Staal raised his right hand.

Karen raised hers immediately after.

Rick Cook didn't look up.

Bob Melville shifted from side to side.

All eyes fell on George Moore, who held the

swing vote, and at Aneyh, who drummed his fingers menacingly on the table. George raised his clenched fist as high as his shoulder. Was he voting or not? Sweat glistening on his forehead betrayed the fear that a vote against his principal held for him. He squirmed, bit his lip, and tugged at his collar. Karen felt sorry for the little counselor. George Moore loathed the principal, but she didn't believe he had the guts for this.

"Well, damn it, Moore," Aneyh bellowed, "we take it you're voting against this idiotic motion."

The evil resonance in Aneyh's voice pushed George over the edge. His arm shot into the air and remained there defiantly. He glanced at the circle of people, took a deep breath, and sat back in his chair. Then George folded his arms over his chest. Years of frustration melted into the smile that covered his face.

"Three to two, a clear majority." Nick affixed his name to the statement with judicial solemnity and handed the paper to Aneyh. "This committee is disbanded." Nick turned and walked purposefully out of the library.

The other members rose quickly and followed him. Robert D. Aneyh stood by himself, the committee recommendation fluttering at his side in a trembling hand.

Karen ran down the hall. She had to get upstairs before David left. He'd never believe this.

twelve

Halls teeming with students were suddenly cavernous as the bell for last hour rang and stragglers dashed for classroom doors. Karen moved through the deserted corridor toward the supply room. She had sixth-hour planning, a time she often used for department business.

Today's headache dealt with missing supplies: two cartons of legal pads, a dozen boxes of transparencies, and eighteen bottles of White-Out, the entire year's inventory for the English department. Central Stores claimed the materials had been sent; Bancroft claimed no one had seen the goods or the invoice. Stuff like this took a lot of time.

Thick, locker-lined walls insulated classroom noise from the halls. But as she passed teachers' doors, little waves of sound dribbled out. A flurry of motion teased her peripheral vision. She noticed David doing his prance. He ranged back and forth between the windows and door, talked, waved his arms, paused midstep to drive home a point. Students' heads followed him across the room.

Mel Lichty's door was closed, the room dark except for a flickering light. He needed a doorknob sign—"Do not disturb. Audiovisual equipment in use." Mel, the perennial winner of the "Revolving Lesson Plan Award," showed a film or a video every day. Years ago someone bronzed an antiquated Bell & Howell 16mm projector and presented him with that trophy at a faculty dinner. No matter. He still rolled 'em.

Alice Cain's voice bubbled from the next doorway. Two hundred and fifty pounds of dynamic energy went into her presentations on economics. Alice had a following. Seniors fought to be in her classes and called her view of money and the national and world economies "Cainseonomics."

She heard the hollow click of chalk from the next room. Bancroft still had old-fashioned blackboards, and the scrape of chalk against slate produced an unmistakable sound. Her pace slackened outside Nick Staal's room. She didn't really want to eavesdrop. That would be a definite taboo, outside the bounds of professional decency. But something about this man made her do strange things. Here she was, snooping at his door.

Karen stood at the side and peeked through the glass window of the half-open door. Every chair in her line of sight was occupied, every eye focused on him. Nick was in Rome talking about class structure—patricians, plebeians, and slaves. Kids asked questions, took notes. When he strolled toward the door, Karen panicked and retreated. Nick Staal really was a teacher, not a dumb farmer as David had suspected. She had not known him well enough to have made that angry judgment in the lounge.

Karen did not walk by his door. There were other ways to get to the supply room.

thirteen

Frank Nolden's wife picked out his clothes. Last year he wore a turtleneck shirt or a sweater every day; this year he wore corduroy. Nolden, decked out in corduroy pants and sport coat, sat at the Lunch Bunch table inhaling a huge tuna sandwich. "You want in on a nasty little rumor?" he asked between bites. "Heard one at the coaches' meeting last night."

"Well, don't keep us on pins and needles." Lydia Fletcher polished a black patent leather purse from which she had taken a plastic zipper bag containing two pieces of broccoli. She didn't eat starchy school lunches but always showed up to keep abreast of news, gossip, and politics.

"Arletti from McGovern says we're headed for a seven-period day next year." Frank talked through a full mouth. "How's that grab you?"

"By the throat."

"Why, Alice? What do you mean 'by the throat'?"

Alice quit spooning soup. "You want another class of 30 kids, Lydia? I have 150 already."

"You don't know you'll have another class," Lydia said with a hint of condescension. "We had the seven-period day in middle school. We made it work, too. Anyway, you don't know you'll be teaching another class. Maybe you'll get another planning period."

"Wanna bet?" Nolden laid down his sandwich and blotted a spot on his jacket. "Everyone in middle school teaches six classes."

"How would you know, Frank?" Lydia flashed a knowing smile. "You've never been in middle school."

"I've never had syphilis either, but I know it's bad."

"See, see! You've never been there."

"Are you nuts? My sister-in-law's in middle school. Downtown duped them with the same crap you're peddling."

"I'm not peddling anything." Lydia folded her polishing cloth and dropped it in her purse. "I just think trashing every new program the way you people do is unprincipled."

"That's because you get off on every new program that comes along."

"I think I'm having a Maalox moment," Alice said.

"OK, Frank," Lydia said quickly. "Let's say for the sake of argument you did have to teach six classes. You could get around that."

"Yeah? How?"

"Tone down your objectives. If you have more students and less time, cut down on the assignments, give less homework."

"Fantastic, Lydia. Then everyone should shut his mouth about last year's buzz words. What were they now?" Frank scratched his head. "Oh, yes! Excellence in education."

"You just don't understand, Frank," Lydia said through pursed lips. "We could offer more electives with a seven-period day. Kids will have a larger menu, more choices."

"Oh, puke."

"I'm wasting my time, Frank. Why do you care anyway? You're just a basketball coach. You don't understand educational philosophy."

Everyone at the table looked up. Frank Nolden was an anomaly among Bancroft coaches, never discussing his sport unless asked a direct question. Although recognized throughout the city as a top-notch coach, Frank looked at basketball as a hobby. American history was his passion, and he could clear a room with detailed accounts about how he presented his subject.

Nolden pointed his sandwich at Lydia with an I'd-like-to-shove-this-up-your-rear look.

"Lydia," he said slowly, "you don't stick with anything long enough to even have a philosophy. I've heard about your playpen up there. You crack more pinatas than books. You don't know why you do anything, what you'll do tomorrow, or next week."

"That's not true," Lydia snapped.

"Anything works for you. Anything to fill up a class period." Nolden slammed the last of his sandwich into his mouth. "Ten years away from here hasn't changed you one bit, except maybe you have a better wardrobe."

"You're really mean, Frank." Lydia resealed one piece of broccoli in the bag, snapped her purse shut, and fled out the cafeteria door.

"Weren't you a little hard on her, Frank?" Alice asked.

"Hell, no. That Pollyanna attitude gets on my nerves."

"Maybe she's right," Alice told him.

"She doesn't have a clue. This isn't about helping kids. The seven-period day is about money." Nolden glanced around at the seven teachers. "They'll cram another class down each of our throats. That's twenty percent more work out of us for nothing! And every class you teach will have at least thirty kids. Think about that! Six of us teach an extra class apiece–they can pink slip another teacher! That's exactly the way it happened in middle school. Even the village idiot could understand that, which puts the village idiot a cut above Lydia."

"Don't you think kids will sign up for another elective?"

"Nope," snorted Darlene McGimpsey. "There'll be a run on study halls. We'll warehouse 'em. Just put 'em on a shelf and keep their mouths shut." Darlene checked the cafeteria clock. "Speaking of which, I've got warehouse duty in five minutes."

Karen drifted toward the cafeteria door, not amazed at all by the typical administrative ploy–a trial balloon wafting on the anguished cries of teachers, who would, as administrators knew, toss the idea around the system. Soon, Aneyh, following a directive from downtown, would descend on the faculty like a used car salesman extolling the orgasmic pleasures of teaching six classes instead of five. The seven-period day was a done deal.

Always more, Karen thought. More classes, more students, more work. "More" in plain English meant "less." Less class time, less time for individual attention. Frank was right. The seven-period day was smoke and mirrors to save money on teachers who were just pawns in an education chess game where all the moves were made by big-time administrators downtown.

Why didn't she have the guts to say no more to more!

fourteen

By a vote of seven to nothing, the Board of Education shipped Jeremy King back to Bancroft without a scratch. No punishment, no expulsion, not even an explanation for their lack of action other than "There are circumstances in this incident that teachers do not understand."

A distraught Alice Cain, perched on the dais like the Colossus of Rhodes, pleaded with Bancroft's members of the Des Moines Unified Teachers Organization to fight back. "We can't shut our mouths about this. We can't just roll over and play dead. What we can do is select a spokesperson to tell these people the truth, how their decision will scuttle morale all over this system. I've called DUTO's executive secretary," Alice fumed. "The board's legally bound to give us a hearing. And we're on the agenda for their next meeting. Someone has got to step forward and tell those fools what happens to discipline when they pull a stunt like this."

"We're on the agenda? For how long?" a teacher in front wanted to know.

"Fifteen minutes," Alice said sheepishly.

"Fifteen minutes? What can you say in fifteen minutes?"

"How 'bout just running them out of town?" offered another.

"Here, here."

"Tar and feather the jackasses."

"How much does a hit man cost?"

"Come on, you guys. One at a time," Alice demanded. "We need something constructive."

"Constructive!" said the teacher in front. "We get fifteen lousy minutes at a board meeting."

"She's right," yelled someone in the back. "If they change their minds, they'd lose face. We're wasting our time."

"You've got to be kidding! Let's not just sit around here on our butts; let's do something!"

"You're right. We've got to make a showing."

Alice tapped the podium for order. "Well, all right, then. We need someone here in this building to lay out our side of the case."

"Let David. He can rip their heads off."

"Yeah, how 'bout David!"

"David?" Alice looked at him beseechingly.

"Can't do it," David answered quickly.

"Are you sure?"

"Yup."

Her eyes stayed on David; he looked away. "We've got to have a volunteer." Alice scanned the group frantically. "We've got some awfully good people in this building. Come on, you guys."

No one stepped forward. The prospect of speaking before the board in open session cooled their passion. The meeting collapsed. As they left, some DUTO members grumbled about the hopelessness of fighting the board. A few gathered in knots around the room castigating the board's stupidity; others mumbled about hiring an attorney.

"David, Karen, wait." Alice removed her bulk from the dais and caught up with them at the door. "David, I wish you would reconsider. Please. You always cut through the muck and get right to the problem."

"I can't, Alice. Come on, you know what would happen. We're talking voluntary suicide here. If you told that bunch of fatheads what they needed to hear, you'd be through in this system." David moved through the door.

"Wait! You could be diplomatic. You don't have to pull the house in on your head."

"Look, Alice, diplomacy with that bunch means grovelling. That's what they expect teachers to do. They think they know more than we do. Go down there begging with hat in hand and they'll think you're sucking up. They might even think you want to be an administrator. I'd rather go to Siberia."

"OK, David. I'll find someone else."

"No, you won't. No one's got the balls to lecture the board, and you know that," he said over his shoulder.

Alice shook her head. "Whew! I misjudged him."

"Yes," Karen said, "but none of that is the reason he won't do it."

"What then?"

"Stick a microphone in David's face and he'd fill his pants. He doesn't have any courage, Alice."

"I don't either, Karen. I'm the building rep. I should make that speech. But I'm too fat. I'd be a blubbering idiot." Her massive bosom heaved with a deep sigh. "I don't know what to do."

"You could ask Nicholas Staal." His was the only name Karen had thought of while Alice pled for a volunteer. "You should have seen him handle Aneyh at the BAG meeting. He says all the things David says, but he says them where they count."

"Staal's a loner, Karen. He wouldn't do it. He's not even a DUTO member."

Karen shrugged. "Who knows. Look, we're talking board members here. You need someone tough."

"Yes, yes, I know."

"Then ask him."

Alice put on her coat and walked down the hall.

Karen could not remember a time when this exuberant, optimistic friend had appeared so defeated. "Alice," she said consolingly, "you did all you could do. Go home. Get a good night's sleep."

Alice appeared at Karen's door at the end of third period and pulled her from the pathway of students passing in and out of the classroom. "Karen, he said he would."

"Who? Would do what?"

"Nick. I saw him early, before school started, and explained what we needed. You know, someone to state our case before the board."

Karen nodded.

"And all he said was 'OK.' That's all. Can you believe that? No hesitation or 'let me think it over.' He just said OK like I'd asked him to hand me a book. Do you think we can trust him?"

"Yes."

"I'm not so sure. Hattie Reins came upstairs after second period and handed Nick a note from Aneyh. He showed me. Aneyh wants to see him after school at three o'clock. You know that dirty louse will tell him what to say. This isn't Aneyh's speech, Karen; it's ours. We really don't know Nicholas Staal. He might betray us."

"You don't know that, Alice. Look, I heard him cut through administrative crap at that committee meeting like he packed a switchblade."

"But this speech is so important. You know how Aneyh is. He might make Nick say…"

"OK, Alice, you give the speech."

Alice started down the hall for her fourth period class. "My reputation's on the line here, you know. I picked him," she said over her shoulder. "This could be a horrible mistake."

"Mr. Staal," Hattie Reins announced with an edge in her voice, "Mr. Aneyh has been waiting for ten minutes."

"Tell him to hold on. I'm just about finished up here."

Nick's voice blasting over the intercom etched a contemptuous scowl on the secretary's face. Hattie Reins relished her power in the Bancroft office. She strutted around her domain like a mother hen clucking instructions to assistant secretaries and student helpers. Few staff members chose to tangle with her. Hattie's usefulness to Robert Aneyh came in her ability to screen appointments and phone calls. Any teacher who fidgeted in front of Hattie's desk waiting for an audience with the head man knew the mission could be compromised by a glance from her in the principal's direction.

This time Hattie had no opportunity to glance or anything else as Nicholas Staal breezed by her desk into the principal's office.

"Come right in, Nick." Aneyh bounced from behind his desk and shook Nick's hand vigorously. He nodded toward a couch across the room. "Sit down. Would you like a cup of coffee? Hattie, bring us some coffee, would you, please?"

His office was a barren room. When he came to Bancroft ten years ago, he made a big deal about rearranging the furniture, and for ten years not one thing had been moved or changed. The room's two couches faced each other, a worn arm chair on one end and a coffee-stained table covered with Phi Delta Kappa magazines in the middle. He called this sterile arrangement of furniture the conversation pit. His desk remained conspicuously aloof at the far end of the room. When teachers appeared at his door, he went into his act of administrative paternalism. He invited them to relax in the pit while he would rise in a studied display of his own humanity, stride benevolently around from his side of the desk, and plop himself gratuitously across from them. David figured this gesture had something to do with removing himself as an authoritative figure, a move Aneyh had probably picked up in Administration 101. Had there not been a garish picture of himself hanging above a vase of plastic roses perched on a Victorian pedestal, this ploy might have worked. But in these surroundings most teachers felt they were in the presence of a third-world dictator.

Not everyone received an invitation to the pit. Those on Aneyh's hit list were upbraided while standing at attention in front of his desk. The faculty called these verbal muggings "crucifixions."

"Nick, you and I have had our little differences," said Aneyh, forcing a laugh. "We need to bury the hatchet. After all, we're playing on the same team. We need to look out for each other."

Nick sat on one couch looking across at Aneyh on the other.

"We have a marvelous opportunity to show the board what a fine school we have here, that the King boy's not typical of our students." Aneyh looked at Nick hopefully. "You've certainly noticed that, haven't you, even in the short time you've been with us?"

Nicholas Staal sat impassively with his hands on his knees.

"Why, yes, yes, of course you have." Aneyh pulled a notepad from his inside pocket. "Now, Nick, I've taken time to jot down some ideas here. You might want to consider them when you prepare your remarks."

He paused to sip his coffee, adjusted his glasses, and began to read.

"First, you should compliment the board members on the great service they're rendering to the system and thank them for the many fine things they've done for us in the past. Second, tell them what a great program we have here, what opportunities we offer kids. Third, when you address them, don't make demands. Use the word 'respectfully' or 'suggestion.' 'Humble' is always a good one. You know," continued Aneyh, loosening the knot of his tie, "the whole city will be watching you. You've got an excellent chance here to advance your career. Have you ever considered administration? If you play your cards right, this might be just the exposure you need."

He paused for a breath. "We thought we were right in this King matter, of course. But there are other points of view. You have to remember that. You have the makings of a fine team player." Aneyh stood and paced between the couches. "Now, Nick, I'll be there. I'll be right behind you. If you need any help, don't hesitate to call on me. I can be of help to you in many ways." He looked at his listener expectantly. "Well, what do you think, Nick?"

During Aneyh's presentation, neither Staal's position nor expression had changed. "Thank you very much, Mr. Aneyh," he said, getting to his feet. "You can be assured I'll consider everything you've said. And thank you for the coffee."

"But you didn't drink any," Aneyh said, looking at Nick's full cup.

"No, I never do, but you were very thoughtful."

"Atta boy, Nick." Aneyh clapped him on the back. "We'll make a good team."

The incident at Bancroft High, covered thoroughly by the media, generated interest across the community. The president of the board, anticipating a large gathering, moved the hearing from the board meeting room to McGovern High, which had the district's largest auditorium. Each session followed a published agenda which on this occasion allowed fifteen minutes to a representative for the teachers.

"Jesus, Alice, you just went through a red light. Why don't you watch what you're doing?" David monitored Alice's driving from the front seat. He, Alice, Karen, and Darlene were carpooling to McGovern High.

"Why don't you shut up. I was halfway through the intersection."

"Halfway? I'd hate to have you divide up the candy."

"Anyway, I'm nervous. I'm the one who chose the speaker."

"How do you suppose Nick Staal feels right about now?" Darlene wondered. "I'd hate to be in his shoes."

"Aw, it wouldn't be so bad."

"Oh, sure, now you change your story, David. When I get this car stopped, I'm going to sit on you."

"Oh, no. No. Not that. Please."

"Will you two quit fighting," Darlene snapped. "I'd like to get there in one piece."

Karen stared at the oncoming cars on the bridge spanning the Raccoon River and the shimmering reflection of lights on the water. The skyline danced and blurred as Alice maneuvered in the traffic. Leafless trees on the streets flashed by like fence posts. McGovern High was on the other side of the city, but Karen was in no hurry. She'd almost made herself sick thinking about Nicholas Staal and his speech all day. Karen knew she could never face the board with the entire city looking on—thanks to the media—not in ten lifetimes. She had a crawly feeling Nicholas Staal was being led to the slaughter and felt culpable because she had suggested him.

All she could do was watch. Like the time her older sister appeared as Emily in the school production of *Our Town*. Karen remembered praying her sister would be a star. In the present case, however, she didn't believe prayers or anything else could bend the minds of these board members once they had issued a decision. Worse, the board might turn hostile and embarrass him. What she wanted to believe was that Nick would prove himself in McGovern's auditorium, which she'd begun to view as a lions' den.

"How could seven intelligent people come up

with a decision like this in the first place?" Karen asked abruptly.

"Maybe 'intelligent' is the operative word."

"No, I'm serious, Darlene. This makes no sense."

David stuck his head into the back seat. "Maybe King caught one of the board members humping a goat."

"You're impossible!" Darlene pushed his head toward the front seat.

"Oh, you want me to get serious. OK. I'll tell you why. School boards used to listen to professional educators. They do damn little of that any more. They paid no attention to the superintendent in this case now, did they? As a matter of fact, they made him look like an ass. The board members want their prying fingers in everything–micromanage–oversee every stinking detail."

"Boy, that's the truth," agreed Darlene.

David unbuckled his seatbelt and stuck his shoulders between the seats. "You know what we've got here? Seven do-gooders who live out there in Ken and Barbie Land. They don't know or care what happens to us. We get our marching orders from a bunch of bleeding hearts who never marched into a classroom."

"That's an old one, David," Alice said.

"Maybe, but it's the truth. Just keep your eyes on the traffic."

"I know parents have changed," Darlene said. "They don't even mess with principals anymore. If they don't get what they want, they go straight to the board."

"That's what old lady King did," David said. "The board thinks we can save every kid who crawls into a classroom, even if he's an asshole."

"We know all that," Alice said. "Why didn't you have the guts to say this stuff to the board tonight, big man?"

David ignored her. "Look at that collection of jerks. They're nothing but elected amateurs. Half of them wanted on the board because they had axes to grind. A couple of 'em are on ego trips. One wants a board experience to put on his resume. He thinks he's going places. Then there's Mrs. What's-her-face, got sick of bridge parties and needed a new game to play."

"My word, look at the cars," Alice said, pulling into the McGovern parking lot. "Good thing we carpooled." She squeezed into a small space and pulled her keys from the ignition. "Now be careful getting out, David. Don't ding the car next—" Alice sat back abruptly. "I just had a horrible thought."

"Yeah, what?"

"Nick Staal. He's late for everything. What are we going to do if he's late for this?"

"I don't want to worry you, Brunhilde, but if he drove all the way to Adair County to feed his cows, then back again, he might be."

"Well, you can quit worrying," Karen said. "Look. Over there—four or five rows over." Parked among some of the car world's latest creations was an old red pickup truck.

The auditorium, which seated around 2,000, filled

rapidly. A conference table bristling with seven microphones stretched across the stage. In the main aisle facing the stage stood a small podium equipped with a microphone and a reading light.

"I can't believe all these people." McGimpsey had picked out four seats. She looked behind them. "The balcony's filling up."

"Hey, look over there," Alice pointed across the auditorium, "by the television cameras and news reporters. It's Aneyh."

"Sure," David said. "He wants his kisser on the late news."

Aneyh, dressed in a well-cut dark suit, smiled benignly and glad-handed acquaintances. A slender woman stood next to him. From across the auditorium she looked stylishly coifed and impressive in a trim navy blue jacket, matching straight skirt, and a shawl-collared white blouse. Each time the woman turned toward Aneyh, her gold hoop earrings gleamed in the auditorium lights. The woman, who appeared younger than the principal, also worked the crowd.

"Who's that?" Darlene wondered.

"Maybe that's Mrs. Aneyh," Alice said.

"You've got to be kidding," David said. "He doesn't let her out in public. This woman's too classy for him."

"They're sitting down together."

"Good, we can keep an eye on them."

The crowd settled down as the board members filed onto the stage with briefcases and stacks of papers. When they finally finished fussing and adjusting their microphones, the board president looked at the crowd and gaveled for attention.

"This meeting of the board of directors is now in session. The Des Moines Unified Teachers Organization requested to be a part of tonight's agenda. That will be the first order of business." She nodded at the board secretary. "Mr. Nicholas Steele, you have the floor."

"Jesus Christ," hissed David, "they can't even get his name right."

"Shush, David," Alice warned.

Karen looked around for Nick. He rose from a seat near the main aisle, stepped behind the podium, and turned off the reading light.

"Why'd he do that?" Alice asked.

Darlene shrugged. "Probably he doesn't have any notes—maybe he doesn't want to look like a jack-o-lantern—I don't know. God, you're more nervous than he is, Alice. Listen."

"I represent not only Bancroft Senior High School," began Nick Staal, his deep voice filling the auditorium, "and the rest of Des Moines' 1,500 teachers, but also those parents who demand and expect a first-class educational system." He held a piece of paper over his head. "I've read your agenda. Thirty minutes allotted for a discussion of dental supplies, a thirty-minute demonstration on improving phone etiquette among employees, fifteen minutes on new silverware for Gates School, forty-five minutes on whether or not a young chap at the traditional school can wear pants with holes in the knees, and an hour set aside for the election of a new board president. You have some weighty educational issues here this evening, ladies and gentlemen. I now understand why the assembled teachers of Des Moines are entitled to a mere fifteen minutes."

An undercurrent of laughter, a smattering of applause rippled around the auditorium. Teachers had been furious all week by such a meager piece of the agenda pie.

"Since time is crucial, we must, then, come right to the point. In the case of Jeremy King, the board has made a grievous error. You must reverse it."

That short sentence brought the excited audience to its feet. Here was a teacher, their spokesman, who knew exactly what needed to be said and said it.

"Go get 'em, Nick!" David thumped the chair back in front of him with his knee until Alice Cain pulled him into his seat by the back of his belt.

As the crowd settled in their chairs, Karen glanced at Aneyh, now slumped in his seat, his head and neck disappearing into his lapels. The woman in navy blue whispered to him and patted his shoulder.

Nick went on. "We're not talking about a kid who threw a spitball. We're discussing a student who willfully pushed Vice Principal Delaney down the stairs, fracturing his collarbone. A student who has subsequently been charged in criminal court. A student who under our uniform code of discipline could be and should be denied further educational privileges in this school system."

Shouts of "yes, yes" and "way to go" punctuated the protracted applause like rifle shots.

"Only the disciplinary code," Nick said, looking directly at the president, "stands between us and the jungle. Three of you sitting on the stage helped shape that code; and one of you sitting there ballyhooed the code in the press as 'a fine document, one that will bring order and stability to our schools.' And now you have violated not only the letter but the spirit of your own code. Why? Your reason, so you say, is because there are 'issues in this case that teachers don't understand.' Well, what are they? Tell us." He paused and waited for an answer that didn't come. "Are the people who implement your rules so incompetent they cannot be trusted? Are decisions such as this to be settled in the House of Lords with no explanation for the common folk?

"I'll tell you what is not understood here. Members of the board, you do not understand that teachers are the only ones who really do understand."

The feverish enthusiasm that overwhelmed the auditorium had little effect on the board. Not one member had yet looked directly at the speaker. Some scribbled notes; some rummaged in their briefcases. The president had reached for her gavel on several occasions, but apparently thought better of using it. And one member, the board's most recent addition, constantly rolled on his chair like a rider with a burr under his saddle. In all, they looked aloof and disinterested, as if they were no part of this proceeding.

"This isn't the Old West. Teachers don't wear guns on their hips although we take them away from students more frequently each year. We have the law. What we need is a marshal willing to enforce it. Ladies and gentlemen of the board, your job is to make the law stick.

"Over the years society has nibbled away at our authority. Oh, do we know that students have rights. We can't tell them how to dress, we can't control their language, we can't make them show up. Sometimes you won't even let us give failing grades for failing performance. You have made us settle for mediocrity. But surely you'll help us stop them from breaking our bones."

From the last row of the balcony, a teacher screamed through cupped hands, "Amen, brother. Hallelujah!"

"Well, there goes the separation of church and state," David laughed. "Jesus, Staal's great. He's bustin' them right between the eyes."

"No he isn't, David. He's a hick and a farmer."

"All right, Karen, so I missed one. But I'm right ninety-nine percent of the time."

Nick went on. "Only two weeks ago the president of this board stood before television cameras. 'Distressful!' Her adjective for the performance of American students when measured against the scores of Europeans and Asians. Her remedy? Bring world class education to this city.

"World class education! Magic words, those. But we can't have world class education by just bringing the words into town. World class means high standards. Academic standards, yes, but also behavioral standards. Standards that cannot be circumvented by every interest group that walks through a school door, or by parents who would rather meddle than make their children behave.

"Board members, you should stand in our shoes. For two decades critics have had their glory years. American teachers have been castigated, maligned, ridiculed, pilloried–Johnny can't read, can't write, can't find Kentucky on a map. The time has come for teachers to scream from the rooftops. This has nothing to do with us. The teaching corps is not incompetent; the system is. This system won't let teachers teach!"

The reaction to this dramatic assertion seemed almost orchestrated. Every teacher was on his feet. Karen, standing with the rest, savored the moment, a memory she wanted to keep. This was the same Nicholas Staal who had taken over Aneyh's committee. Now, this triumph brought tears to her eyes.

Karen scanned the crowd. At this moment she felt ecstatic for the Des Moines teaching corps. At long last, they had a mouthpiece, a man on a white horse, who in the presence of the board and under the glare of television cameras, championed a cause they knew was right. And they were responding. This was more than a speech; this was a release of their frustrations, a collective catharsis.

The board president, gavel in hand, glanced nervously at her watch, indicating that Nicholas Staal had exceeded his time. He ignored the body language.

"At the same time you people sitting on the stage blather about world class education, you also co-opt teachers' time and content by forcing them into the laboratories of social experimentation. European and Asian teachers couldn't do any better in Des Moines than we do. Let's beam over fifteen hundred of them, the creme de la creme, endow them with the gift of English, then dump on them what you have dumped on us. Multicultural non-sexist training, drug abuse prevention, death education, suicide prevention, child abuse awareness, global education, teenage pregnancy prevention, alternate lifestyle sensitivity, students at risk awareness, study hall, ticket taking, pep assemblies, chaperoning, sexual harassment prevention, lunch room supervision, overcrowded classes, hostile students, and the list goes on.

"Those foreign teachers would be pulverized by the sheer enormity of these diversions. European and Asian parents don't expect teachers to cure the evils of society. They expect teachers to teach. If you saddled European teachers with the social architecture of our curriculum, their patrons would scream to high heaven. I can see it now: German citizens storming Unter den Linden, fuming with Teutonic rage. 'Ach, mein Gott! Johann can't find Berlin on a map!'"

"You're the man, Steele. You're the man," shouted someone sitting close to the podium.

Nick stepped back as a deafening roar of shouts,

whistles, and clapping filled the auditorium.

"Oh, Karen," Alice yelled through the din, "this is marvelous." She pointed to the seven board members. "Look at them sitting there like a bunch of zombies. You know they've got to be boiling inside."

"Alice. Ssssh."

"Members of the board, when you leave this hall tonight, this decision will touch your lives no longer. But the teachers of Des Moines will wrestle with its consequences every teaching day. If you let your decision stand, you're allowing every student one free whack at a teacher."

The gavel crashed upon the table several times in rapid succession. "Mr. Steele," said the board president curtly, "you are out of time."

"Madame President," Nick shot back, "what you say is prophetic. We are out of time. This is the eleventh hour for public education. All around us private academies with their strict codes of behavior and high expectations are chipping away at our talent, our money, and support. Talk of school-choice and vouchers is rampant. Maybe it's too late. The teachers sitting here don't think so. Ladies and gentlemen of the board, you give us the tools, and we will give you world class education."

Nicholas Staal turned on the podium light and returned to his seat. The board president rapped her gavel for order as the applause continued for several minutes. Finally, most of the teachers filed out of the auditorium. The stoic expressions on board members' faces had not changed.

Quiet returned. The president was at her microphone. "Thank you, Mr. Steele. Next on the agenda our report on dental supplies."

"Christ," David said. "The board's gonna have to read the morning paper to find out who spoke here tonight. They don't get anything right. Come on, let's get out of here."

The excitement spilled into the lobby where teachers, exuberant at hearing the board lectured by one of their own, slapped backs and gripped each other's hands. The consensus emerging from conversations throughout the lobby seemed to be that finally someone had artfully articulated their problems in straightforward, hard-hitting prose. David and the three women listened for awhile as reporters taped interviews.

"Look, there goes Aneyh," David said. "Boy, does he look pissed. Let's follow him out."

"Where's Mrs. Aneyh?" Alice wondered.

"Ah ha! That wasn't old lady Aneyh," David said. "He wouldn't have left her in there."

"I'll bet he wishes he could do this over again." Darlene held the foyer door open. "If he'd known what the board was going to do, the King case would have never left the building."

Alice and Karen followed behind in the chilly night air as the four walked between parked cars. Alice, relaxed and cheerful, was satisfied with what had happened inside. "Nick was so good, Karen. Surely the board members will change their minds now."

"You never know about that bunch."

"I did something wonderful when I picked him, didn't I, Karen?"

"Yes, Alice, you did something wonderful."

"Oh, Karen, don't you just love Nicholas Staal!"

Karen was stunned by how Alice's off-hand exclamation struck her. Alice meant love in the platonic sense, of course. But how did she, Karen Merchant, mean the inane "yes" that jumped from her lips in response? Her perception of Nicholas Staal as a boor seemed light years ago.

Each day Karen made several aimless trips by his classroom, and she felt giddy at his rare appearances in the cafeteria. The sound of his voice created a feeling in her different from any other emotion she'd known. Truthfully, she did not know what was happening to her, if anything was happening, or what to do if it were. This man had become an important part of her life whether she wanted him to be or not.

"Hey, David!"

"Hi, Roger."

"Who's that?" Alice asked.

"Roger Selby from Castelar."

"Some speech," Roger shouted. "Where'd you people find that guy, anyway?"

"We brought him up from the farm team."

"Tell him the teachers at Castelar want him to run for office. Nicholas Steele for President!"

"Damn it, Roger, it's Nicholas Staal."

"Oh. Who cares what his name is. We still want him for President. See you later, buddy."

David waved.

"Wait! What's the matter with me?" Alice stopped in her tracks. "I must be in a daze! I'm so excited I forgot all about Nick. That's terrible. Let's go back in there and congratulate him. We should take him out for a drink or something. Come on, you guys."

"It's too late, Alice," Karen said. "Look, his truck's gone."

David stared at the empty space. "Who was that masked man?"

fifteen

Six ugly concrete columns guarded Bancroft's cafeteria like silent titans. They supported a reinforced floor of concrete and steel for the woodshop directly above. Anyone resting against one of these could feel the vibrations produced by table saws, band saws, and drill presses, but the industrial racket never seeped into the eating space below. An assortment of noises coming from five hundred students each lunch period along with a jukebox threw up an acoustical barrier.

On this day, not every student laughed or talked. David studied a pensive couple close to the Lunch Bunch table staring blankly at the grey Formica tabletop. A sly smile creased his lips. "Lydia," he announced, "you owe me five bucks."

"I do not." Lydia pawed at a piece of broccoli. "I've never borrowed any money from you. You never have any."

"Do you welch on bets?"

"What are you talking about?"

"You bet five bucks she wouldn't get pregnant."

"Who?"

"Ms. Hormone."

He nodded at the couple, and Lydia watched them for a few moments.

"You don't know that. She doesn't look pregnant to me."

"Lydia, Lydia, Lydia." David assumed his professorial manner. "Listen and learn."

"Oh, God," Frank Nolden said. "I feel a lecture coming on. Alice, do you want the rest of those french fries?"

"Take 'em."

"Observe," David went on, "Monsieur Le Gearhead. See the doleful look like his dog had been shot. Notice the absence of bravado, of small talk, of all talk. What you have here are two deaf mutes languishing in mutually imposed celibacy. A month ago when the scent hit his nostrils, he rutted around her like a goat in heat. The wanton urge went from his brain to the crotch of his greasy pants in a nano second."

"Man overboard!" Frank said.

Lydia shook her head. "You're cruel, David. They're just a young couple in love."

"What the hell do they know about love? Shitty diapers, that's what they're thinking about, a squalling, screeching kid, no money, and how the hell to break the news to their parents. And he's trying to figure out how many women he could have screwed if it weren't for this god-awful mess."

"I've heard enough." Lydia turned toward Karen

and Darlene with a rescue-me look.

"Ask Nicholas Staal, Lydia. You think he knows everything. He could tell you when a heifer's stuck."

"Listen." Lydia turned to face him again. "If you think that pitiful analysis is going to con five bucks out of me, you're crazy."

"Fine. I can wait."

"You'll have to," Lydia snapped with a tone of indignant outrage. "You have no expertise in these matters."

"Here comes a guy full of expertise." Darlene nodded toward Hal Delaney, just entering the cafeteria. An outsider at the Lunch Bunch table would immediately sense the respect this klatch of teachers held for him by simply watching their faces brighten.

Alice pulled out a chair. "Hal, we'd offer you something to eat, but Frank's cleaned up everyone's tray."

"Thanks, I'm not hungry." Delaney sat beside her. "I've got some bad news. Jeremy King will be back tomorrow. The board wouldn't budge."

"God."

"No, no."

"Can't you do something, Hal?"

"I just came from the principal's office, Alice."

Delaney stared at them like a man who had just had a knife shoved in his back. "The boss told me there would be no more incidents, he meant like this one, that would bring discredit or negative publicity to Bancroft. He told me that this incident was my fault, that I'd handled it poorly. He's making a full report for my file. I don't fit in any more, Alice. I don't understand these New Age administrators. They want to help kids over every little puddle. I choke on their educationese and their smiley-face stickers."

"He can't do that to you," Alice said.

Delaney got to his feet. "Alice, you've been around here long enough to know that Robert Aneyh can do whatever he wants to do." The vice principal smiled. "One thing has emerged from all of this. I've learned who my friends are." He winked at Alice. "I want to thank you, people, for everything you did for me. I'll never forget it. You're one hell of a group."

He slapped Frank's shoulder. "I'd better get out of here before this gets maudlin. But if any of you ever have a problem, get your butt to my office. I'll do everything I can." Delaney picked up a solitary french fry from Frank's tray, popped it into his mouth, and headed for the exit.

"I can't believe this," Karen said. "Aneyh just turned on Hal Delaney."

"Here's a hypothetical." Alice made a steeple out of her fingers and rested them against her lips. "King smashes a student's face or rips a girl's blouse off. Delaney's credibility is gone. What's he do? Bow and say, 'As you wish, sir'?"

"No, he lets Aneyh handle it."

"Right. He'd form a committee."

"We haven't got at the real demons yet," Darlene told them.

"Who?"

"The board. Aneyh's a butt-covering sycophant. If the board had jerked King out of here like they should have, Aneyh wouldn't punish Hal. He'd kiss his behind."

"Don't waste any bile on them," David harumphed. "The board's legally blind. They just overlooked an assault on an administrator. Now tell me, what would it take for them to get rid of a kid? Murder? A ninth grader at McGovern, a real bitch, told a teacher to go fuck herself last week. She wasn't even suspended."

"Don't get graphic, David."

"Go to hell, Lydia. Kids can say 'fuck' or anything else they want to. So why can't I?"

"Because you know better."

"Hey, you guys," Karen said quickly, "we don't need a fight over this."

"These kids will never know better unless they're punished."

"David, please, they're just kids."

Frank Nolden, who hadn't uttered a word since Delaney left, suddenly became agitated. "Lydia, you're a guileless little snit. You're part of the problem. And everyone else like you. Why don't you quit this job and run for the board. 'They're just kids,'" Nolden mimicked. "You make me want to puke. In God's name, when are these kids going to be held responsible for something? For anything? Tell me, Lydia. When?" Nolden's fiery eyes burned into Lydia Fletcher.

"I'm fed up with this liberal shit. Where in the

hell have you been, anyway? Public schools have turned out two generations of slobs. But you wouldn't have noticed—you're too busy chirping about the latest educational gimmicks. Do you understand what the board just did to Delaney? They don't give a damn about us! No one out there's got the nuts to get us off this highway to hell. And, Lydia, you don't even care!"

Nolden tossed a napkin on his tray. "David, take this back for me, will you." He hurried through the student tables and stiff-armed the cafeteria door.

Lydia Fletcher's face turned red. Student laughter and the clang of trays being emptied in the kitchen bore down on the silent table.

Highway to hell. Dante's *Inferno,* this week's focus for her Advanced English classes, played with Karen's mind. "This swamp that breeds and breathes the giant stench that surrounds this place of sorrow, which now we cannot enter without anger."

Karen added her own corollary: And teachers shall have no dominion over education, saith the board.

sixteen

"Sixty-five trees." The classroom clock clicked to quarter after six in the morning. "Sixty-five trees every semester to feed this paper waste. They should make these forms out of corn. I'd be rich." Nicholas Staal scribbled grades and names on Form 13s, the numerical euphemism for failing slips. "Copies in duplicate, in triplicate, in quadruplicate. Now let's see. The white copy to the parents, the salmon-colored copy to the vice principal, the registrar gets the blue, the canary-colored to the counselor."

He looked up.

"How long have you been standing there?" Nick said, flipping his pen to the desk. "How's the counseling racket?"

"All right." George Moore smiled sheepishly from the doorway. "I didn't want to interrupt. I enjoyed your monologue."

"Damn it, George, you shouldn't eavesdrop on a guy talking to himself."

The little man pushed his glasses to the bridge of

his nose. "Are you alone?"

Nick looked over his shoulder, then out at the empty room. "Yes," he whispered, "I'm alone."

George stepped backward into the hallway, looked both directions, and ducked through the door. "How many chairs in here, Nick? This room is packed."

"Thirty-five. You know how many. You funnel 'em in here. Thirty-five in every class except one. The extra kid in fourth hour gets to use my desk. Five periods a day. One hundred and seventy-six kids."

"It's not my fault, Nick. I divide 'em up evenly. We need more teachers."

"Yeah, right."

George slid into a student chair in front of Nick's desk. He traced the pencil trough with his finger. "How were your crops this year?"

"You didn't come in here to talk about the price of corn."

George left the desk and walked toward the windows with his hands in his pockets. After staring outside for a few moments, he turned around and leaned against the window ledge. "I'm going to come right out with this, Nick. Someone in this building's after you."

"Hmmm. What's she look like?"

George paced away from the window nervously. "Now listen, this is important. I'm trying to help you."

"Oh? Go ahead."

"Well, I was here until five o'clock last night

waiting for my wife to pick me up—my car's in the shop—I'm looking out of the office windows—do you understand?—trying to get a glimpse of her so I can run right out there—there's no parking in front."

"I'm still with you."

"No one knew I was there. Now, Aneyh's door's open, and I hear him get on the phone. I'm not spying or anything—I wouldn't do that—but I overheard him. I couldn't help it." George paused and looked directly at Nick. "Aneyh said, 'I'm going to get rid of that son of a bitch.' You've got to be careful, Nick."

"How do you know he wasn't talking about you, George?"

"He didn't mean me; he meant you."

"Do you think I'm a son of a bitch?"

"Now quit that, Nick! I don't know who was on the other end, but Aneyh talked about that speech you gave. He said, 'I'll get rid of that bastard before this year's out.' Nick, I'm telling you, you've got to be on your toes," George said passionately. "I've been here twenty-five years, ten years with Aneyh. He's meaner than snot. What do you think you can do?"

"Nothing, George. I'm already a terminal case."

"How do you mean?"

"They want to get rid of me. They've shoved me around to seven schools hoping I'll quit."

"They can't get rid of you, Nick," George said indignantly. "You're an outstanding teacher. All the kids tell me that."

"That doesn't have a damn thing to do with anything." Nick boosted his feet on the desk and leaned back on the chair. "They don't care what you do in the classroom, whether you're good or awful. They don't care as long as you don't bring parents down on them screaming like banshees, as long as you don't send too many kids to the office. And for Christ's sake, keep your mouth shut. Don't argue with an administrator or you'll be branded a troublemaker. How dare a teacher think! Board members know things. Administrators and consultants know things. Teachers? They're just grunts and damn well better learn their place." Nick looked at the clock. "I'm making another speech, George. I've got to get these forms filled out before the kids get here."

"I know all that, Nick. I know this system stinks. They've ruined public education. Look at me. I do everything but counsel. Aneyh's made a mouse out of me. Every time he snaps his fingers I squeak. I'm afraid of him." George shuffled his feet again and looked at the floor. "I know there's guys around here that laugh at me, talk behind my back. For ten years I've hated to come to this building—every day I've hated it—until this year." George looked at Nick. "I've gotten some courage from you." His voice quavered. "You made me feel important at that committee meeting—like I had a job to do—like a real man. For the first time in ten years I felt good about myself. I came in here to tell you this 'cause—well—I don't want you to leave."

George abruptly ended the dialogue and moved quickly through the door.

Nick heard the little man's footsteps tapping

down the hall. He jumped from his chair and hurried to the door. "Hey, George," Nick yelled at the retreating figure. "You're one hell of a guy."

Nick watched him disappear around the corner. From the doorway he surveyed the thirty-five chairs packed into the small classroom and the mountain of forms covering his desk. He wondered about what George had said, not what George had heard Aneyh say, but why Aneyh would toy with the spirit of a good man like George Moore.

seventeen

After eighteen years behind the desk, George Moore had escaped the drudgery of grading geometry proofs night after night by earning a counseling degree. His decision to leave the classroom had not come without soul-searching. He enjoyed interacting with young people and did not want to lose that contact. Counseling gave him an out; he escaped the blizzard of papers and yet retained the personal contact with students that meant so much to him. Because of this choice George looked forward to the remaining years of his career.

During Robert D. Aneyh's first year at Bancroft, George suspected Adam Boresi, a tenth-grade counselee, of malingering. He missed two out of every four school days. But Adam always returned to the academic wars armed with an excuse from his mother. Adam had a sore throat, Adam had diarrhea, had a headache, backache, bellyache. George scheduled five appointments with Adam, whom he had begun to call the artful dodger, but the dodger was always gone on appointment day.

An impatient man with a gravelly voice had picked up at Mrs. Boresi's work number. No. He had not seen her, and he made one thing very clear: she would mend her ways or he would damn well can her.

George had no idea how many times he rang the Boresi home before he caught the mother. She peppered him with parental woes, the high cost of doctors' fees, the price of food, rent, electricity, what she had to pay for cablevision, and what she had to pay in general to rear children in this economic climate. George squeezed in a suggestion, an evaluation of Adam's illnesses by the district medical team, at no cost to her.

Thirty seconds of indignation spewed along the wire, followed by a loud click. George sighed and washed his hands of this case by dropping the matter in the truant officer's lap.

The day after parent conferences in November, the new principal summoned George to his office to participate in an incident that the faculty later dubbed "The Crucifixion," an incident which gave them a preview of the governance that they might expect from their new leader.

Aneyh sat at his desk. His finger tapped a sheaf of papers. "Moore, you've been harassing a parent."

"What?"

"That woman cornered me last night. Thanks to you, she's fed up with Bancroft. She's pulling her kid out of here and sending him to St. Mary's."

"Mr. Aneyh," said the confused counselor, "I don't know which mother you mean."

"Mrs. Borsesi," Aneyh shot back.

"Oh, you mean Boresi." Now George knew what the principal was talking about. "Let me fill you in on that."

"You badgered that woman on the phone about her son's attendance. She knows the boy is sick. And what in the hell is this about a district medical evaluation?"

"The boy's name is Adam, Mr. Aneyh. He's absent two or three days a week." George tried to focus. "I just thought perhaps they needed help finding medical assistance."

"He's sick all right. He's been diagnosed, school phobia. If you'd been doing your job, you would have known that. His records state that clearly, and I have them right here." Aneyh roiled the air with the sheaf of papers. "He has a condition that makes him afraid to come to school. He cries if teachers won't let him leave class. What's the matter with you? Don't you check your students' records?"

"I've never seen those records, Mr. Aneyh," George said, looking at his feet. "There's always a lag time when kids move up from middle school. I don't know where you got them, but..."

"Those boxes have been in the registrar's office for a week. All you had to do was dig through them. I had Hattie do that this morning."

"Well, we don't have much help in our office, and..."

"So what's wrong with you? Can't you do anything on your own? You're not a cripple."

"I tried to solve this problem, Mr. Aneyh."

"Yeah, right. You accused that woman of being a poor mother."

"No, I didn't."

"Of not getting medical help for her boy. I won't stand for that in my school. This incident is going in your personnel file."

"It wasn't like that. I don't know what to say."

"You've said too much already. Now it's my turn. You get that kid back in this school. He transfers out of here, then you go with him." Aneyh flicked his wrist toward the door. "Go get it figured out. I've got work to do."

George Moore backed out of the office and slouched toward the counseling center. He tried to make sense of this, to recreate the events as they really happened. The principal had given the whole thing a sinister spin. George was now to blame for Adam Boresi's poor attendance.

George had a friend who knew the principal's past, which made this tongue lashing an even more bitter pill to swallow. Aneyh's dossier, barren of credentials one might expect in a resume of a secondary principal, showed a five-year stint as a special education teacher and five years as facilitator of the district's federal programs. George knew Bancroft's new principal had never shouldered a full load of academic classes, and yet, with this limited experience, an administrative certificate in his hip pocket, and a sponsor in the good-old-boy network downtown with whom he had played football, Robert Aneyh landed at Bancroft, a high school housing 1,900 students and a teaching staff of 130.

As educational leader, he spouted the new philosophy that schools accept responsibility for society's problems and the onus for individual educational failure. "Conditions" such as school phobia or attention deficit disorder and many more conjured up by professional educators gave students and their families a conduit to funnel away the blame.

George Moore was no fighter. He resolved to coax Adam Boresi back to Bancroft, no matter what was really best for the boy.

eighteen

"Ms. Merchant," hissed the wall box PA exactly seven minutes into the period.

"Yes."

Pencils and pens flew as her fourth period class labored on an essay test over *Crime and Punishment;* interruptions like this poisoned the atmosphere.

"Please send Susan Fatka, Angela Ulvestad, Kathy Thelen, and Ellen Nilsen to Mr. Delaney's office before they go to lunch," wheezed the box.

"All right," Karen said quickly.

"He needs to see them before 11:30," said the box.

Sixty student eyes were glued to the box as if it were a huge pair of lips.

Trouble! This meant trouble! She had changed from second to fifth lunch period for one day. Second lunch was split-ten minutes of class time, thirty of lunch, then forty-five minutes of class. Fifth lunch had a complete class session with lunch afterward, a full block of uninterrupted test time without a forced march to the cafeteria in the middle. Effecting a change in a lunch schedule, even if for only a day, meant pleading your case with Hattie Reins, who officiated ad hoc in such matters. Karen always left these negotiations feeling she had promised her first born.

"But we've changed lunch periods," Karen blurted. "We're trying to take a test up here."

A muffled discussion ensued in the background. She was on hold.

"Well," came the reply, finally. "I'm sorry, but this is important. These are the Kiwanis students of the month, and they need to get passes for early dismissal tomorrow."

"All right. All right. I'll come down and get them."

She ducked through the door, down a flight of stairs, and flew into Delaney's office. Students wouldn't cheat during her absence; this wasn't that kind of test. She stood impatiently in front of the reception desk in the vice principals' outer office.

"What do you want?" asked the clerk, a less menacing but equally exasperating version of Hattie.

"I'm here for those passes for the Kiwanis students of the month."

The clerk dug through her desk. "Well, do you know they have to have parental consent forms, too?" she sermonized as she handed over four pink pieces of paper. "Why don't you send those kids down here right now? I'll show them how to fill 'em out."

Karen's mind reeled. "Look, Mrs. Meredith, my

class is trying to take a test. I'll send them down after class."

"Oh really?" The clerk arched an eyebrow. "If you're down here, how do you know they're not cheating?"

Karen grabbed the passes.

She heard a loud voice coming from her room. A young man in the front row jabbed a finger in the air at the wall box. A call-in host hyperventilated about strip joints in greater Des Moines. "Miss Merchant, can't you shut that thing up?"

Several students holding their hands over one ear continued writing. Others waved both hands, fists clenched, in a frenzy. Some smiled and winked about the topic.

"I'll try, Jake." She punched the call button.

"Yes?" demanded the box.

"You left the radio on in my room," Karen yelled. "Could you please turn it off."

Click. The noise ended abruptly. Order restored.

She walked the circuit of the desks. Interruptions from the office were not a sometimes thing; they were as relentless as water torture—one after another after another. Like the bell just now ringing for second lunch, one of the thirteen bells that tolled during fourth hour defining the five lunch periods.

She dropped into her desk chair and smiled as students checked the clock. This was an opportunity to watch them work. A student wrestling with a complicated idea looked at her with a furrowed brow and turned his eyes away under her gaze. She had crafted this test to prevent the regurgitation of facts; it measured the students' ability to use the concepts in the work to support their opinions. She was anxious to see how it all came together. Karen glanced at the morning classes' papers, mentally calculating the hours she'd spend reading.

B-r-r-r-ang. B-r-r-r-ang. The fire alarm bell in the hall jolted them to attention. She grabbed her grade book and peered into an empty hallway–all the other classes in her hall were at lunch. As inept as the office staff was, they wouldn't stage a fire drill during lunch period. This had to be a fire.

Students trained by years of practice moved toward the door and spilled into the corridor heading for the fire exit.

"Excuse me," boomed Hattie Reins over the PA. Her voice echoed in the nearly empty hall. "This is not an official fire drill. The alarm system has malfunctioned. I repeat. This is not an official fire drill. Return to your classes immediately. Return to your classes."

An impish young man walked into the room with Karen. "Who does Reins think she's kidding? What you have here is a perfect fire drill–Chinese."

"We're not going to have enough time to finish," several students complained.

"You can do it. We have twenty-eight minutes left. Look," Karen said, responding to the desperate glances, "if you don't finish, you can stay through lunch. I can give up mine if you can. Don't talk. You're wasting time."

She heard the heavy steps of people in a hurry

clattering down the hall. The stocky form of Aneyh loomed in the doorway while the bald head of Sam, the head custodian, peered over the principal's shoulder.

"Any of your students been in the hall?" Aneyh barked before she even reached the door. Sam stepped back and looked up and down the corridor. "Well?"

"When?"

"Just a few minutes ago. Some kid yanked that fire alarm. I've got reason to believe it was in this area."

"We were all in the hall a few minutes ago, Mr. Aneyh, responding to the fire alarm." She pointed to the alarm lever–untouched–on the wall next to David's room.

Aneyh gaped over his large glasses. "Well, listen," he said at last. "I want you teachers to be more aware of what's going on out here during classes. We look pretty silly when a student yanks a fire alarm and gets away with it. Come on," he said to the custodian. "It's got to be in the other upstairs wing." Aneyh trotted around the corner with Sam drafting behind, skidding around the corner like a character in a cartoon.

Karen sank into the desk chair. This wasn't a learning environment; this was a zoo.

Click. "Ms. Merchant? Please tell Bill Krause his grandmother left his gym clothes in the office."

nineteen

Brook Fielding prowled Bancroft's halls preaching the mysteries of the universe. No one escaped. He cornered teachers in the office and ambushed them in the halls. He even got them in the men's two-holer, where, separated by a thin metal panel, an unwilling captive had to endure his chatter.

Slight, dark, and bearded, Fielding was Aneyh's fair-haired boy, handpicked to coordinate a federally-funded program called SWEET, a saccharin acronym for School Work Everyday Experience Team. Robert Aneyh shoehorned himself into administration via the SWEET program, and he had integrated this federal plum into Bancroft's curriculum. In his own mind, programs with names made him an innovator, a man to watch. He counted on Brook Fielding to make him look good. Fielding dealt with about twenty students. He found them part-time jobs for wages and class credit. None of this took much time.

Brook often dressed for school in jeans or a jogging suit. He did thirty laps in the gym and without a shower claimed squatter's rights in the lounge all afternoon. The communal lounge phone hummed with his personal calls for political or environmental causes. He often yanked students from teachers' classes to pursue his activist agenda; he called these activities "Fielding trips."

One bitter day in December, Brook, late as usual, found no parking space in the teachers' lot. He ignored the yellow warning lines and parked his car beside the old brick smokestack by the back door.

The years had taken a toll on the brick and mortar of this ancient incinerator which spewed forth the effluvium of discarded paper and other debris. On that very morning a solitary brick, loosened by years of freezing and thawing, plunged 150 feet into the passenger seat of Fielding's illegally parked car by way of the windshield. The near miss and scattered glass strewn about his car unhinged the SWEET man. Toting the brick like a loaf of bread, the shaken Fielding stomped through the building to Aneyh's office. Teachers checking their mailboxes heard his painful yowling through the closed door.

The next morning waiting in each mailbox was a questionnaire marked CONFIDENTIAL across the top. It contained a single question: Should parking spaces be assigned in the faculty lot? Please circle "yes" or "no," fold, and submit to Hattie Reins.

"The stinking little jerk!" Frank Nolden held court in the men's lounge. "I'd like to shove that brick up Fielding's ass. Like he needs another perk."

"Another perk?" asked Dan Tennant, still trying to unscramble Bancroft's pecking order.

"Fielding doesn't have any classes," Frank said, "but he pulls kids out of ours. And did you ever see him in the cafeteria?"

"Nope," Tennant answered.

"Right. The little bastard eats out every day. Try that sometime, Tennant. You can't do it in 27 minutes." Nolden banked a paper cup off the wall into the wastebasket. "You won't see him in faculty meetings either. He schedules phantom home visits and cuts out."

"What's he got on Aneyh?" Tennant asked.

"He hasn't got anything on him. They just came from the same litter. Aneyh's even got the little prick working on an administrative certificate," Nolden growled. "You watch. In three years he'll get Fielding a school of his own. Can you imagine working for that little son of a bitch!"

"You work for Aneyh, don't you?" David emerged from the restroom drying his hands on a paper towel. "Fielding couldn't be any worse."

Bob Melville leaned against the wall with a pop can in his hand. "You don't have to worry about the parking lot. Nothing's going to change. No one I talked to voted for it."

"No one should," Nolden said. "First come, first served."

"How else could he do it?" Tennant asked.

"I'll tell you exactly how." David put a foot on an empty seat. "There are 162 spaces out there. Aneyh'd claim he put everyone's name in a hat and drew 'em out blindfolded. Brooky—boy would get one of the first three spots. And so would Hattie Reins. He'd shit on everybody he didn't like—stick 'em at the end of the lot—and sprinkle everyone else in between."

Melville thumped David's back. "You don't have to worry. Nobody's voting for it."

"Yeah, but Hattie Reins can't count." David headed for the door.

Tennant pulled Frank Nolden aside as the lounge emptied. "I've got to tell you something, Frank. When I went up to the counter to hand Hattie my ballot, Nick Staal stood there writing on his. I looked over his shoulder."

"What'd he say?"

"He wrote, 'If parking spaces were assigned commensurate with the amount of work one does in this building, Brook Fielding would be parking out in Madison County.'"

"I wish I'd said that."

After school Nick Staal walked out of the restroom door straight into Brook Fielding whose hands shook as he waved a paper in Nick's face.

"All right, Staal." Every head in the lounge turned. "Did you write this?"

Nick glanced at his parking lot ballot protruding from Fielding's clenched fist. He shrugged his shoulders. "I don't know. What's it say?"

"You know what it says."

"You're damn right I do. It says 'confidential' right

across the top. Doesn't that mean anything to you? How the hell did you get it?"

Nick brushed by Fielding and dropped into a chair, slinging one leg over the armrest. Brook followed close on his heals and planted himself in front of the chair.

"You listen to me, Staal."

"Simmer down, Fielding," Frank said. "No one in here is hard of hearing."

"Stay out of this, Frank. This is between Staal and I."

"Between Staal and me," Nick said with a grin.

Guffaws swept the lounge.

"That's the trouble with you, Staal," Fielding ranted over the laughter. "You think you know everything. And where do you get off saying I don't do anything around here?"

Nick's lips curled in a wry smile.

"Oh, so you think that's funny, do you?" Brook wadded up the ballot and slammed it into a wastebasket by Nick's chair.

"You want to know what I think, Fielding. I think if you'd get your ass out of bed in the morning like the rest of us, you'd have a legal parking spot. You wouldn't be picking bricks out of your car. And, no, you don't do anything around here. You jog on school time, haul your sweaty carcass in here for the rest of the afternoon, and make this room into your personal office."

"You wouldn't understand this, Staal, but you don't have to make kids sit in rows and behave all day to be an educator."

"You couldn't do that, Brook."

"What?"

"Make kids behave. A few days ago, I saw a kid leading you down the hall by your tie with two more pushing from behind."

"Well, sure, that's just horseplay. Kids need fun."

"Oh." Nick stared. "Which end of the horse were you?"

Fielding's face reddened, his upper lip shook, and his fists clenched at his sides.

"Now, now, Brook," said Frank Nolden. "Don't get too exercised. Nick's taller than you are when he's sitting down."

Brook turned to look at the other men. "You guys are really the shits, the whole pack of you. You don't appreciate a damned thing I do. I get these disadvantaged kids jobs, boost their self-esteem, build their futures, and you don't even care."

"Why should we," Nick said. "They work 39 hours a week all night, then come over here and sleep all day."

"They need the money," insisted Fielding.

"Yeah, for cars," Nick said. "Cars own them. Monthly payments, insurance, gas. School doesn't mean anything anymore; they couldn't stay awake if it did."

"That's right."

"Right on, Nick."

"You guys always listen to him, don't you?" Brook whined. "Let me tell you something about this guy. He's no professional. He's a freeloader, a scab. He spouts off about professionalism, but he doesn't belong to one professional organization."

"I'm president of the Adair County Cattlebreeders Association," Nick said.

"Come on," Fielding crowed, "why aren't you man enough to admit it? The rest of us are proud to pay our share. And goldbricks like you reap the benefits."

"Who cares," Nolden said. "I don't belong to any either."

"Then you're no better than Staal, but he won't admit it."

"Brook, Brook," Nick said smiling. "I'd join the local if I didn't have to join the state and national. You get that fixed, I'll be a member."

"See what I'm telling you guys? He is a scab. He's such an expert on world class education! Well, the NEA's our best hope. He not only won't join, he makes fun of it."

"Oh, for Christ's sakes." Nick got out of his chair. He towered over Fielding. "Boy, do you need a wake-up call. You want better education? Trash the NEA. And while you're at it, dump the federal Department of Education. You and the other special programs are the only ones that get any money out of it. The rest of us just get paperwork."

"Get rid of the NEA? That makes no sense at all."

"Hell it doesn't! Education's just a hobby with them. Their business is political correctness. Go read one of their reports, Fielding. They're so damn busy bashing political appointees and the Boy Scouts, they've been so wrapped up with causes like South African divestment and the Sandinistas, they haven't done a thing about class size, discipline, or anything else that's dragging us down."

"Now you wait just a damn minute," blurted Brook.

"No, you wait. I'll tell you what guys like you and the NEA want. A fleet of semis, a backhoe, and access to the federal treasury. Then we'd have five or six more federal tits in every building, and these kids could suck around the clock. And more guys like you would have cozy little jobs. But that wouldn't help education or raise any test scores. They're social workers, Fielding, just like you are."

"I'm going to tell you something, Staal."

"No," Nick said, "you're not." He took a step toward Fielding. " Get out of my face!"

Fielding's eyes darted about for an ally. "Staal, you're awful." He stamped toward the door. "You're a disgrace to the profession." The glass in the door rattled.

"Whew," Frank said. "You took care of him. Someone needed to cut him down a few notches, and it ain't going to be Aneyh."

"Frank," Nick said, looking disturbed, "what kind of man would allow access to ballots that he, himself, labelled confidential?"

The answer came soon.

The following Monday morning astounded staff members pulled from their mailboxes an official memorandum from the desk of Robert D. Aneyh. "To all teachers: A tabulation of the ballots in re-assigned parking for our 162 spaces indicates that a majority of teachers have voted in favor of a new arrangement. These spaces have been drawn by lot. A list of names and spaces is attached." Rick Cook drew space number one. Space two went to Brook Fielding. And space three belonged to Hattie Reins. Karen Merchant had space sixty-eight, David one twenty-four. In space number one hundred sixty-two, at the very end of the lot, was Nicholas Staal.

twenty

Karen peered through the classroom at a grey December afternoon. A cold west wind moved the branches of leafless trees, and the tink-tink of icy mist pelted the window, audible even over the racket of giddy students in the hall. They were loose, and so was she. Winter Break, the politically correct designation for Christmas, Hanukkah, Kwanzaa, New Year's, et. al., had finally rescued a weary faculty. She slipped into her coat and boots, slung her bookbag full of student work over her back, and peeked outside once more. No ice, please. Why not the white Christmas the Varsity Choir had sung about for the past three weeks?

"Treats for all the good little boys and girls?" David yelled from across the hall. "You're crazy to take all that stuff home."

"Tell Kathy and the kids to have a Merry Christmas." She didn't want to acknowledge him.

The corridor was awash in color—ski coats, scarves, mittens, earmuffs, stocking caps. Through this kaleidoscope of flesh and cloth, Karen spotted Darlene McGimpsey's brown square-shouldered jacket. McGimpsey, an imposing figure at an even six feet, waited for Karen at the top of the main staircase.

"New Year's Eve at my house," she barked. No trouble hearing McGimpsey. If Karen didn't know Darlene, she'd be afraid of her. "You can bring your significant other."

"Fat chance. Would you settle for chips and dip?"

"Sure. I'll furnish the liquids." Darlene glanced at students streaming down the stairs toward the front door. "I've got to go remind Alice. Merry Christmas, hon." Darlene leapt down the stairs two at a time and disappeared into a mesh of kids.

The lower hall leading to the parking lot was mostly deserted. Karen plodded toward the back door, listening to Christmas music piped over the PA. "Frosty the Snowman." A sign of the times. Years ago the fare would have been "Silent Night." Now "I Saw Mommy Kissing Santa Claus" or a bunch of dogs barking out "Jingle Bells." Thank God for McGimpsey's New Year's Eve bash. Pointed hats, noisemakers, champagne toasts. That never changed.

Karen wrestled with the coat button under her neck, put on her gloves, and rubbed at the frost covering the glass of the back door. Snow was falling now, horizontally.

"Let me help you with this." The voice startled her, but she knew without looking who was there. Nicholas Staal lifted the bookbag from her back. "I'm glad I'm not an English teacher. This paperwork would drive me nuts."

"You don't have to carry that. I can manage."

"I know that." He held the door for her. "But I'm going your way. Since I won Aneyh's parking lottery, I'm going everyone's way."

She hadn't spoken with Nick alone since the morning of her apology in the lounge, but in her pretend conversations with him, she was always articulate and brilliant. Now her brain went limp. Something stupid was going to come out of her mouth.

He cradled the bookbag in his arm. They walked past rows of cars, their feet crunching in the fresh snow.

"Do you hate this new parking arrangement as much as I do?" Karen asked.

"Yes. Aneyh wasted a lot of paper with his phony referendum. He should have done what he wanted to in the first place. He would have looked better. Where are you?"

Karen pointed toward her tan Cavalier. "I'm sixty-eight. For a week I kept looking for my car in the first space."

"You really missed something. Right after school on the first day of the new system, this lot looked like a movie set for the Keystone Cops. Aneyh stood right here poring over a clipboard with everyone's name and space number. Quite a few people had gotten into the wrong slots in the morning, which screwed up the whole arrangement."

"Really."

"We have some good actors on this faculty, Karen. They wandered around, scratched their heads like Stan Laurel, and bumped into each other."

"What did Aneyh say?"

"He got mad. I cupped my hands and yelled, 'Has anyone seen a '68 Chevy pickup?' Frank Nolden was on the other side. He rolled down his window and screamed, 'Yeah. I've seen your pickup, Nick. Looks awful. It's w-a-a-a-y down there–clear at the end of the lot. W-a-a-a-y down in space one sixty-two. I think that's the last one.'"

"You guys are merciless."

"Aneyh smashed the clipboard against his leg and stomped toward the building."

"Did he come back out?" Karen shivered and pulled her collar higher.

"Not while I was there. You're getting cold. Where do you want this?"

"Trunk." Karen had the key in the lock, but the lid wouldn't open. "Must be frozen."

Nick pushed on the lid until it popped open. "See. I could do things for you."

She was momentarily rattled and responded with a perfect non sequitur. "How far do you have to drive?"

"Forty miles west, twelve south." He slammed the trunk.

"Doesn't that get tiresome?"

"In weather like this."

"Well." He still held her keys. "Thanks for helping me. I hope you enjoy your vacation."

"You, too," he said, unlocking the door. "How are you going to spend it?"

"You just put my Christmas vacation in the trunk. But I'll be at my mother's Christmas Day. My brother's family will be there." Karen threw her purse onto the passenger seat. "Will you be with your family?" she asked, buckling her seatbelt.

"Yes. Eighty-five head of Herefords. Cattle are easy to entertain. They go to bed early New Year's Eve."

Karen watched him brush snow from the windshield, come back to the door, and rest his gloved hands on the car's roof. Snow fell into the parking lot, building up on cars and the unsanded driveway. Cold air whipped through the open door. She needed to get the engine started, the heater going. But not while he was standing there, not while he was paying attention to her. She should ask him inside, but her heart thumping through four or five layers including a scarf and heavy coat would give her away.

He looked down at her strapped in the seat for several moments, shut the door, and mouthed "Merry Christmas" through the closed window.

Blurred by the swirling snow, Nicholas Staal appeared in her rearview mirror, moving toward the old Chevy. He unlocked his truck, which made Karen smile. What cargo could that dilapidated old wreck possibly carry that demanded lock and key? As thick, vaporous exhaust formed a cloud in space one sixty-two, Karen quickly went through what was becoming a mental ritual. Was he lonely? Did he have a live-in?

What was his place like? Who kept it clean? Did he fish, hunt, read? And what did he really think of her? Did he like her looks? And, perhaps because cosmic justice demanded that she seek intellectual legitimacy from one she'd accused of getting his words from a feed sack, did he think she was smart?

The old truck backed out and headed for the driveway, but she didn't put her car in gear. Very quietly, she whispered, "Merry Christmas, Nicholas Staal."

twenty-one

Some Iowans regard snow driven in by howling winds as the state's only affliction. Karen Merchant was one of them. She gagged on the products of those early American authors who described snowdrifts with lines like "ermine too dear for an earl." In her mind, the old poets had hidden away by the fireside behind too many tankards of warm ale, concocting goofy lines about a ravage of nature of which they were totally ignorant. Who cared how many sides a snowflake had, anyway, or that no two were alike? They'd never frozen their ears, worn out a back at the end of a shovel, or waded up to their butts in the stuff! Karen fought back by scapegoating John Greenleaf Whittier, upon whose head she heaped her considerable disdain for all of their simpy musings about the wonders of snow, refusing, as a matter of fact, to teach old Greenleaf's "Snowbound."

On the Wednesday evening after Christmas vacation, TV weather charts and Doppler radar predicted an affliction of six or more inches, single digit temps, and raw winds. The image of a heap of swirling snow descending like a mushroom cloud on a woman armed only with a shovel sent Karen immediately to the utility closet to hunt for her weapon. She set the shovel by the front door, searched drawer bottoms for warm, heavy clothes, and loaded her bookbag.

By 8:30, the skies surveyed from the kitchen window only added to her apprehension. The storm had started. Snowflakes danced crazily in the yard light. The wind was rising; Karen cracked the window and listened as it whistled through white pines at the rear of the yard. Her mother's phone call, during which Grace twanged out a list of no-nos to be aware of if, in fact, it snowed, was more than she could handle.

Karen went to bed early and slept in bits and pieces as the house throbbed with strange noises. She twisted restlessly, shedding bed covers, and half-awake, tugged them back where they belonged. A recurring dream often visited her on stormy nights, eerie pictures in black and stark white, in which she heroically freed her car from huge drifts and drove through blinding snow in an ethereal race to reach Bancroft before the tardy bell rang.

Karen awoke with a start before the alarm to a bedroom bright with reflected light. She yanked the cord on the bedroom curtains, revealing a bleak, silent landscape of endless snow. The word "deep" escaped from her lips in a whisper. Here in the benign stillness of her home, away from the wretched cold, the view was serene and harmless. But in a matter of moments she would be out there throwing snow from the sidewalk and driveway.

The storm door didn't move against at least eight inches of the white stuff drifted on the front stoop. Karen escaped onto the back patio with her shovel and labored inside heavy clothes along the side of the house. The air was frigid, and snow was still falling. A half-hearted yowl from the neighbor's dog assured her that there was still life on the planet.

Karen rested her chin on the shovel handle and peered at her car, an igloo with side mirrors, and proceeded to arrange her priorities. She needed to clear a path to that forlorn looking piece of machinery, denude it of snow, crank up the engine and heater, and retreat to the radio inside in case the superintendent had the good sense and cojones to call the whole thing off.

Snow began to fly. The screech of steel against concrete was a sound she had really learned to loathe.

"Greenleaf, you old bastard," she said in low, funereal tones, "I wish you were here."

The house was warm and the kitchen smelled like coffee. An announcer on Des Moines' fifty-thousand watt "Voice of the Middlewest" plowed through a mound of school closings. Karen longed for those magic words "No school in Des Moines today. Pack it up, kids. Go back to bed." Even "School will be delayed for two hours."

"Come on, you guys!" she pled. "Every burg within a hundred miles is shut down. How 'bout us?

Oh, you fools, you damn fools!" The newscaster had delivered the body blow: "School as usual in Des Moines."

Karen punched the radio's off-switch, unplugged the coffee pot, and wearily buttoned her heavy coat. The path to her car was drifting in again. Deep snow on the unshoveled driveway rubbed against the floorboards as she slowly eased onto the street. Bancroft was one mile away, a distance she didn't mind walking when the weather was good. Snow hit the windshield from all directions, and even though there was no traffic, cars parked along the street loomed as menacing obstacles.

Tires grabbed at the snow on the final turn to Bancroft. Only four more blocks! Her confidence soared. "Jesus!" She strained to see through the swirling snow. A pile of a man wrapped in fur and topped with a Dr. Zhivago hat suddenly appeared in the headlights. His huge bottom smothered the seat of a garden tractor with an attached snowblade. With jerky stops and starts, he pushed snow from his driveway onto the street. "Damn you to hell, you! There's a law against that!" she yelled through closed windows. Karen braked and felt the car fishtail and crunch to a stop next to the curb on a snow ridge winnowed up by the garden tractor. Shifting between low and reverse didn't work; the smell of overheated tires seeped into the car. She was stuck. The dashboard clock read 6:35. She stuffed her purse into the bookbag, stepped onto the snowy street, and locked the car door. In the murky light around her, she wasn't able to see anyone, not even the malefactor and his garden tractor. "Hey, where are you?" There was no answer to her plaintive call toward his house. Perhaps she'd imagined the whole thing.

Karen pulled the straps of her bookbag over her shoulders and plunged ahead into the gloom and cold. She followed what appeared to be the middle of the road, orienting herself by the houses on either side. And every house with a light beckoned as a refuge where she might escape the pain that attacked her fingers and toes. But she didn't knock on any doors. Stubbornness drove her on.

Suddenly the area in front of her brightened. A car was plowing through the snow from behind. She quickly dove headfirst into the drifts at a right angle from the approaching vehicle. She rolled onto her side just in time to see it pass within two feet of her boots. Karen's frightened cry hung in the silence around her. A perverse impulse to make a snow angel was overwhelmed by reality. Snow packed the insides of her boots and clung to her face, hair, and coat. She had to get up. She had to get to school. Karen struggled to her feet and waded to the middle of the street, where she found an ironic comfort in following the ruts carved out by the car that had almost killed her.

After what seemed like a million steps, the Bancroft parking lot, an unbroken field of glistening snow, twinkled in the distance. The irony was inescapable: "School as usual," yet a school bus would disappear in those drifts. Karen avoided the lot and inched her way along the side of the brick building into the biting wind toward the front door. Her hopes of survival depended on that door: it had to be open. "I'll freeze to the handle if the door's locked," she muttered through thick lips. "I'll be an ice sculpture, a sacrifice to stupid administrative decisions. Maybe they'll rename this place Karen L. Merchant Senior High School. How 'bout that, Martha? They'd already have my statue."

Eyelashes stiffened, cheeks burned, and mucus gelled beneath her nose. Dysfunctional feet jabbed at the drifts. There was no feeling in her right foot at all. Her shadowy figure turned the corner along Bancroft's front façade. Decorative evergreens beneath classroom windows looked deformed and grotesque under inches of snow, and frozen halyards chattering against the giant flag pole impressed on her dulled senses the danger of the situation.

In front of the massive triple doors, a square patch of gray concrete lifted her spirits; someone had cleared this snow away recently. Karen lunged for the door handle and stumbled into the building. Her nightmare was over.

The office door was closed, the halls empty. The shadowy figure of the janitor waving something overhead appeared at the far end of the main corridor. "I'm coming with the keys," he yelled.

"That's OK," Karen yelled back. "I'm going upstairs. I'll just wait in the lounge."

Her cold face stung as she reached the top step and entered the small room. "Incredible!" she gasped.

Nicholas Staal sat in his usual place, smoke curling over his newspaper. "I can't believe this. How did you get here?"

"I started around 4:30 this morning." He folded his newspaper and looked at Karen closely. "What happened? You look awful."

"Thank you very much." Karen shed her coat and flung it toward the couch. "If you really want to know, you'll have to wait."

She sloshed into the bathroom and stood before the mirror. Nick was right: painted cheeks, big lips, matted hair—she did look awful. Karen shook the snow from her boots into the toilet, blotted her hair with a paper towel, and walked back into the lounge. Her wet socks left tracks on the tile floor.

"Can I do anything to help?"

"No," she said quickly. "Ever heard of Nanook of the North?"

"Yes."

"Well, I met him this morning on a garden tractor." Karen collapsed on a chair close to Nick. "Nanook had the street blocked. I got stuck and walked the rest of the way."

"Really?"

"Yes, really. I fell down twice and almost froze coming up the hill. My head aches, my face burns, and this...well, my foot is numb. I guess I needed old Greenleaf out there."

"Greenleaf?"

"John Greenleaf Whittier. He's a minor poet. No one ever reads him."

"I did."

"You're kidding. Why?"

Nick shrugged.

> " 'And when the second morning shone,
> We looked upon a world unknown,
> On nothing we could call our own.' "

He got to his feet and stood in front of her.

> " 'No cloud above, no earth below,
> —a universe of sky and snow!
> The old familiar sights of ours took marvelous shapes:
> Strange domes and towers rose up where sty or corncrib stood,
> Or garden wall or belt of wood;
> A small white mound the brush pile showed,
> A fenceless drift was once a road.'

What do you think?" Nick asked, smiling.

"I can't believe you."

"Do you want more?"

"No. Why do you know those lines?" Karen wiggled her toes. She still couldn't feel them.

"Family tradition."

"What do you mean?"

"My parents and I lived on the farm with Grandpa. Great old guy. He was smart as a whip, and somewhere along the line, none of us ever figured out why, he committed 'Snowbound' to memory."

"The whole thing?"

"Every syllable," Nick said with admiration. "He even knew where the commas and semicolons went. Every year Grandpa waited for the first heavy snow and then took over the kitchen. Of course, he had a captive audience. He recited and we listened. We sat around the warm stove while he paced to and fro like a Shakespearean actor. The kitchen windows and the snow piling up outside were his backdrop."

"Did he teach it to you?"

"You just heard all I know. I learned those lines because they talk about a corncrib." Nick sat next to her. "You may not like Whittier, Karen, but you'd have liked Grandpa's finish. It was the same every year. He delivered the last ten lines with his back to us, arms raised at his sides, peering through the window into the storm."

"Well," Karen said, "maybe I'll have to reevaluate old Greenleaf. Did your grandfather like snow?"

"Yes, but not for aesthetic reasons. He believed nature dealt everyone challenges. Snow was his, something he had to deal with and whip. Keeping livestock alive during a blizzard in those days was no simple task."

"You come from his gene pool. Do you feel the same way?"

"Are you kidding," Nick laughed. "I drove fifty miles through this crap, hating every minute."

"You know, if your grandfather had been with me this morning, I'd have let him accept the challenge of carrying me those last four blocks."

"Hell, I'd have done that," Nick said quickly. "If you'd let me."

What Nick had just said caused not even a ripple in a head that ached with pain. Karen didn't want to talk anymore. She moved across the room, and when Nick disappeared behind the newspaper, she pulled off her wet socks and wrapped her scarf around her feet. Her head throbbed like a woofer on a cheap stereo. Her mind disappeared in the horrors of the snowy morning as she gently rubbed her temples with her fingertips.

Suddenly a strange sensation gripped her withered leg. She dropped her hands and stared directly into the eyes of Nicholas Staal. Karen had heard nothing—no footsteps across the room, no rustle of clothes as he knelt in front of her. He appeared as suddenly as an apparition. She gasped at the sight of her thin right leg enveloped in his large hands and sensed an impending disaster. Her first impulse was to jerk her leg away.

"You know something," Nick said softly.

Karen remained immobile and silent.

"When I was a little kid my mother rubbed my legs just like this." He kneaded the flesh of both legs from the knees down to the ankles. "I'd freeze my ass off in the snow and sit in the kitchen until she rubbed life back into them. God, it felt good!" Nick untangled the scarf from her feet. His fingers surrounded her toes, squeezing rhythmically, gently. "Doesn't this feel better?"

No man had touched her since that horrible afternoon in Charleston. That thought streaking across her memory made her shudder.

"You're still cold. You're shivering. Isn't this helping?"

"Yes. Yes. Thank you," she blurted.

Nick continued talking, but his words tumbled about her incoherently. Karen was in and out of the conversation like a drunk struggling to be lucid. She focused on what he was doing, not on his words. Karen had traveled a torturous path on her way to trusting this man, but this frightened her. He touched and caressed a leg that she herself could barely look at. What was going on here would either revolt him or he would feign the sort of pathetic sympathy that she could never tolerate. So why didn't she pull away or tell him to stop?

Karen wallowed in an utter state of confusion, agitated and frightened and yet inert, enthralled by the compassion in his eyes, the warmth of his hands, the sonorousness of his voice. This was like one of her dreams.

Finally, Nick stood and tossed her wet socks into the microwave. "When they're warm, don't eat 'em," he laughed. "Where are your shoes?"

She pointed toward her bag.

"Do you want to put these on until your socks are dry?"

Karen didn't answer. He slipped one on each foot, first the left, then the right.

The lounge door rattled. Darlene McGimpsey, swathed from head to waist in a knitted muffler, stormed in. "Did you hear they've delayed school until 9:00?"

"No, I hadn't heard that," Nick said, moving toward the door. He grabbed his paper and touched

Karen's shoulder with it. "Hope you're feeling better," he said on his way out.

"So, what's that about, Karen? Has Mr. Blue Eyes been hittin' on you?"

"Please, Darlene."

"Did you two spend the night here?" McGimpsey thought that was funny.

"Darlene, really." Karen's face flushed. "My car is stuck. He was just sympathetic, that's all."

"Your car's stuck!" Darlene roared. "Not to worry! I'll dig you out after school."

"You're on." Karen retrieved her socks from the microwave and left the lounge wondering what had just happened there.

twenty-two

After the announced two-hour delay, the superintendent's assistant for public relations, the on-air spokesman in times of confusion, informed the city at 9:00 a.m. that since school buses were unable to run and that city snow-removal crews were just then making a dent on the main arteries, school in Des Moines was, in fact, canceled for the day.

Darlene and Karen, along with five other marooned teachers, waited until 10:30 when a city plow carved a channel past the building. McGimpsey's Blazer, powered by 180 horses, burst onto the open street and charged for Karen's stranded car. The snow had stopped, and a bright sun glistened across the drift tops. Darlene bathed her in a stream of the machine's features, how it performed in mud, rain, sleet, and, of course, snow. She glanced at McGimpsey, an imposing figure behind the wheel, confident and in control, a perfect match for the Blazer because she was also powered by at least 180 horses.

The snowplow had swerved around the car,

leaving an impacted drift up to the windows. Darlene pulled a shovel from the backseat and attacked the drift like a hungry dog digs for a bone. She refused Karen's attempts to help, allowing that this was a job for a big, ugly ox like her. Karen had always vacillated about whether Darlene or Alice Cain was her best friend. Right now McGimpsey had the upper hand.

The walks at 1233 Castle Drive had drifted in again when Karen finally got home. Inspired by Darlene's scooping frenzy, she decided to end the day the way she had started. She cleared away all the snow before going in. Even though the task was no more enjoyable or less difficult than earlier, from this day on, whenever she picked up a shovel, Karen would think of Nicholas Staal's grandfather's recitation of "Snowbound" and smile.

On her way to change into sweats, Karen stopped before the full-length mirror on the closet door, tossed her clothes in a heap on the floor, and surveyed a body clothed in pants and a bra: proportioned breasts and hips, a narrow waist. People had told her she was pretty, a possibility she almost believed when looking over her left shoulder where a perfectly shaped leg covered that frightful limb. "If I looked like that over both shoulders," she whispered absentmindedly, "I'd go after Nicholas Staal." She turned the other way; her eyes fastened on a stick where a normal leg should be. How could anyone overlook that ugliness?

Karen sat on the bed and stared at her sweat pants and wondered what his wife's legs had looked like.

Maybe she had thick, ugly ankles. No. He would never pick someone like that. She ran her hands up and down both legs. This was what he had felt. But what did he think? She would have to be a bigger fool than she felt that she was to imagine that that leg made no difference.

Since her accidental discovery that she resembled Nicholas Staal's wife, he had played in all of her dreams, exotic adventures set in the damndest places—parks, row boats, foreign countries, the back seat of a car. Always, he filled her needs as a friend, confidante, and companion. She dreamed of him as lover, too, in situations so sensual that sometimes she was jarred from her reverie by her own embarrassment. If he even suspected the secret life she had concocted for them, she would die. But perhaps a more disquieting fear came from the realization that in her life, Nicholas Staal would always be only a dream.

Karen dressed, entered her book-lined study, and clicked on the TV for background noise. She made a few inane observations about the day in the direction of Martha Y. Bancroft's picture and sat at her desk piled with student papers, where she worked until hunger drove her to the kitchen.

The smell of soup wafted in the air, and in the small room, the clunk of a sharp knife slicing vegetables on a wooden board sounded loud and hollow. She lifted a jar of homemade salad dressing from the refrigerator and glanced at a picture of her sister and her sister's husband magnetized to the refrigerator door. They lived in North Carolina. And this snapshot of a summer camping trip in the green foothills of the Appalachians caused Karen to forget, for the moment at least, the blizzard she had waded through earlier that day.

The phone rang.

"Oh, Mother, not when I'm just ready to eat." She leaned against the wall and picked up the receiver. "Hello."

"You're home."

A man's voice. Men didn't call Karen to chat; they called to sell her something or ask her something.

"Who is this?"

"Nicholas Staal."

The soupspoon dropped on her bare foot.

"I called to make sure you got home safely."

"Oh...well...yes. I did. I'm in a warm kitchen getting ready to eat."

"Who dug your car out?"

"Darlene McGimpsey."

"By herself?"

"She wouldn't let me help."

"Sounds like McGimpsey. Are you walking to school again tomorrow?"

"No. I don't want to, anyway. But it isn't supposed to snow, at least I didn't hear that it was, but then I haven't checked lately." She rambled. Talking to him on the phone was so personal, so intimate.

"Well, I don't want to interrupt your dinner. I was just worried about you."

"My mother always says that when she calls,"

Karen said breathlessly. "I thought you were she. I mean, when the phone rang I thought Mother was calling me."

"Your mother always says she doesn't want to interrupt your dinner?"

"No, that she's worried about me."

"Then I'll get off the line so she can get through."

"Oh, no." Karen sucked in air. This conversation had to go on. "What do you like to be called? Nicholas? Some of the men just call you Staal."

"Nick."

"I want to be correct."

"I've noticed that."

"Have you noticed anything else recently?" Karen twisted the phone cord around her wrist. Here it comes, she thought. He had held her flaw in his bare hands that very morning, and she had now steered the conversation into a corner where he had to comment. Nick did not play games. He always said what was on his mind whether people wanted to hear or not. And she had to know.

"Have I noticed anything?" repeated Nick. "You hang back. Never get in on the action."

"I guess not. I fall and slip a lot. You may have noticed that, too." She wasn't making sense. Why wouldn't he talk about her leg?

"You mean literally?"

"No. Well, yes. I fell in the snow this morning."

"I'll tell you something I've noticed. It has nothing to do with falling on your behind. My father used to thunder a lesson at me when I was little like a preacher fuming from the pulpit. 'When you're up against it, son,' he'd say, 'whatever the obstacle is, don't run and hide. Face it! Stare it down! Grab it by the throat until you have the upper hand.' I've seen you do that, Karen. Like your apology to me in the lounge. I know that was hard for you. Or when you voted for my resolution in the BAG committee with Aneyh breathing fire on your neck. You don't run with the crowd, Karen. I like that."

Her eyes teared. No one had ever told her such things. Did he really believe them?

"Your father is a wise man. Does he still give you good advice?"

"Yes, he was wise. He's dead now."

"Oh, my goodness. I'm sorry. I didn't..."

"Karen, you asked an innocent question. You don't have to be sorry. My father died years ago when I was in fourth grade. Karen? Are you still there?"

"Yes. I always ask the wrong questions."

"No, you don't. Ask anything you want. Karen? Look," Nick said decisively, "I know your mother is trying to get through. I'll talk to you tomorrow."

The dial tone ground in her ear. He was gone. The salad looked wilted and drab. The disposal knives dispatched it to the city sewer. Karen wandered around the kitchen aimlessly, kicked the spoon across the floor, and stared blankly for a moment when the phone rang.

"I'm here, Mother."

"You wanted me to talk about your leg, didn't you?"

She squirmed in her chair. "Do you want to talk about my leg?"

"Yes, I do. But not before we get something straight. Do you know what you did to Frank Nolden last week?"

"I don't know what you mean."

"He complimented you on your hair. You don't even remember, do you?"

"No."

"You looked like you'd been hit in the belly with a corn shovel. You didn't even acknowledge him. You do that to me now and your mother can have this line. Did you hear me?"

"Of course. I wouldn't do that."

"We'll see. Have you read *The Glass Menagerie*?"

"Yes. I've taught *The Glass Menagerie.*"

"I was afraid of that."

"Why?"

"Because I know you. You think all men are disingenuous. When you hear this, you'll say I plagiarized that from Tennessee Williams. That I don't mean a word of what I'm saying."

"No, I won't."

"Doesn't matter because this is what I really feel. I like you, Karen. Your leg doesn't diminish that. Not one bit. No more than Laura's did in *The Glass Menagerie.*"

She stared at the stove. Tears welled again.

"Do you believe me?"

"Yes, I guess, but..."

"Don't 'but' me. I don't even know how to tell

you this without arousing your suspicions. I'd like to be your friend. I'd like to talk to someone like you. But, Jesus, every time I get close you crawl into your shell."

"I want to be your friend." An aching lump swelled in her throat. "There are so many things I'd like to tell you."

"You can tell me anything. Anything."

"I'd like to believe you."

"Damn it. There you go. You can believe me. And there's something else, too."

"What?"

"Your hands."

"My hands!?"

"Yes. You're so obsessed with the one thing, you've missed everything else. You should watch your hands some time when you talk, Karen. They're the most graceful hands I've ever seen attached to a woman."

"You can't mean that."

"The hell I can't. I've been looking at them. For a long time now. See you tomorrow."

twenty-three

A copy of *Slaughterhouse Five* rose and fell on Karen's stomach as she slept, fully-clothed, on the living room sofa. On the floor, five stacks of student papers were visible evidence that she had completed a big project. The papers were as strictly arranged, alphabetically and by period, as was her schedule when loaded with a project of this magnitude. There had been 145 papers last Friday when she'd gathered them. She'd used every tick of the clock over the weekend and Monday, Tuesday, and Wednesday evenings to analyze these student themes, pausing only for short breaks and calls of nature. On Wednesday, as if the weight of those stacks had lifted from her shoulders, Karen lapsed into a fretless sleep.

Brrrang. The phone dimly entered her consciousness. She stumbled toward the kitchen. Through heavy eyelids, Karen squinted at the stove clock. 10:30. Or was it 11:30?

"Hello?"

"I woke you up."

"Who is this?"

"Nicholas Staal."

"I think I'm awake, but not very much."

"Do you know who Aneyh is?" Nick asked.

What was wrong with Nick? Karen thought. "You tell me—who is he?"

"Spell his name backwards."

"Backwards! I can't spell his name forward—took me three years to learn how to pronounce it. I hate his name, his voice, his…what do you mean 'backwards'?"

Laughter echoed in her ear. As dopey as she was, Karen realized that this was the first time she had ever heard him really laugh. "Please, Nick, I'm only half awake. What are you talking about?"

"Do you have paper and pencil handy?"

Karen turned over a recipe card lying on the counter. "Yes."

"Write 'Aneyh.'"

"Okay."

"Now, spell his name backwards."

"H-Y-E"—her hand froze in mid-letter. "Hyena!" The fog enshrouding her somnolent brain cleared instantly. "Hyena!" she yelled. "This is glorious!"

An arpeggio of laughter slid along the phone lines until Karen, wiping tears from her eyes, managed to gasp, "How did you stumble on to this?"

"I don't know. Maybe I'm dyslexic."

"Can you imagine what David will do?" Karen was giddy. "How can I ever look at Aneyh again without seeing beady eyes and sharp yellow teeth?"

"How 'bout a drink Friday after school?"

"A what?" Karen wasn't laughing now.

"Let's go for a drink after school Friday."

"Oh," she said quickly.

"Do you have something on?"

"Well, yes. I'm wearing a blue sweatshirt and sweatpants."

"No, no, Karen," he said, laughing again. "What do you have on after school Friday?"

"Oh! Nothing. Shall I meet you someplace?"

"No, I'll pick you up at four o'clock. We'll go to the Forty-second Street Pub."

Karen told Alice who told Darlene who told David who told Frank who told the janitors. Everyone knew. From that day forward, Bancroft High caged a resident hyena. Of course, his title and station demanded "Mr. Aneyh" in formal settings. But winks, nods, and stifled grins followed this ravenous carnivore wherever he prowled. Teachers could not have invented a more delicious epithet than what accidentally fell into their laps.

twenty-four

January 29 was an important day in Karen's life. She had a date, a meeting, whatever it was with Nicholas Staal. The strange dichotomy of her feelings about him in which a nagging contempt had fought mightily with her growing admiration now included something new. How could she, Karen Merchant, gimp and old-maid schoolteacher, withstand the what-in-the-hell-is-he-doing-with-her looks? She had not told a soul, not Alice, Darlene, or even confided before the Victorian portrait of Martha Y. Bancroft, whose sensible approach from the past would mock her with "Give it up, honey."

But why worry? The fickle deities that controlled her life would never permit the consummation of this date. The earth would yawn and she would topple into the maw, or the rapture would carry her away in a feathery cloud. After all, a drink in a third-rate bar hardly mattered in a universe messy with real problems.

Nevertheless, Thursday night Karen was possessed

by a cleaning frenzy. Nothing escaped, not even the closets. Tub, sink, and stool glistened under the bathroom lights. She stood straddled over the john to check what he might see from that position. If Nicholas Staal entered her house, he would be impressed by her cleanliness and organization.

Karen fidgeted her way through Friday's classes. She had her coat on before the last plaintive echo of the dismissal bell died in the hall, straightened her desk, and planted generic lesson plans for Monday in plain sight. She might not survive this weekend.

On her way to the office to pick up her check, she passed Nick's room. He wasn't there. Strange. She hadn't seen him since his Wednesday night call. Could he be avoiding her—kicking himself for making this date? Karen sucked in a contemplative breath and worked her shoulders into a shrug. No, he would never make a misstep like that.

The drive to the bank was a blur, a fantasy land of red and green lights, stop signs, engine noises, and a gratuitous compliment about her coat from a "have a nice day" type in the teller's cage. By the time she got home, Karen was a nervous wreck. She plowed into her study, deposited her bookbag on the desk, and posed a disjointed question about a bath in the direction of Martha Y. Bancroft's likeness. She checked her watch. 3:45. "You're right, Martha. I don't have time." Karen washed her hands and sprayed her neck and wrists with perfume.

"No!" she screamed at the ringing phone. "He's going to cancel on me!" Her trembling hand grasped the receiver. "Hello?"

"Karen?"

"Mother! What?"

"Is something wrong?"

"No! What do you want?"

"Well, why don't you come over for dinner tonight. I'll fix your favorite, pork chops and rice."

"I can't. Why didn't you call me earlier?"

"What?"

"Mother, I've got to go. I've got to go. Someone's knocking on the door. I'll call you later tonight."

She smoothed her hair and peeked through the window at Nicholas Staal on the front stoop. He wore a black overcoat. A gray Beretta parked in the driveway gave her a slight pang of disappointment. She really wanted to ride in a farmer's working vehicle.

The Forty-second Street Pub was a neighborhood tavern that also offered brats, dogs, and burgers. Karen had been there once with Darlene, or, at least, inside. They had stopped for a drink, but the ambiance of clacking pool balls, cigarette smoke, and a sizzling, greasy grill drove them away thirsty. She puzzled over why Nicholas Staal would take her there. Her old intellectual friend, Dean Dawson, would rather die than be caught in such a place. Neon bar signs, a wall lamp with a paper shade at each booth, and the afternoon sun stabbing through grungy venetian blinds provided the pub's only illumination. A few people drank at booths and munched popcorn from small plastic baskets. Near the rear where a jukebox twanged out country-western, a tall, slender man with a short, fat cigar clamped in the corner of his mouth fretted over a pool shot.

Nick hung their coats on a rack fashioned from an old wagon wheel and guided her toward a booth where they sat on hard pine benches across from one another.

"Do you like country-western, Nick?"

"Sometimes." He threw a pack of cigarettes and a lighter on the table. "I like all music except hard rock. Do you?"

"Do I what?"

"Like country-western?"

"Not really."

"Well, we'll talk over it."

"Nicky!" A shrill voice coming from the bar startled Karen. A fortyish woman in black leotards covered to the knees by a tan skirt raced toward them. A black scoop-necked blouse revealed a large expanse of bosom. Strands of frosted hair flopping on each temple framed a face that the man with the cigar would call sexy.

"Nicky! Where in the hell have you been?" She bent over the table with parted lips and bestowed a resounding smack on Nick's cheek. "I haven't seen you in over a year."

"I work on the other side of town now, Shirley. I don't get in here any more."

"Tell me about it. I've missed you, Nicky. As a matter of fact, none of your old gang comes in here much any more. Oh, Nicky," she glanced at Karen, "I was so sorry to hear about your wife."

"Thanks. This is a friend of mine, Shirley, Karen Merchant. And, Karen, this is the best cocktail waitress in Polk County, Shirley Garland."

"Hi, hon. Nicky will have a bourbon and water. What's your pleasure?"

"Light beer. Draft. Nice to meet you."

Shirley patted Nick on the shoulder, looked at Karen, and went after the drinks.

"Look, Karen," Nick confided. "Now that we're in here, I'm embarrassed about this place." He glanced at the bartender-slash-cook moving hamburgers around on a sputtering grill, a huge man in a black t-shirt embossed by a Harley that stretched across his meaty chest. A dirty white nail-apron with compartments for salt and pepper shakers was almost pushed to his knees by a distended belly.

"Teachers from Crescent used to stop on Fridays for a drink. I'd forgotten how bad this place smells."

Shirley set the drinks, napkins, and an ashtray on the table.

"Did you bring your wife here?" Karen asked.

"Several times."

"What did she think of it?"

"She thought it was quaint."

"So do I."

Nick lifted his glass and examined the bronze liquid inside. "How 'bout a toast?" he asked. "Got any ideas?"

"To the demise of the hyena and all his ilk."

"Great. He deserves a dump like this."

Glasses clinked across the table. Suddenly, Karen lunged for her beer glass, which had slipped from her hand. She watched helplessly as it toppled over the table's edge onto Nick's lap. He leapt to his feet. A wet spot the size of a soccer ball circled the crotch of his pants.

"You baptized me in the name of the hyena," he said, smiling.

"Oh, God." Karen frantically sopped at the table with a napkin. "I am so sorry. I didn't mean…"

"You're wound too tight, Karen. Just sit right there. I'll go to the can and take care of this."

Karen watched Nick stride toward the restroom. "Sit tight?" How could she sit tight? This wasn't a casual faux pas; this was an unmitigated disaster—not a blot on his pants but a blemish on an evening that she had so carefully rehearsed.

Shirley appeared with a sponge and towel. "You a little edgy, hon?"

"No, I'm not edgy. I'm just clumsy."

"Oh, come on now. Nicky's a good man. I'll bet he thinks it's funny."

"How could he?"

"I'll bring you another beer."

"No. Please, Shirley. Just let it go."

Nick returned with a fistful of towels.

"Shirley's already cleaned up." Karen reached for her purse. "Nick, I've ruined your evening and your pants. Why don't you just take me home."

"Don't be silly," Nick told her. "I've had beer spilled on me before."

"You're trying to make me feel better. You can't sit here in wet pants."

Nick slid into the booth and pushed her purse against the wall. He gripped her forearm. "Now you listen to me. I've waited a long time for this. And now that I've got you, you're not going anywhere." He squeezed her arm tightly. They stared at one another across the cigarette-scarred table until her stern expression slowly melted into a smile.

"God, what's wrong with me? Why can't I lighten up?" She took a breath. "I've wanted to do this, too. If you ever asked me, I knew exactly how I would be. I practiced in front of the mirror. 'Oh, Karen,' I'd say to myself. 'You must be genteel. Avoid hackneyed phrases. Impress him with your mind. And at exactly the right time, lay your keen wit on him. Make him think you're clever.' Now look at me, Nick. I've scuttled my own script. And what's worse, here I sit spilling my guts."

"And I'm listening."

"What I don't get is why you asked me. You could do so much better. Shirley would snap you up in a minute."

"Get serious." His fingertips brushed the top of her hand. "You know what your problem is?"

"What do you think?"

"When you hold a hand mirror to your face, you see a leg. Then you proceed to define your appeal by a viral accident over which you had no control. If you didn't view life through that post-paralytic prism, you wouldn't tie yourself in knots like this."

She fell silent. "If you wore my shoes," she said finally, "you'd understand."

"I understand that you need another beer." Nick got Shirley's attention and pointed at Karen. In a matter of moments the waitress set a beer and a straw in front of her.

"She thinks I'm a klutz," Karen said.

"Shirley wouldn't waste her perverse humor on someone she doesn't like." Nick lit a cigarette. "This bothers you, doesn't it?"

Karen glanced at the layers of greasy haze striated by the venetian blinds, the pillars of the smoke billowing over booth tops. "What difference could it make here."

Nick smiled. "Have you always taught at Bancroft?"

"Seventeen years. I'm an institution in that institution."

"You're not old enough to be an institution." Nick traced the rim of his glass with his finger. "Did you always want to teach?"

"It was expected."

"Expected?"

"My father wanted to be a teacher, but he laid bricks for a living. He never had the money to go to college." Karen sucked beer through the straw. "So he was determined one of his children would be a teacher. My sister got married right out of high school, and my brother refused to do anything other than lay bricks like Daddy. Guess who fulfilled his dream?"

"Chalk one up for education. You're good."

"How would you know?"

"I've listened at your door. I wanted to come in and sit down."

"What was I talking about?"

"Slaughterhouse Five."

His admission immediately absolved her guilt about snooping at his door. Karen threw down the straw and took a huge gulp of beer. "I'll bet I can tell you why you're a teacher."

"Go ahead. Try."

"You were little. Your friends wanted to be policemen, firemen, pilots. That wouldn't do for you. You had to be different. You hitched up your short pants, pulled your beanie with a propeller on it over one eye, lowered your squeaky voice, and told them, 'I wanna be a teacher!' You were as independent then as you are now."

"Pretty close."

"I was kidding."

"I went to country school," Nick told her. "Our school marm was Old Lady O'Brien. But Miss O'Brien wasn't old—probably right out of normal training. We should have called her Wonder Woman. She had us little twerps right under her thumb. Eight grades in one room. She got everything out of us that was gettable. High school was a breeze because of her."

"Think how hard she must have worked."

"I admired that woman. I wanted to be just like her. I peeked at her from my desk whenever I could and expected that at any time she'd rip off that old smock and there'd be a red and blue uniform with 'Wonder Woman' emblazoned across her breast."

"Was she pretty?"

A wistful smile crossed Nick's face. "I had a horrible crush on her. I watched her all day and thought about her all night. Eight years inside those red clapboards with that remarkable woman, and suddenly the curtain came down. No graduation ceremony. No certificate of achievement. She just said, 'Good-bye, Nick,' and kissed me on the cheek. 'Good luck in high school.' My throat got thick. I ran home, my eyes so clouded with tears I couldn't see the road or the fence posts."

There was a brief silence. "Did you ever see her again?"

"Once or twice. She got married and moved out of Iowa."

Shirley set two more drinks in front of them.

"Could you teach in elementary?" Karen asked.

"Are you kidding? I'd quit first."

"You'd quit?"

"I've built a reputation in this system, Karen. I argue with principals. None of them want me. I'm just a scab they'd like to pick off and flick away." Nick fussed with his napkin. "Bancroft's my seventh building. Banishment to elementary would push me over the edge."

"Why?"

"Because. An elementary teacher has the toughest job in America. Except maybe for a lion tamer."

"Tougher," Karen said. "A lion tamer can crack the whip."

Nick smiled. "You've taught nearly half your life. You must like it."

"Yes. Well, I did for the first five years. But you know what the job has become. You made a speech about that."

"Sure."

"I'd like to try something else. But Daddy really sacrificed to put me through college. Quitting would seem like a betrayal."

"He wouldn't be happy if you were miserable."

"Perhaps. Maybe I'm not capable of doing anything else. 'Those who can't teach,' remember?" Karen twisted the straw around her index finger. "And then there's Mother. My quitting this job would put her in bed. Every time I nibble at the edges of this subject, she turns to stone." Karen grabbed Nick's lighter and absentmindedly lit and extinguished flames.

"Why do you get uptight when you talk about your mother?"

The lighter dropped on the table. "You don't want to hear this."

"I don't ask a question if I don't want an answer."

Karen leaned against the hard booth. "Well, Mother and I went through a lot together. She dragged me back from the edge of despair by willing me to walk again. My mother's taken on a lot of guilt for what happened to me. That's ridiculous, of course. But right now, she's at peace because she thinks I'm content and set for life."

"Maybe. Why don't you ask her."

"Ask her?"

"What she thinks about a career change."

"Because that would force her to say things she doesn't want to say."

"Like what?"

"Like 'Look, Honey Bunny,'—that's what she calls me—'you have a handicap. You've got a safe job, respect of the community, medical insurance, and you're invested in a pension plan. You want to throw that away? For what, a pig in a poke? Be sensible; stick with something you know you can do.'" Karen paused. "She's probably right. Maybe this is all I can do."

"You're an expert at underestimating your capabilities, aren't you?"

"You really think so?"

"What I really think is that you underestimate your mother. Did she remarry?"

"No."

"Sounds to me like your happiness is more important to her than her own. You said it, Karen. She pulled you through polio." Nick expelled smoke into the smoky room. "I own a reserve champion bull. I'd bet him on this, that if you decided to chuck this job, your mother would be there with pompons and hurrahs."

Karen placed her elbows on the table, clasped her hands, and looked beyond him. A sudden calm descended on the Forty-second Street Pub as the jukebox fell silent. Now no one needed to out shout the doleful drama of country-western balladeers. For awhile, conversations became muted and private. Karen reviewed the dingy décor and the Toulouse-Lautrec images around them. Here in these prosaic surroundings, she had already revealed to Nicholas Staal more private corners of her life than she had ever told another. He seemed like Father Nick and this booth a confessional. She felt the tension drain from her body and mind as they talked for over an hour. He listened without a trace of the arrogant judgmentalism that had scarred her conversations with Dean Dawson. Nicholas Staal made everything right. Even the Pub's foul air was becoming salubrious.

They devoured burgers and salads. Karen watched Nick drag fries through a pile of catsup. Couples labored at the Texas Two-step, and the cook, with a spatula stuck in his hip pocket, argued with Shirley about stock car drivers. At the pool table shouts of joy and profanity charted the battle's ebb and flow. Nick fit right in. When she entered the Pub an hour and a half ago, these characters looked clownish and unreal. But now she felt like a living piece of this human mosaic.

Shirley, her face lit with a devilish smile, approached the table. Several dollar bills peeked from inside her well-defined cleavage. She bent toward Nick. "Here's your change, Nicky."

"Just hand it to me, Shirley."

"You haven't changed a bit, Nicky. Always a gentleman." She placed the money on the tabletop and winked at Karen. "I never could get him to take money from there. Maybe you'll have better luck, hon." She shifted her weight to the other foot. "Listen, Nicky, don't stay away so long next time. And bring your lady back, too. You make a great looking couple."

As Shirley headed toward the bar, every negative thought Karen had about this woman was scrubbed from her mind by that one delicious phrase—"a great looking couple."

Nick stared at Karen from across the table. That same look she had seen that day in the lounge. "I would," he said.

"Would?"

"Yes. I would take that money from your cleavage, Honey Bunny."

twenty-five

Grace Merchant filled her home with collectibles. She designed her displays to fit holidays and seasons and crammed the overflow into cupboards and closets. Still, she never missed a crafts show and often coerced Karen to go along in case she needed a pack mule. Since the shelves in her own basement already stored some of Grace's extras, Karen's hidden mission on these excursions was to put the brakes on her mother's penchant for doodads and knickknacks.

On Saturday morning, she drove her mother to the annual collectors' extravaganza at Vets' Auditorium, but her mind was not on the stuff piling up in Grace's shopping basket. Instead, Karen rewound her conversation with Nick from the time he appeared at 4:00 until he dropped her at her door at 8:45. She had earned many "A"s as a student, but in her mind, a report card on her performance last night at the Pub would have read "incomplete." Karen was good at dubbing sentences into dialogue after the fact or deleting embarrassments that she could have avoided. What she needed now was another chance. Instead of admiring racks of pressed glass and primitives, she hatched schemes that would give her just that: another chance.

Karen froze in her tracks. A foot-and-a-half-long model of a country school, complete in every detail down to the miniscule strips of white clapboard siding, sat on an antique table. "Harrison Township School" read the small letters over the vestibule. Even though the model, priced at $150, wasn't red, and Karen had no idea of the whereabouts of Harrison Township, she intended to own that schoolhouse. As Karen approached the dealer, Grace Merchant suddenly assumed the role of a consumer ombudsman.

"$150 for that?" Grace pointed at the model. "Maybe for the antique table it's sitting on, but not for that!"

"It's my money, Mother."

"I know that, and you've earned every cent." Grace set her basket on the counter. "But you shouldn't waste money on something like this."

The eager dealer, wearing a flapper dress and feather headpiece, reached for her receipt book.

"What are you going to do with this?" Grace asked.

"Doesn't make any difference. It reminds me of somebody." Karen ran her fingers along the miniature siding.

"Must really be somebody for $150!"

"Mother, please."

"Well, who does that white elephant remind you of, Karen?"

"Mother, look at your basket. It's full to the handle. You've got six or seven items in there. I only want to buy one." She stopped short of adding "you hypocrite."

"Karen, those six items only come to $20."

The flapper closed her receipt book.

Karen smiled at the dealer. "I guess I haven't made up my mind about this. I'll just take one of your cards."

That night the computer fan hummed. Karen needed an outline for Monday's new unit. Nothing came. Her fingers danced over the keys in a fit of electronic doodling. "The quick brown fox jumped over the little red schoolhouse...little Nicholas Staal wore bib overalls and read about Dick and Jane...Miss O'Brien's Emporium of Knowledge...the last of the red hot marms...Nicholas Staal+Miss O'Brien..." Her fingers stopped. She suddenly knew what to do. She'd write about Nick's little red schoolhouse and the relationship between Miss O'Brien and him!

The screen glowed into the wee hours until Karen hit "save" and stopped for the night. Sunday, except for breaks to rummage through the refrigerator or to down another cup of coffee, she never left the computer chair. She moved words, moved sentences, moved paragraphs, edited, and reedited until at last she felt she had captured the simple relationship between a country teacher and her students. "We could learn so much from the little red schoolhouse," she ended and signed the essay "Voice in the Wilderness." She wanted him to figure out who wrote this.

Karen fastened the papers together and went to bed. She'd have to get up early to place her essay in Nick's mailbox before he got to school.

Monday morning Nicholas Staal unloaded his school mailbox. He sifted through announcements and absence slips. Intrigued by three typewritten pages, he lingered at the top of the stairs, leaned against a locker, and read.

Long strides carried Nick to Karen's room in a matter of moments. The start of the new week found her disorganized and unready. Karen stood at the chalkboard trying to put together the week's reading assignments. She thumbed through the four open books and her lesson plans lying on her desk beside the pile she'd unloaded from her mailbox.

"You're hard at it," Nick said from the door.

Karen dropped the chalk and pressed her hand against her throat. "You scared me."

"You entertained me." Nick took her hand and led her to the desk chair. He sat on the edge of her desk and dangled three papers in front of her.

Karen glanced at her essay. "How do you know I wrote that?"

"Because you're the Voice in the Wilderness type," he told her. "You know how to write, Karen. This piece is vivid and tight, not a wasted word." He put his hand on her shoulder. For a moment she felt the urge to jump from her chair and throw her arms around him. Nick had no idea how his touch resonated throughout her nervous system. "I want to do something if you'll let me," he said.

"What?"

"I want to run this off and put a copy in every teacher's mailbox. They all need to read this."

"No. I don't want anyone knowing I wrote that."

"No one will. 'The Voice in the Wilderness' wrote this. We'll hide your light under a bushel."

Nick's hand slipped from her shoulder, and he disappeared into the hall.

One duplicating machine in a small room served the entire Bancroft staff. All day long this room droned with the sound of a Risograph slapping papers into a steel tray. Teachers, with the smell of hot ink in their nostrils and their eyes blankly fastened on the copy-counter, impatiently waited their turns. Paper jams and other mechanical glitches meant a change of lesson plans for those who put off making copies until the last minute. The only way to avoid this morass was to get there early.

Wednesday morning, Nicholas Staal entered the room at 6:30 to duplicate a quiz, only to find George Moore at the machine.

"What's going on, George? Counselors giving tests these days?"

"No," George said nervously. "This is for my wife."

"Oh, doesn't her school have a machine?" Nick asked. "Maybe they're out of paper, huh?"

George's body shielded the copy holder. "I'll be done right away."

"Don't sweat it." Nick peered over the small man's shoulder. "Is that the essay we got yesterday on the little red schoolhouse?"

"Yes. And this is my own paper, too. I paid for it."

"What are you going to do with the copies?"

"My wife read this last night." Moore wrenched the sheets from the tray and straightened them on the table edge. "She wants every teacher in her building to have this."

"You're spreading the essay around, eh? You must like it."

"Yes, I do." He tucked the papers under his arm and smiled faintly at Nick. "Did you write this? Sounds like the things you say."

"No, I didn't."

George walked toward the door, paused, looked both directions, and melted into the hallway.

Karen fumbled for the phone.

"Hey, I've got a great idea."

"Nick? What time is it?"

"I don't know. Midnight, maybe."

"Midnight! Must be some idea."

"Listen," Nick said, "you hit a homerun."

"What?"

"Yesterday I watched people read your essay. Frank Nolden amen-ed every paragraph. Alice Cain's

213

ready to drag the school system kicking and squealing backward into the age of the little red schoolhouse. And George Moore ran off a copy for every teacher on his wife's faculty. I think we've got something here. We should go public. A newsletter—district-wide, sent to every teacher and administrator."

"Have you been drinking?"

"No. I want to publish a newsletter. Will you help me?"

"Wait. Wait. I don't want my name connected to anything."

"Why? Don't you want anyone to know what you believe?"

"Yes, of course. But I've seen people ruined in this system for speaking out. Look at you! You hardly get comfortable in your chair before they send you packing."

"Okay. We'll go underground."

"Underground? Like *The Free Press*?"

"Sure."

"I can't do that, Nick. I don't have time, and I don't have that much to say."

"Then we'll get more people."

"Who?"

"David."

"David! Come on, Nick." Karen pushed her back against the headboard and flicked on the light. "That weasel would never take any chances."

"No. He wouldn't. Not in public anyway. But David's clever. He could fire shots from the shadows. And Alice Cain is disgusted with this system. You know she's worried about education. You could just mention this to them tomorrow. Plant the seed. Teachers have never had a real voice in this town, Karen. Don't you think they deserve one?"

"But, Nick…"

"I know you're tired, and I apologize for waking you. I'll call you tomorrow night—at a decent time. Work on it."

Karen stepped into her slippers. She poured a glass of milk in the kitchen and wandered into the study. Piercing eyes glared at her from the wall above the desk. She could almost see Martha Y. Bancroft's lips move.

"Why, you little fool! You hatched schemes all weekend that would throw you together with him. He's just made it easy for you."

The following evening, Karen stayed close to the phone. She had sheepishly broached the possibility of an underground paper to Alice and David as Nick suggested and was amazed at their responses. Alice glommed on to the idea immediately. And David, after a series of legalistic demurrals involving his liability and his cover, agreed to participate only if Nicholas Staal understood that if the crunch came, he, David, would deny "three or fifty times if necessary before the cock crowed" any connection with the project. With this list of caveats on the table, he deluged Karen with a wave of ideas and headlines that would, in David's words, "knock teachers' socks off."

Karen grabbed the phone before the first ring stopped.

"Nick, I'm so excited. Let's do it!"

"Oh." Silence on the other end. "I must have the wrong number. Excuse…"

"Mother, wait."

"Karen, is that you?"

"Yes."

"Well, you had me confused. I thought…who's Mick?"

"His name is Nick. A man I know from school. He's going to call me. What did you want?"

"Nothing really. Do you know him well?"

"He teaches at Bancroft. And, no, I don't know him that well."

"Karen, you said 'Let's do it.' What were you and Nick going to do?"

"Just something for school. That's all."

"Is he a nice man?"

"Oh, Mother."

"I'd like to meet him. You should bring him over sometime."

"Mother, this is not that kind of relationship."

"I see."

"No, Mother, you don't. What did you want?"

"Just checking in. Good night, Honey Bunny."

twenty-six

David followed Karen to her room. He closed the door behind them and unleashed a torrent of questions.

"David, you need to calm down. You're going to blow our cover before we get started."

He rested his weight on her desk. "All right," he said gravely. "Tell me. What in the hell has Staal been doing? Where are the papers?"

"In the district bag mail."

"What! You mean he dropped them in the district's own bag mail!" A vein pulsated in his temple as he paced. "That's stupid. If anybody saw him, downtown could trace this right back to us." David stepped in front of her chair. "You told me they'd be mailed."

"That was the plan, David. But stamps are expensive. 1,800 copies cost at least 60 bucks. Nick decided…"

"Nick decided!" David yelled. "When did you start trusting him? If Aneyh finds a clump of 1,800 papers in Bancroft's bag mail, he'll blow the roof off. I told you—if Staal gets nailed, I'm out."

NEWTON & GRETCHEN KAUFFMAN

"He didn't put any in Bancroft's bag mail," Karen assured him. "Nick visited his six old buildings Tuesday. When no one was watching, he dropped about 300 at each of those buildings. The paper should show up here tomorrow." She stood and poured the remains of her coffee into the philodendron on top of her filing cabinet. "This saved money that we need for paper and stuff. Anyway, sending them in the district's bag mail is wonderful irony, don't you think?"

"I don't like this," David said. "Staal always plays on the edge. That's his business. But he shouldn't involve us."

"Well, I am involved," she told him. "If you don't have the nerve for this, you can drop out any time."

"Maybe that's just what I'll do." He headed for the door.

The district bag mail, an in-house delivery service, unwittingly served as mailman for the first issue of the underground paper. Every certified employee in the Des Moines school system, as well as seven board members, opened an envelope and unfolded an eight-page paper whose masthead screamed *THE EMPEROR'S NEW CLOTHES*. The moment the copies hit Bancroft, no one spoke of much else.

Michelle Valder, Bancroft's non pareil among French teachers, accosted David and Karen in the hall right after second hour. "Monsieur et Mademoiselle"—her French appellations always made David want to puke—"there's something wonderful downstairs." She smiled and held up a copy of the paper. "Magnifique!"

"What is it?" Karen asked coyly.

"Look in your mailbox." Michelle drifted away into a sea of students.

"Let's go, David. We sent copies to ourselves. We have to make this look natural."

A dozen or so teachers were rumaging through their boxes until each found a personally addressed, legal-sized envelope. Hattie Reins, hands on hips, watched the assault on the mailboxes from behind the counter. Alice Cain, trying her best to dissolve into the background, observed this spectacle from the telephone stand while she picked dead leaves from a plant.

David sidled up to the co-conspirator. "Would you look at that, Big Mama," he muttered from the side of his mouth. "Hattie's bewildered. She puts all the mail in these boxes. She'd shit if she thought she'd delivered an underground paper."

"She would, indeed." Alice tried to ignore him.

"So, Brunhilde, what do you think? The teachers like what they're reading?"

"Yes, look at them. David, guilt's spread all over your kisser. Go back to class." She turned her back on him and glanced at a copy of the paper over a teacher's shoulder.

The Emperor's New Clothes
Once upon a time there was a big school district in a little state. Over the years the district survived the baby boom's rapid growth, school construction and expansion, open spaces, cadres, declining enrollment,

magnet schools, grade shifting, affirmative action, school closings, boundary changes. During much of this time, the powers that were remained in the palace downtown, quietly reviewing measurable objectives and negotiating contracts. But one day, a new emperor arrived on the scene: the great sovereign Public Relations. "Excellence in Education" became the motto: "Selling the Schools" became the method. The administrative palace wore a new coat of paint and sacrificed its windows to central-air. The board room overflowed with state-of-the-art, high-tech equipment poised to disseminate information to the masses. Soon the media were full of test scores, personnel reports, volunteers in the schools, programs for all manner of special needs, and statistics used to support any number of contradictory conclusions. But all was not excellent; in fact, much was mediocre. The right hand didn't seem to know what the left hand was doing. Sometimes the two even slapped each other! Most statements made by administrators and board members didn't even address the business of educating. Out in the vast reaches of the kingdom, the teachers in the schools, the ones truly involved in the profession, decided that they, too, needed to relate to the public. "Enough of this!" they cried. "We have had enough of the BULLetin and other sanctimonious tracts that gloss over and say nothing. Let us hear the naked truth. The teachers need to be heard and will be heard." And here is their voice—*The Emperor's New Clothes.*

Nicholas Staal opted for lunch in the cafeteria. The Lunch Bunch table was a sounding board where teachers, uninhibited by administrators, said what they thought, and Nick hoped for a candid appraisal of the underground paper. He set his tray by Frank Nolden, who turned pages of *The Emperor's New Clothes* with one hand and shoved food in his mouth with the other.

"Nick, have you seen this?" Frank asked.

"Seen what?"

"An underground newspaper, apparently." He dropped his sandwich and flipped back to page 1. "Remember that dippy mission statement the superintendent crafted a few years ago?"

"Sure." Nick grabbed the tip of his napkin and rolled the silverware onto the table. "'The Des Moines Independent Community School District will provide a quality educational program to a unique and diverse community of students in which all are expected to learn.'"

"Lord, you know it by heart."

"Of course," Nick told him. "I take this job seriously."

"Get a load of this. 'MISSION STATEMENT: The 21 missions established by Father Junipero Sera

221

and his successors were the strongest factor in developing the Spanish territory.'"

Laughter engulfed the Lunch Bunch table. Students nearby winked and watched the normally sedate faculty dive into the newspaper like vultures scrambling for the bloodiest bits of meat. Dan Tennant played with his moustache and peered over steel-framed glasses. "Listen to this," he said in stentorian tones. " 'The education vandals are not at the gates. They are inside the walls raping, pillaging, overwhelming the educational and cultural traditions that propelled this nation to center stage as a world power.'"

"Who do they say the vandals are?" Alice asked.

"Read page 4," Tennant suggested. "Great editorial."

"These guys are good," Nolden said.

"Here's one elementary teachers will love." Darlene McGimpsey patted her lips with her napkin. " 'When the Des Moines School System computes the teacher-pupil ratio, they think we believe them. Come on! We know they count teachers like precinct captains count votes in a Chicago election. They toss in the special ed staff, counselors, associates, a janitor or two, and a few teachers looking down from that great classroom in the sky. No matter! With all these arithmatic gymnastics, we still lag behind. In a recent international survey, even Libya, homeland of that noted educational savant Muammar Qaddafi, had a lower teacher-pupil ratio than America. Teachers read in the Bulletin that Des Moines' teacher-pupil ratio is 1-15 and then look into a sea of 35 faces waiting for the day's reading lesson. Give us elementary classes with 1 teacher to 15 students and we will roll down the highway toward world class education.'"

"Who are these guys?" asked Frank Nolden.

"Maybe Muammar Qaddafi's publishing this paper," David said. "His image needs some help."

Alice Cain glanced at him and said under her breath, "Shut up, David."

"Nobody from downtown's doing this," he went on.

"How do you know?" Lydia asked.

"Look at the subject matter," David told her. "You think they're going to hoist themselves on their own petard? Anyway, none of those fools down there can write."

"Whoever did this, well," Lydia tapped her fingers on the paper, "some of this seems a little disrespectful."

"Look," Frank said, "when you're sticking swords in the gasbags that run the public schools, you expect a little odor." Nolden finished off his sandwich. "We've needed something like this. This paper's got some naked truth in it."

"Like this, for example." Tennant adjusted his glasses. " 'ASS CLASS: Educators scouring the landscape like scientists on a microbe hunt have discovered a new virus—attention span syndrome (ASS), which, according to their findings, infects a number of the nation's children. We expect the prognosis soon—a federal program loaded with money in which the diagnosed will have 50 classes a day, each lasting for 5 minutes.'"

Karen watched Tennant's head and shoulders shake with laughter. The paper seemed to be an elixer pumping new life into her old teacher. This was not the same man she had watched since late August condemned to serve out the rest of his sentence behind Bancroft's massive triple doors. This was the teacher she remembered in front of her ninth-grade class, engaged, animated, confident. Could *The Emperor's New Clothes* resuscitate Tennant and others whose days in the profession focused on crossing squares off a calendar? No doubt the paper had captured Bancroft's staff. But she wondered about McGovern, South, Washington, Poe, and Irving High Schools and the rest of Des Moines' 65 schools. What did those teachers think?

Karen's memory raked up her twelfth-grade composition teacher, who ended each writing assignment by clearing her throat and intoning, "Remember, class, the pen is mightier than the sword." Karen had no illusions. *The Emperor's New Clothes* would not make the earth move. Nevertheless, her pen had moved the Bancroft staff. That was worth something. And, since the only education diet served up to teachers came almost exclusively from the administrative food chain, she hoped the underground paper, which presented a different point of view, might force those in positions of power into an honest dialogue. Whatever direction this enterprise took, Karen could not recall since becoming a teacher a more exciting day. And she was sharing this day with Nicholas Staal.

twenty-seven

George Moore poked his head into the upstairs lounge, approached the room's only table, and parked himself in a chair across from Nicholas Staal. He folded and unfolded his hands on the tabletop.

"You're lost, George. The last time you got close to this place, you wouldn't even come through the door."

"I know where I am." His eyes swept the room. "I never noticed before. This lounge has the same kind of furniture as the one downstairs."

"Uh huh."

"This place is really small and drab."

"Yup."

"That door over there lead to the bathroom?"

"Damn it, Moore!" Nick tossed his newspaper across George's nervous hands. "Do you ever get right to the point? Did you come up here to redecorate this room?"

"Nick, I want something."

"Well?"

"Uh…I know you're doing that paper."

"What paper?"

The Emperor's New Clothes.

"You don't know anything of the kind."

"Yes, I do—and I want to be part of the effort."

"Wonderful, George! But you're talking to the wrong guy."

"I couldn't write anything," George continued. "Well, I can write, but, as a matter of fact, not as well as what's in your paper, which, to tell you the truth, is great material." He leaned toward Nick. "But I could be your gofer—address envelopes, lick stamps, sharpen pencils, anything."

"George, listen to me." Nick stared into his face. "I know nothing about that paper."

"Don't do this to me, Nick. You're the only person in this whole system who's got, if you'll pardon my saying so, the balls to write stuff like that, then send it out in the district's own bag mail." George became deadly serious. "If you don't want me, just say so. That's all right—but you're not fooling me."

Nick leaned his chair back on two legs, hands clasped behind his head. "Moore, you're a real piece of work. You think you've got this figured out, don't you?"

"I know I do."

"You know where Karen Merchant lives?"

"No, but I could find her."

"Be there Friday after school, 4:30."

George stood up and shook Nick's hand.

"George?"

Moore stopped at the door. "Yes?"

"Keep your mouth shut."

"You can count on me. My lips are sealed."

Nick knew George would peer down the hall both ways before he left.

twenty-eight

On Friday, school ground to a halt. Students had a day off while teachers throughout the district were required to assemble in carefully orchestrated continuing-education workshops. "Students at Risk" screeched from the programs handed to the Bancroft staff as they entered the little theatre for In-Service Day.

Once a problem such as students at risk hit the national scene, methodologies to solve that problem dropped in from university education departments, freelance consultants, professional journals, the Department of Education, and the National Education Association. Even the nation's smallest districts were in the loop with information percolating along this pipeline. And federal money flowed into the coffers of any district that could harvest students that fit the "at risk" label.

Teachers had some skepticism about programs such as these because they often fizzled out. For example, the year before, newspapers, talk shows, and coffee klatches roasted the public schools because their products butchered the English language when they entered the business world. Des Moines' answer to these criticisms was WAC—Writing Across the Curriculum, a program conceived, nurtured, and buried within one school year. Follow-ups evaluating the success or failure of these periodic forays proved inconclusive and, in fact, were seldom conducted since the boards had to be erased for next year's crisis.

Karen took her usual seat in back for the general session. Robert Aneyh hovered around the podium. He lavished attention on a woman dressed in a black power suit and high heels who stood directly in front of him. She held a coffee cup in one hand, a manila folder in the other, and smiled at teachers filling the front seats.

"Who the hell is she?" David collapsed into the seat at Karen's side.

"How should I know. Someone from downtown, I suppose. Here to observe Aneyh's style and round out her education. Beats work."

David grunted. His eyes were glued to the body language around the podium. "Disgusting."

"What?"

"The hyena fawning around her like he wants to jump her bones."

"David," Karen said coldly, "this is going to be a long day. Don't make me vomit before we get started."

David continued to study the pair at the podium. Suddenly he grabbed Karen's knee. "You know where we've seen her before?" he gasped.

"Where?"

"McGovern High. That's the babe Aneyh sat with the night Nick made his speech. Darlene thought she was Aneyh's old lady."

"So what? You're suspicious of two administrators sitting together in a public place? Give me a break."

"All right, I'll drop it." He slumped in his seat. "Bet you ten to one he's doin' her."

"Stop!"

"Okay, okay. We've got to pick up the mail for *The Emperor's New Clothes* tonight right after this circus. You forget?"

"No, but don't talk about that. Someone might hear you." She still feared David would leak their secret. Not intentionally, but she had seen him buckle under pressure before.

Aneyh stepped to the microphone. "Welcome," he roared. "Welcome to our annual in-service day. I'm pleased to introduce Dr. Edwina MacIntosh."

MacIntosh, an administrative intern, was climbing the career ladder. She had that company glow that enshrouded most career educators and a smile that seemed stuck on her face. Teachers understood that that smile expressed relief; she had escaped the rigors of the classroom.

"Dr. MacIntosh will be serving as interim director of the district's new dropout prevention program for students at risk." Aneyh grinned as if he had dropped an education bombshell. He waited. Applause came in dutiful spasms. "Dr. MacIntosh will be spearheading our campaign to keep kids in school." His fingers drummed the podium top.

"Listen," David whispered, "Bancroft's going to be a beacon."

"Here at Bancroft," Aneyh bellowed, "we can be innovators. We can build a program second to none. We can be a guiding light for the rest of the district and state. Dr. MacIntosh is here to help us light that lamp. We are so fortunate to have her. And now may I present Dr. MacIntosh. Edwina?" He positively beamed as she approached the podium.

"Thank you, Bob."

"Did she say 'Bob'?" David squirmed in his seat. "Nobody calls him Bob. What did I tell you, Karen?"

"Shut up."

"I'm pleased to be here today," said the doctor, "to launch the newest program in the Des Moines Public Schools, something designed to help each and every student reach his or her fullest potential."

Karen glanced toward Nick. He always sat in front with Frank Nolden. Nick never sought her out at school. That was OK. She wanted theirs to be an extracurricular relationship.

"I'm announcing today the implementation of a pilot program, one in which Bancroft can be a leader, just as Mr. Aneyh said. We're calling it MENTOR. Let me spell that for you. M-E-N-T-O-R. That stands for MAXIMIZE EDUCATION NOW THROUGH OUR REARING."

Giggles from the rear wiped the Buddha-like grin from Aneyh's face. The principal's eyes swept across the room. If looks could kill, 150 teachers would have been vaporized where they sat. The mini-rebellion collapsed immediately. Teachers viewed acronyms as an affliction. Rule of thumb: if they're cute, they won't work. And this one, a gem set in a sterling silver -ize verb, dropped from the lips of Edwina MacIntosh like a watermelon from the second story. Karen pictured the ashes of Mentor, teacher of Oddyseus, spinning in his Grecian urn at the profane use of his good name by the doctor of education.

"When we use the term 'at risk,'" MacIntosh went on, "we are talking about students who are not reaching their full potential. They are failing to find success in school. Their primary and secondary needs are not being met. We need to make all students feel that they are valued, that they count, that we believe in their capabilities, and, in some cases, that we believe in them as persons but not in their behaviors."

The faculty listened in stony silence.

"We invite you to be a part of this program." She flashed that smile again. "You'll be paired with a student who is not succeeding. These students may be facing school-related problems, but most of them will be exhibiting antisocial behavior or other characteristics caused by economic needs, physical health problems, mental health problems, dysfunctional families, what have you."

"What about acne?" David whispered.

Karen smiled.

"Your participation will be voluntary," the doctor said. "But we know you will all want to take part. Our social work and psychological support teams have identified 58 Bancroft students at risk. Bob will fill you in on that. Thank you so much for your enthusiastic attention." She retired to the rear of the dais amidst no applause.

Aneyh stepped to the podium again. He slowly scanned the room, obviously upset by the faculty's lukewarm reception of MacIntosh and her new program. He nodded toward her. "I can promise you, Dr. MacIntosh, that Bancroft will be the leader in this area." He glared at his staff. "We have too many failures in this building. And when a student fails, it's your fault."

A "What?" got away from someone in the middle of the group.

"You heard me," Aneyh thundered. "Your fault. And that's exactly why we're instituting this program. MENTOR will help you meet your responsibilities. I expect total cooperation and participation. Now, after our break you will meet in rooms for small-group work. Pick up your assignment sheet as you leave. The sheet contains room number, committee members, your group's facilitator, and a list of 58 at-risk students. We need to come up with insightful ideas that will save these kids. At 1:30 this afternoon, we'll meet back here and discuss the strategies you've come up with."

The faculty left the theatre in a surly mood. They walked in clusters toward lounges and assigned rooms. Karen followed Alice Cain and Michelle Valder. Madame Valder was a babbler. Teachers avoided her conversations—rather, her monologues—since no one could slip in a word. Right now, she explained to Alice that today's session was meaningless to her. After all, she taught French to college-bound students. No one in her classes was at risk.

Karen ducked into 211, her assigned room for small-group work, and studied the list of 58 students at risk. Trouble makers all. Jeremy King's name jumped at her. And this committee was supposed to save him? She checked for Nick's name on her roster. Not there. Mel Lichty, Alice Cain, Dan Tennant, Frank Nolden, Gordon James. "Oh, God!" Karen exclaimed, "Michelle Valder." The group's facilitator was Eldon Carpenter-Olson, an itinerant school psychologist assigned to Bancroft on alternate Thursdays. He was the only male Karen had ever heard of with a hyphenated name. She had received his memos but had never seen him and often wondered whether he was Carpenter or Olson.

Committee members filed in and took their seats in front of the desk. Suddenly, a man toting a briefcase, with thinning hair, leather patches covering the elbows of his cardigan sweater, and eyes magnified by thick glasses, bounced through the door. "Hi, I'm Eldon Carpenter-Olson, your facilitator." The man in the flesh was younger than Karen thought he'd be. He opened his briefcase on the desk, removed several transparencies, and faced his captives.

"Before we get started," he said smiling sweetly, "why don't we just go around the group, tell who you are, some history about yourself, and what each of you expects to take away from this session. This can be our little icebreaker. You, sir," he nodded at Frank Nolden. "Why don't you begin."

"Look, Mr. Eldon," Frank said.

"Actually, it's Carpenter–Olson, but you may call me Eldon."

"Sure, Eldon. I see these people every day. We teach together, eat together. I know more about them than I want to. We don't need an icebreaker. Why don't we just get on with this."

"Well," said the facilitator, a little cowed, "if that's the way you feel."

"That's the way I feel," Frank said.

"Then." Carpenter–Olson cleared his throat. He pressed a button. A statement printed in red uppercase letters and titled "STUDENTS AT RISK–PHILOSOPHY" appeared on the wall. He read the statement to the group. He enunciated very carefully, pointing at underlined words along the way. "RECOGNIZING ITS PART IN THE COMMUNITY OF EDUCATORS, THE STAFF OF THE DES MOINES PUBLIC SCHOOLS WILL, THROUGH THE MENTOR PROGRAM, JOIN THE URBAN SUPERINTENDENTS' CALL TO ACTION TO PREVENT DROPOUTS BY NURTURING, CARING FOR, AND EDUCATING EVERY MEMBER OF THE COMING GENERATION."

"So help us God," muttered Frank Nolden.

"I think this mission statement sums up our job quite well," remarked Carpenter-Olson. "Now, if you will please review this next transparency for a moment, you will begin to understand some of the mentoring practices we'll use to alter these kids' destructive behavior." A new transparency, a list of suggested mentoring techniques, flashed across the wall.

1. Give your mentoree a wake-up call once a week to show you care.
2. Discover his or her hobby and show an interest. Share your own hobbies and interests.
3. Turn a shopping trip with him/her into an educational experience.
4. Check progress with his/her teachers. He/She will respond when you show that the student's academic well-being is important.
5. Hold an after school volleyball game. Mentors v. Mentorees would be a good idea. This type of camaraderie sometimes returns lost sheep to the fold.
6. Try a pizza party. Many of these students never have a chance for experiences like this.
7. Mentors, using Bancroft's home ec facilities after school, could teach mentorees how to bake cookies.
8. Sit with your mentorees at athletic contests. Help build school spirit.
9. Hold after-school sharing sessions.
10. Take your mentoree to a movie. Be sure to check rating.

The group members exchanged glances and squirmed in their chairs.

"As you studied these techniques," said

Carpenter-Olson, pushing ahead officiously, "you probably noticed several that fit in well with your methodology, but we need to pick your brains, so to speak. Your job, committee, is to add to this list, come up with some fresh, innovative techniques of your own. You're the ones out there in the trenches, and we expect some insightful input from you." Carpenter-Olson became expansive. "Later in the afternoon we will convene in the little theatre, and Mr. Aneyh will share with everyone the contributions of each committee. When you enter the little theatre, just place your completed list on the table by the podium. If we can turn some of these 58 students around, this program will be a great success."

Carpenter-Olson hoisted himself upon the desk. "Well, what do you think?"

Silence.

"We can't solve problems without your input."

"Are you serious?" asked Frank Nolden.

"Serious? I don't know what you mean, sir. Sorry, I don't know your name. You vetoed our introductory icebreaker."

"My name doesn't matter. Are you serious about that simpy list of activities? Who put that together, anyway?"

"A very competent task force of administrators, consultants, and parents. I was a member."

"Any teachers?"

"No."

"Figures," Frank said.

"Sir," Carpenter-Olson said uneasily, "this

MENTOR program is voluntary; you don't have to participate."

"That's not what Aneyh just said."

"Well, that's the way it is. And all of these activities are designed to take place outside the school day."

"Like we don't have enough to do already?" Frank said.

"You don't have to be a part of it, sir," said Carpenter-Olson. "This program is for the doers in this system."

"Mr. Carpenter-Olson," Karen said. "I teach five classes of English. I couldn't tell you how many hours I spend outside class time with papers. If I don't get involved with this program, by your definition, I'm not a doer."

"That's not what I meant."

"That's what you imply," Frank shot back.

"People, people," Carpenter-Olson protested. "You're getting the wrong message here. Let's calm down and get to the task at hand. We need to come up with some suggestions. Surely you have some good ones."

"Grease their skids," Frank said.

"Sir?" asked the psychologist.

"You wanted a suggestion. I gave you one. Grease their skids. Get 'em the hell out of here. Read that list of 58 kids. You wouldn't know them, Olson. You don't have to teach trash like that. They're a disruptive, profane bunch of hedonistic brats. You could bake a thousand gingerbread boys with any one of them. Wouldn't change a thing."

"Now, now, sir," cautioned Carpenter-Olson.

"Look at number 47 on your rogues' gallery there. Jeremy King! Pushed Hal Delaney down a flight of stairs. Want to go shopping with him, Carpenter? He'd swipe anything he could get his hands on. And you'd end up getting booked for aiding and abetting a criminal. And while you're paying his bail, he'd be out in the parking lot siphoning your gasoline."

The facilitator raised his right hand, palm toward the group. "You're right. We lost this young man over the years, and we need to bring him back into the program to make the school better."

"Want to make this school better? Get rid of these sleazes. They don't want to be here. They drag everybody else down."

"What did you say your name was?" asked Carpenter-Olson.

"I didn't, but my name is Frank Nolden."

"Well, Mr. Nolden, I don't think you grasp the educational psychology around the MENTOR program."

"Oh, I don't? For pity's sakes. Let me put it in the educationese of an honest teacher, Mr. Eldon. The psychology of this program sucks."

"That's simply not true, Nolden. The MENTOR program will nurture academics at Bancroft."

"Nurture?" Frank was livid. "Why don't you lay caring and sharing on us while you're at it. Let me tell you how bad things are here. A Barbary ape could enroll at Bancroft and earn a diploma. Even if he watched eight hours of TV every night."

"Mr. Nolden, we're getting away from our task, and I'm sure you're in the minority. You, Ms." Carpenter-Olson nodded at Michelle. "Do you share his views?"

"None of this means anything to me," Michelle said. "I teach French to college-bound students. I don't have any students at risk."

"Well, aren't you the lucky one," Frank said sardonically.

"What do you teach, Nolden?" The facilitator's voice had become adversarial.

"American history. I've had half the kids on that list. They won't bring books, paper, anything. Study? You've got to be kidding me. Fail one of these slobs and Aneyh accuses you of messing up his self-esteem."

"Well, I've heard enough of this," proclaimed Carpenter-Olson. "You're a very bitter man. We don't need people like you in this profession."

"That's what you guys always say," Frank said quickly. "Here's one for you. Instead of dreaming up crap like that," he pointed to the wall, "why don't you grow a backbone and demand standards of these kids?"

"I think you're insubordinate," said Carpenter-Olson. "And your ideas on how to improve public education are impractical."

"I only mentioned one, but let me give you another. Round up all you psychobabblers that come up with stuff like this and ship them to Japan and Europe. Then we could teach something for a change."

"You've missed the whole point, Nolden! This program will help you bring these kids back. This program will make you a better teacher."

"How many years did you teach before you got into counseling, Eldon?"

"Two."

"Two? I've been doing this for two decades. Where do you get off giving me advice on how to be a better teacher?"

Carpenter-Olson snapped off the overhead, crammed the transparencies into his briefcase, and slammed it shut. "There's no way to work with a group such as this," he said. "You people are on your own." He left the room in a huff.

Alice Cain tapped her pencil on the desktop. She finally broke the silence. "God, Frank. What a performance! You know he's going straight to the hyena."

"I'd bet on it," Frank said.

"He'll be all over you. Is that what you want?"

"No." Frank got up. "But I don't want some yuppie scout leader getting in my face with crap like this, either. For Christ's sakes, he's taught two years. Probably in some finishing school. And he wants me to exchange cookie recipes with a gangster like King." Nolden walked across the room and stopped in the doorway. "I'm sorry if I embarrassed any of you. Maybe you see some value here. I just see this stuff as another symptom of a hellish problem." His hand went to his forehead in a limp salute. "Aneyh would never accept any of my contributions to that list. I'm going to my room and check papers."

Committee members arranged their chairs like settlers circling the wagons. With the exception of Michelle Valder, who inventoried the contents of her purse, this group appeared hell bent on adding to the district's list of mentoring techniques. The dispute between Nolden and the facilitator inspired them. And the energy that poured from the circle of chairs would have convinced Carpenter-Olson, had he peeked at them through the open door, that he had carried the day despite Nolden's condemnation.

Alice Cain, the elected chairperson, carried the unsigned fruits of their labor to the little theatre. After only 30 minutes, they had produced a week's plan, a regimen for combatting at riskism.

WHO'S AT RISK?
OR
HOW TO SAVE A FEW AND LOSE THE REST

Monday, greet them at the door. Roll out a red carpet embossed with smiley faces.

Tuesday, pat their little cheeks. Tousle their little heads. Give them hugs and warm fuzzies.

Wednesday, wipe their little noses with Kleenex, Puffs, or cotton balls, or your own handkerchief for a more personal touch.

Thursday, pat their little butts. But not suggestively. Remember, this is mentoring not molesting.

Friday, smoke doobie with them behind the gym.

Saturday and Sunday, lend them your credit card, car, and wife or husband or significant other.

twenty-nine

The Emperor's New Clothes, for all its excitement, was also dangerous. And since the conspirators had pled for money and stamps on the paper's last page, Alice Cain, in order to protect their personal identities, rented a post office box in a substation downtown.

David insisted he would be the first to pick up the mail, an act that he saw as his red badge of courage in the eyes of the other three; but after a week of bravado, paranoia crept in. Fears often assailed teachers who took positions outside the administrative cocoon, and David's mind was a fertile ground for worst-case scenarios: the district's henchmen lying in wait at the mailbox, Robert D. Aneyh sniffing the trail for his scent, the cloying fear of being outed by a member of his own cell.

When David climbed into the passenger seat of Karen's car in Bancroft's parking lot after In-Service Day, he wrestled out of his parka and into a trench coat, pulled a baseball cap over his brow, and looked at her through a pair of Ray-Bans.

"What are you doing?" Karen asked.

243

"We're going after the mail, aren't we? I'm protecting my identity."

Karen put her head on the steering wheel. "David, this is crazy. You drive. I'll get the mail."

"No," David said grimly. "I said I'd do this, and I'm going to do it."

Karen shrugged and headed for the downtown substation. "OK, David, remember, there's no parking. I'll circle the block and pick you up at the corner of 4th and Walnut."

"Where'd you say the box was?"

"Alice told you, David. Right in the middle. Waist high. Number 206. The number's on the key." Even though he had asked the question, Karen could see David was too nervous to hear the answer.

He pushed his Ray-Bans to the bridge of his nose and tugged at his cap. They drove in silence to the substation, where she dropped him at the curb. After her fourth trip around the block, David emerged from the substation door with bulging pockets and loped toward her car.

"My God, Karen," he exploded, once inside, "didn't Alice check this place out?"

"What happened?"

"That box—right in front of the window! Anyone could have seen me!"

"Who would know you in that get-up?"

"And that television camera on a swivel trained on my every step!"

"Grow up, David. That camera's part of the security system."

"Exactly. Part of the security system. My picture's on record."

Karen laughed and merged into the traffic.

"Not funny," he snapped.

"Come on, how 'bout the mail? Did we get any?"

David unloaded his pockets and piled the mail in the space between them. He removed his shades and ripped an envelope open with the mailbox key.

"Stay out of those, David. We're not looking at any of them until we get to my place. Nick and Alice deserve to be in on this."

"Bull! I risked my neck to get these."

Karen snatched the envelope from his hand. "Well, poor baby! Just lie back and rest. You've had a very scary day."

"Oh, hush up, Karen. Just get me back to my car."

The gang of four assembled in Karen's living room at four o'clock. Alice, parked on the couch, held the contents of their secret mailbox on her massive thighs. Nick straddled a kitchen chair backwards, his forearms resting on the chair back. Karen carried in a tray with four mugs and the coffeepot, wondering why Nick had asked for the extra cup—she knew he never drank coffee. David paced with his hands in his pockets and his eyes riveted to the carpet. He continued to juice up the dangers of the mail-run until finally he stepped over the threshold of Alice Cain's tolerance.

"OK, Don Quixote," she said at last. "Let's face it—you are a colossal wuss."

"Well, Big Mama, next time you get the mail."

"Anything to shut you up. I'd rather listen to Edwina MacIntosh."

"Let's settle the mail problem later," Nick said. "I want to discuss another matter."

The edge in his voice got everyone's attention.

"I believe only one person has figured out who's publishing this paper."

"Oh, no!" Alice gasped.

"Who?" David demanded.

"George Moore."

"Oh, crap," David blurted. "Moore doesn't even know he's alive."

"He confronted me in the lounge," Nick told them. "He knows."

"That little bastard may run straight to Aneyh," David said.

"He wouldn't do that," Alice assured him.

"You don't know him, David." Nick fixed David in his gaze. "He has courage. George Moore won't be running to Aneyh. He wants to help us. He wants to be a part of this paper."

"No! I don't want him," David said. "What could he do, anyway?"

"Maybe he could go get the mail," Alice said. "That seems to scare the pea-wadding out of you."

"What do you think, Karen?" Nick asked.

Karen looked over her coffee cup. "I'm all for George Moore. He's one of my favorite people."

"Alice?" Nick asked.

"If David's against him, I'm for him."

"Look," David paced again. "George Moore's afraid of his own shadow. The hyena terrifies the little twerp. The odds for our being found out go up exponentially with every new person we take on."

"Not with this person." Nick shrugged. "Anyway, too late. He'll be here at four-thirty."

"We should have voted on this, Staal," David said.

"You'd have lost three-to-one," Alice told him. "Let's just check out the mail."

David fell onto the couch next to her muttering to himself.

"I wonder how many of these will be complimentary?" she went on. "The first one's addressed to 'The Emperor.'"

David snatched the envelope and ripped it open. "The address doesn't say Empress. Listen to this. 'I applaud your paper. I am one who saw many years ago that the Emperor was, indeed, shamefully naked. But no one heard my cry. Yet we teachers are the ones held responsible for the sad state of education locally and nationally. Give us more. Signed—a fan.'" A ten-dollar bill fluttered to the floor. "There's your answer, Alice. They love us!" He scooped up the ten and handed it to Karen. "Here! Keep track of this, a log or something. We need to account for every penny. We're going to be these people's mouthpiece. Teachers all over the U S of A are madder than hell, and WE DON'T HAVE TO TAKE THIS ANYMORE!"

Alice gave him the whites of her eyes. "Can't you come up with something original?"

"Come on," David said. "Pass those envelopes

around, you hog. Whoops!" He slapped his mouth in mock embarrassment.

Alice handed each of them a fistful of envelopes, ignoring, as she always did, David's fat jokes, an indifference that she knew played with the comedic image he had of himself. She ceremoniously opened an envelope. " 'Four dollars,' the letter says. 'I opened my billfold, and you get all I had.' No return address."

"Here's a return address," Nick told them. "Council Bluffs."

"Really! How would they get access to our paper?" Karen wondered.

David shrugged. "What difference does it make? They have the same problems we do. Put this paper in the teachers' lounge in Buzzard's Breath, Wyoming, and they'd think we were writing about them."

"We've got a name here, too," Nick said. "Sibyl Christensen. She wants every issue. Her letter is signed by 25 teachers at Noah Webster High School in Council Bluffs. 'Dear Editor: Your paper, *The Emperor's New Clothes,* was right on the mark— entertaining, timely, and painfully correct. Our faculty wishes you success and wide-based support. We wait for your next edition.'"

"Any money?" David demanded.

Nick held up a twenty and two tens.

"Lord." David patted Alice's shoulder, a tactile peace offering for having called her a hog. "What do you think, Alice? Maybe we should syndicate, go national."

Three taps on the front door interrupted Alice

Cain's answer. Nick opened the door. George Moore stepped in and removed his hat. Karen viewed George Moore's observance of early-twentieth century manners as an endearing anomaly. He was quiet, demure, kind, always a gentleman. If for no other reason, she despised Robert D. Aneyh for his contemptuous treatment of this inoffensive little man.

George took several steps forward. His eyes moved from Karen to David to Alice.

"Surprised to find out who's in on this?" Alice asked.

"I'm not surprised to see you here, Alice." He fiddled with his hat. "I suppose I should say something. You'll never know what this paper means to me. I admire what you're doing, and—uh—I'm really happy," he cleared his throat, "that you all let me…"

"Sit down, George," Nick said. "Have some coffee and listen to the mail. Pretty good stuff."

"Not this one," David said. " 'I read your first issue with great interest. It was obviously written by someone with very good writing skills. I suppose it wasn't one of our high school English teachers.'" He thumped the letter with the back of his hand. "Now isn't that the shits?"

"Doesn't bother me. I don't teach English," Alice said. "Read the rest of it."

" 'Nevertheless, your paper was concise and witty.' I forgive him. Two books of stamps in here." David put the letter down.

Alice turned to George Moore. "Let me tell you

what's exciting. Everyone and his dog is trying to figure out where this paper came from."

"Oh, that's so true. My wife's faculty's been crazy all week. But don't you worry, Alice; I'll never tell her I'm helping you." He forced a grin. "She wouldn't believe me anyway."

"I'm not worried, George."

"Listen to this!" Karen waved two pieces of blue paper. "I could have written this letter. Ninety percent of the teachers who are afraid to open their mouths could have written this letter."

"OK, OK," David said. "Don't analyze the whole teaching corps. Read the damn thing!"

"'I opened the envelope and was momentarily puzzled by its contents. But your red-hot publication soon made me whoop with delight. I think those whoops mark me as one of you minus most of your courage. The whoops, however strong, may not be memorable, coming as they were from a teachers' lounge, but the little dance I tapped out certainly will stick in the minds of co-workers. At this point in paranoia, I refuse to be identified further, even among you. You understand the feeling, of course. It's the big one that bonds so many Des Moines teachers, but also holds us down together. I expect that there will soon be those who claim you should be ignored because you write/publish under cover. "No credibility without identification," they may scream. Please, ignore them. I would hope that you just go on writing, publishing, raising hell. Don't play their game; play your own. Remain underground. Just lie low and keep hurling those cannonballs.'"

Euphoria engulfed Karen's living room. If the fledgling staff needed legitimacy, they found it in what Karen had just read. The writer's painful abdication of courage, the spirited entreaty to fire more broadsides became their mission statement. Later, Karen matted and framed the letter, which found a home on the wall next to the sepia-tinted picture of Martha Y. Bancroft.

The clock said 6:00 straight up when Nicholas Staal, still straddling the kitchen chair, slowly withdrew an envelope from his pocket as if he had happened on a propitious moment to reveal its contents. George and Alice were preparing to leave. Karen was removing cups from the coffee table. And David, his head resting on the back of the couch, was crowing about the $468 in money and stamps.

"Before you leave," Nick began, "we have one more letter—probably from a crackpot."

"Who's a crackpot?" David asked.

"This letter doesn't pass the smell test—could have been sent from someone like Aneyh to frighten us."

Alice came back from the front door. "Read it."

" 'I urge you to protect your anonymity.'" Nick glanced at David. " 'Rumor has it that the central office and some principals are working hard to discover the identities of those behind this paper. I have a very reliable source. Supposedly your PO box is being watched and bag mail deposits monitored. In a few buildings, envelopes were intercepted and deliveries prevented. Watch your backsides!'"

David pushed himself forward. "You don't know that a crackpot wrote that letter, Staal, or what his motives are. Sounds to me like someone who knows damn well what he's talking about."

"You're right. I don't know."

David stared at Alice Cain. "What'd I tell you? You sat there and belittled me with that Don Quixote shit. You heard the letter! Do you still think I'm tilting at windmills?"

"Yes, I do."

"You don't get it. My picture's on that PO tape."

"The FBI couldn't figure out who you are," Karen said. "You should have seen his disguise."

Nick pulled his chair closer to David. "You wrote a terrific article in this first edition, David. Bet you've waited awhile to get all that stuff off your chest. Felt pretty good, didn't it?"

"Well, sure."

"Didn't say anything immoral or libelous, did you?"

"What are you getting at, Staal?"

"The First Amendment. Doesn't matter how many tapes your picture's on. What you're doing here, what we're all doing here, is perfectly legal. We'd all be better off writing in the open. If someone tried to shut us up, the free press would crawl all over them. But you won't do that, will you, David? If you can't stay in the closet, you won't play. In deference to you, we've all agreed to anonymity, and you're still quaking in your boots." Nick leaned toward him. "What was the title of that article you wrote?"

"'We Need the Courage to Change,'" David said sheepishly.

"Oh, yeah, that's right. You had some great lines in there, too, like the one where you called teachers who failed to speak out shameless toadies. So," Nick asked him, "how is it that a man who writes about spleen heads for the hills at the first blush of danger? I don't fear being discovered, David. I fear being a hypocrite."

"I hear you," David said. "OK. OK." His lips tightened and he stroked his chin. "But I'm not going back to that mailbox again."

"You don't have to. That will be my job." Everyone looked at George Moore, who sat erectly on the front of his chair. His hands resting on knees held tightly together gave him the appearance of a bird on a perch. "I've been sitting here wondering what I can do to help this cause. You folks concentrate your talents on content. I'll be the mailman."

"You don't have to do that, George," Nick told him. "We'll take turns."

"Oh, yes, I do," George insisted. "A face like mine on a post office tape would never arouse suspicion. Maybe a little pity," he grinned. "But not suspicion."

Nick shrugged. "Everyone still on board?"

"Of course," Karen said.

"You couldn't blast me out," Alice replied.

"Yes," David said, "as long as Moore's the permanent mailman."

thirty

Jeremy King sat on a street corner half asleep, his back against a mailbox. The vacuous stare etched on his face indicated his total disinterest in the sights and noises around him. He waited for Lydia Fletcher, who had adopted him through Bancroft's MENTOR program. At school, King had been only mildly defanged for his attack on Hal Delaney: Aneyh demanded his participation in the MENTOR program as the price for avoiding permanent detention. A municipal judge, however, viewed King's conduct as a serious breach of law; the judge revoked his driver's license for one year and imposed a $500 fine.

Lydia beckoned from her car and soon found herself crowded inside the small space with her charge. Nothing could dampen her enthusiasm. The MENTOR program was her cup of tea, and she intended to demonstrate for the program's detractors what marvelous results could be wrought through total involvement. Turning Jeremy King around would not be easy. She understood that. But Lydia ate and slept the philosophy that building a student's self-esteem was the most notable educational achievement of all.

"I'm glad you're going to work for me," Lydia told him. "I'll pay you minimum wage, of course. You can use the money for your fine."

King grunted.

Lydia glanced at him. "My husband loathes yard work. Will he be surprised when he gets back!"

"Oh."

"Do you have brothers or sisters, Jeremy?"

"Yeah."

Lydia didn't like conversational lapses. "Tell me about them."

"Three brothers. No sisters." He watched the well-kept houses in Lydia's neighborhood fly by.

"Are they still in school?"

"Nah." He scratched himself.

"Where are they?"

King shrugged.

Lydia employed every trick she knew to draw out her mentoree. But he persisted in monosyllabic answers. She entered her driveway. "Let me guess," Lydia smiled sweetly. "I'll bet your parents are really proud of you for landing this job."

Another shrug. He opened the car door and stepped onto the pavement.

The mild March day was ready-made for yard work. King, like a clumsy, overgrown dog, followed Lydia around the yard. She nodded at last year's leaves under the shrubs and those impacted in the bottom of the chain-link fence. Her arm moved gracefully away from her body, demonstrating the proper way to broadcast grass seed onto bare spots. In all, Lydia's tour revealed seven specific areas that needed attention.

King leaned on a rake while Lydia hovered. She explained the possibility of future employment—mowing, spot painting, moving rocks—if he completed the day's projects successfully.

"Now I must leave," she told him from the car. "I'll be back around 3:00. We can have a little snack before I take you home. Have a nice day, Jeremy." She backed into the street and yelled through the open window, "The side door is unlocked if you need anything. You know, the bathroom."

Rap music boomed through the side door when she returned at 3:10. Her eyes swept the yard. Leaves still quilted the chain-link fence and surrounded the shrubs like so many scarves. The rake lay on the exact spot where King last leaned on it. Lydia hurried up the three steps to the kitchen. Cigarette smoke and the reek of beer raked at her nostrils. No one smoked in Lydia Fletcher's house! Her husband sneaked cigars on the back porch or in the garage.

She placed her purse on the kitchen table alongside an empty beer can, closed the refrigerator door, and followed the music to the family room, where she found her noble experiment in fitful sleep. The room was a shambles—the couch, which barely contained King's 6-3 frame, resembled a raft adrift in a sea of debris. Magazines, tapes, beer cans, and pretzel bags littered the floor. Some of the pretzels were ground into the carpet. Ashes and butts despoiled her favorite porcelain dish. Deafening bass notes spanked the sides of the entertainment center, enshrouding the family room in a surrealistic aura, the centerpiece of which was a boy in a man's body, an inebriated felon with a trail of saliva dribbling from the corner of his open mouth onto his neck.

Lydia cut off the stereo in a panic and faced the consequences of her social experiment gone sour. "Wake up, Jeremy! Wake up!"

King licked saliva from his lips and rolled onto his side. Lydia grabbed the boy's massive shoulders in an effort to shake some life into him. Groggy and disoriented, he blinked at her through bloodshot eyes. "Get out of here, you drunken sot!" She pulled his arm, trying to raise him from the couch.

"What in hell's the matter with you?" he said sloppily. "You invited me in and told me to use anything I needed."

"You are drunk! I want you out of this house immediately!"

King grabbed Lydia's wrists and pulled her on top of him. A menacing laugh forced through beer befouled breath brought bile to her throat. "Jeremy," she screamed, "you're hurting me! You let me go this instant!"

"Jesus, Miss Fletcher, you've got big tits! How 'bout I lick 'em for ya."

"Why, you bastard! How dare you do this to me!"

Her blouse ripped and her hip brushed against a bulge in the crotch of his pants. He wrestled her to the floor and pinned her wrists to the carpet with one hand while he choked off a stream of "dirty bastards" from her mouth with the other.

A messy flood of images washed over Lydia's mind. *Molested in my own home by a mentoree . . . All I wanted to do was help this boy . . . My husband's in Chicago . . . My daughter's at ISU . . . Aneyh's mentoring program put this creep on top of me . . .* All ending in the terrifying realization that there was no exit.

Lydia lay helpless, unable to move. The ceiling fan in her own family room swirled indifferently above. Jeremy King, like a frantic animal, kneed her legs apart and rutted against her pelvis through four layers of cloth. Brassy drops from his loose lips fell on her forehead. She watched his eyes glaze over, his nostrils flare. Primitive noises gurgled in his throat until, at last, the rhythmic pounding stopped and a sickly grin rolled over King's face. The death grip on her wrists and mouth weakened. He toppled onto his side like a tranquilized gorilla.

"You dirty bastard," she screamed, struggling to her feet. She stumbled toward the kitchen, where her trembling finger punched in an unrelated series of numbers. A sweet, courteous voice advised her that she had misdialed, that she should hang up and try again. For a frightening moment Lydia felt faint, but the loathsome figure of Jeremy King looming in the kitchen doorway snapped her back to reality.

Lydia held her torn blouse together and grabbed

the teakettle from the stove. "You get out of here this instant!" She waved the teakettle in front of him.

"Tell you what, Miss Fletcher. Pay me the twenty-five bucks you owe me and I'll leave."

Lydia hyperventilated. Words stuck in her throat.

"You better pay me. Or I'll be back again next time your husband's gone."

Lydia pulled objects from her purse: lipstick, a nail file, finally two twenty-dollar bills landed on the table. King grabbed them, stumbled down the three steps, and turned at the side door. "Don't I get a ride home?"

"Get out before I call the police!"

King grinned. "See ya Monday, Miss Fletcher. I had a good time."

thirty-one

Hattie Reins handed each teacher a copy of the faculty meeting agenda; the backside doubled as a scratch pad for wandering minds. The agenda varied little from meeting to meeting: I. Announcements, II. State of the School, III. Hip Hip Hooray. But something new, item IV. FONE logs, sent teachers to their seats buzzing.

Karen took her usual place beside David in the back row.

"FONE logs, with an 'F'! I don't like this," David said.

"You worry about everything," Karen told him. "Might be something educational."

"Educational, my ass. An acronym means another committee." David nodded toward the door, which Hattie Reins had just closed behind the principal. He charged the podium and plowed through a welter of announcements, which had already been in the weekly bulletin or read over the PA, as if anyone cared to hear them again. Suddenly, four words tumbling from Aneyh's lips electrified the yawning gathering of doodlers: *The Emperor's New Clothes*. Pencils stopped in mid-doodle; three hundred eyes riveted the man on the podium.

"We are monitoring the bag mail. Never again, I'll reiterate once more, never again will these hacks disseminate their libel by that means. We will track down the perpetrators, and they will be dealt with. I know you agree with me that we cannot run a healthy school system with traitors nibbling at our guts from within." Aneyh inspected his audience, clasped his hands, and rested his elbows on the podium. "I know I can count on your help. You people are as devoted to quality education as I am. If you know who's involved in this illegal publication, or anything about it at all, I invite you to come to my office for a chat. Be assured I would never violate a confidence. There might even be a reward in it for you."

There was no outward reaction to what the faculty had just heard but, rather, a sinking feeling down to the last teacher that the principal had just ruptured any remaining bonds between them, a sense that words such as "honor," "ethics," "integrity" did not exist in this man's moral code. And, as a final insult, their chief stood at the podium oblivious to the possibilities that he had tampered with any of these concepts.

Karen felt like she needed a shower. She glanced at her friends. Color drained from David's face; his right leg jiggled. Alice's head moved almost imperceptibly from side to side. A sly smile bunched up George Moore's lips. And Nick, who always sat in the front row with the coaches, looked like a high-stakes poker player.

Aneyh moved to item III, Hip Hip Hooray, a ritual that allowed him to stroke teachers of his own choosing. "Let's have a hip hip hooray for Brook Fielding, Marcie Reynolds, and Lydia Fletcher," he bellowed. There was a rustle of applause. "These are the first staff members to sign on to the MENTOR program. Will you three please step forward." He pulled three certificates of achievement from the podium shelf, but only Lydia Fletcher, splendid in a tailored linen dress, approached the podium. Aneyh cocked an eye at Hattie Reins, who informed him that Ms. Reynolds was attending a district meeting and that Mr. Fielding was on a home visit.

"Well, Mrs. Fletcher," he crowed. "Since you're getting all the attention, why don't you give us a testimonial for the MENTOR program. I understand you're working with Jeremy King." He beamed at her like a proud parent. "I'm sure the faculty would like to hear about your experiences."

She whispered "thank you," grabbed the certificate from him as if she were pulling a weed, and hurried back to her chair.

The faculty exchanged glances. Lydia Fletcher never gave up an opportunity to trumpet progressive ideas. Whispers rose to a drone before Aneyh rescued the awkward situation. "Well, Mrs. Fletcher, I must say your modesty is charming. Perhaps we can hear from you at some other time." He removed his glasses. "As pleased as I am with you, frankly, I'm disappointed with the rest of this faculty."

Karen's mind swam. Contradictions flowed from this man's mouth like water. He was disappointed in them! Moments ago, he had painted them as devotees of quality education.

"I told Dr. MacIntosh," he continued, "Bancroft would be the leader for the MENTOR program. Apparently, I was wrong. These three people are the only volunteers. While the rest of you sat on your hands, two more at-risk students have left Bancroft. Mrs. Fletcher can't save these kids all by herself.

"Item IV." The principal nodded at Rick Cook, who tromped through the aisles handing each teacher a paper headed "FONE log" with five columns: Student, Phone Number, Date, Time, Strategy. George Moore winked at Alice Cain, but mostly teachers sat in restless silence as Aneyh explained that the city-wide MENTOR program now had a homegrown adjunct, FONE—Faculty Oversees New Enthusiasm, a powerful concept, according to the principal, which had sprung from the brain of Brook Fielding.

Aneyh carefully outlined the new responsibilities. Participation in MENTOR was now mandatory. Three teachers had been assigned to each one of the students on the original at-risk list. These three teachers would each call the assigned student's home once a week. A report on the content of the call and suggested strategies would be submitted each Monday to Hattie Reins. The animated principal concluded with a flourish. "Let me tell you what these FONE logs are designed to do. They will, in short, track the outcome of your input."

No one could remember the last time George Moore sought recognition in a faculty meeting, but there he sat, hand straight in the air, an impish twinkle in his eyes.

"Moore," Aneyh barked.

"Mr. Aneyh, could you tell me what the outcome of our input is supposed to be."

"Perfect attendance, of course! This program may be beyond your experience, Moore. Stop and think for a minute. A reluctant, perhaps angry child gets three phone calls every week from concerned, caring faculty members. Do you have any idea what that might mean in his life? What lights might go on? What doors might open? We have a powerful weapon here, Moore. All we have to do is use it. The FONE program will lure these kids back to class. Now, doesn't this make sense to you?"

"Well, I guess," George said.

"Any other questions?" the principal asked.

"Yes," George said. "What makes you think a few phone calls from caring teachers will get these kids back here when truant officers can't?"

"Because we are going to pay them for attendance."

Aneyh's statement drew gasps from the faculty.

"Pay them?" The twinkle faded from George's eyes. "How much?"

"Perhaps I used the wrong word. We're going to

reward them. Truant officers use the stick. We will use the carrot. Brook Fielding found corporate sponsors willing to donate products like tanning sessions—kids love those, you know—or passes to the waterslide park, things like that. Weekly prizes to at-risk kids for perfect attendance. And," he smiled, "I should admonish all of you against announcing this to the entire student body. They might feel left out." Aneyh picked up his papers, carefully stashed his glasses inside his suit coat, and prepared to adjourn the meeting.

"Mr. Aneyh."

He frowned over the podium at Nicholas Staal. "What do you want?"

"I know you are always concerned with propriety. I'm wondering, however, if this might not be construed as a form of bribery on the same level, perhaps, as paying students a dime or fifteen cents for learning new words."

"You know something, Staal, your comment is impertinent. I don't go off half-cocked. Dr. Pagano, Interim Director of Secondary Education, in case you've forgotten, has examined this, as well as Dr. MacIntosh, and I might add both have endorsed the plan whole-heartedly. Their area of expertise is interacting with disturbed children. They know what's best for kids."

"That's reassuring," Nick said. "When would we make these FONE calls?"

"Whenever you can get through. Outside the school day, wouldn't you think?"

"That's my point. I live 40 miles west of here." Nick paused. "Will the Des Moines Public Schools or Bancroft High School, specifically, pay my phone bills?"

Aneyh loosened his tie. The glassy smile evaporated. "If you lived in this district like you should, these calls wouldn't cost you a damn cent." The room got quiet enough to hear that cent drop. Each curving tier of chairs ascended to a higher level from which the faculty, like patrons in the ancient coliseum, looked down on Staal and Aneyh, two gladiators on the floor below, stalking one another for advantage.

"If I understand you correctly," Nick said, "you're saying that all school personnel should live within the district."

"Exactly. The taxpayers of this district pay your salary, Staal. We taxpayers are the stakeholders. By living out in the sticks, you take from the district and you don't put anything back. You're a freeloader. And that should make perfect sense even to someone like you."

"Yes," Nick said quickly. "You're certainly right. And may I suggest, the next time Dr. MacIntosh addresses this faculty, you introduce her as a freeloader. She lives in Indianola. And I would let Dr. Pagano know he's taking from the district and not putting back. He lives 35 miles north in Ames— probably doesn't know he's a parasite."

"Why, you son of a," Aneyh caught himself. His meaty hands clutched the podium's corners. The moment lengthened into several, a freeze frame, while their words resonated in the dead air. Aneyh's eyes blazed into Nicholas Staal as if the principal expected the teacher to incinerate under his withering glare. The silence approached embarrassment.

"Mr. Aneyh," Nick said calmly, "why spend so much time and energy on kids who don't even want to be here?"

No response.

"How 'bout the good average kids who show up every day. How do we reward them? Bury them in a class with 34 other kids while we make phone calls and write strategy reports?"

Still no response.

"Why don't you concentrate your talents on reducing class size or selling the board a strategy on how to raise academic and behavioral standards?"

"If you want a committee to raise standards, Mr. Aneyh," blurted George Moore, "I'll serve as chairman."

"I'll be on that one," offered someone in the back.

"Me, too."

Suddenly Aneyh released his grip on the podium and pointed a finger at his tormentor. "Staal, you're a disgrace to the profession—the most impudent, unprincipled teacher I've ever encountered. You don't have a clue of what it takes to run a school of this size. We'd all be better off if you'd stay out there on that farm and slop your hogs." He scooped his papers from the podium. "None of what you're babbling about is on the agenda. We're talking here about FONE logs. Period. You and everyone else in this room will make your calls, suggest your strategies, and hand them in each Monday. Beginning right now."

Aneyh left the stage in one giant step and rushed through the door, which Hattie Reins barely opened in time. Clusters of people gathered around the room. The real faculty meeting was on. FONE logs, threats about *The Emperor's New Clothes,* a rejuvenated George Moore, Aneyh's histrionics—they had plenty to talk about.

"Hey, Nick," Frank Nolden yelled. "These people over here want to know. Are you going to do those FONE logs?"

"Of course," Nick said. "He's the boss."

thirty-two

Darlene McGimpsey harrumphed from the doorway.

Karen looked up from a book. She had turned in her third-quarter grades and was waiting for the dismissal bell that signaled the beginning of Spring Break.

"Better strap on your bulletproof vest, hon."

"That sounds ominous."

"May be." Darlene came to the front of her desk. "Do you know what next week is?"

"Spring Break."

"Not if you're a football player," Darlene told her. "Next week is national letter of intent signing."

"So?"

"You're about to be summoned. Rick Cook's giving you holy hell in Aneyh's office as we speak—about the 'D' you gave Lance Moffat."

"I didn't give him that grade. He earned it." Karen slapped the book shut. "He's lazy and usually unprepared. The work he did turn in was awful. How would Cook know anyway? I turned in my grades not ten minutes ago."

269

"Shows you how things work around here," Darlene said. "Cook has a direct line to the registrar. The minute you left, he got the grades and went straight to the hyena. If Moffat doesn't maintain a 'C' average, he'll never be offered a scholarship." Darlene raised her eyebrows. "Aneyh told Cook he'd get you to change the grade."

"He did what?"

"That's what I meant about the flack jacket."

"How do you know all of this?"

Darlene sat on the corner of Karen's desk. "I was there when Cook came in. Aneyh wants me to read Moffat the ACT."

"You're not thinking I should change a grade, are you?"

"Of course not! I just came up here to warn you. Don't you budge an inch!"

"Ms. Merchant," the wall speaker said. "Mr. Aneyh would like to see you in his office."

"OK." Karen pushed herself up. "I don't need this, Darlene. All I want is Spring Break."

"You want me to go with you?"

"Thanks, but no. This is between the good old boys and me."

Lance Moffat played center for the Bancroft football team. He had been heavily recruited by Iowa State University in spite of his dismal academic performance. His eligibility for each week's game literally hung in the balance right up to kick-off time. To enter ISU, Moffat had two hurdles to jump:

maintain a "C" average and qualify on the ACT. In order to boost his beefy center over the first of these hurdles, Coach Cook had plucked an exotic from his bag of trick plays. Since Moffat had badly mangled the ACT on two previous occasions, Cook had finagled "special ed" status for his star. This meant that a special ed teacher could read him the ACT, and he would be allowed extra time to complete the exam. But the coach had not figured that Moffat would stumble over a third-quarter grade in Senior English.

Principal Aneyh greeted Karen from the conversation pit with a broad smile and indicated that she should join Rick Cook, who sat glum-faced on the sofa across from him. Karen sat down as far from the muscular coach as she could.

"I'll get right to the point, Karen," Aneyh said. "Lance Moffat's third-quarter grade. You know that he'll be signing his letter of intent next week. This dedicated young athlete has a chance to continue his education at ISU on a scholarship next year."

"So I've heard."

"Then why do you want to destroy a promising football career?" Cook demanded.

Aneyh frowned at the coach. "Rick, simmer down. I'll take care of this. Karen, surely you understand what having one of our graduates playing football for Iowa State would mean for Bancroft."

"No, I really don't, Mr. Aneyh."

"Of course you wouldn't," Cook snapped.

"What does this have to do with me, Mr. Aneyh?"

"Since I've been principal, Karen, you've had the

best schedule in the English department—four Advanced Placement classes and one Senior English. You are aware of that, aren't you?"

"Yes," Karen said quickly. "I remember when Mr. Wilken retired. He recommended me as the most qualified teacher in the department for Advanced Placement. You told me that yourself."

"Schedules can change," Aneyh said.

"I do a good job. At least eighty percent of my students who take the Advanced Placement test earn college credit. That's the best record in the district."

"I don't want to change your schedule, but I do need a little cooperation here with Lance Moffat's situation."

"Are you telling me to change his grade?"

"Let's don't put it that way, Karen. We all know that we sometimes make mistakes. Why, I wouldn't be surprised that if you check your records, you might find a mistake in adding points or maybe you forgot some extra credit—something like that."

"No. I check every grade very carefully. There is no mistake."

"Oh, for Christ's sakes!" Rick Cook pushed himself to the front of the sofa. "What difference does it make! It's just a pissy-assed grade in Senior English."

"Coach," Karen said, "I don't tell you how to run your football team, and you're not going to tell me what grades to give."

"Maybe you don't understand, Karen." Aneyh's eyes narrowed. "Next year instead of having topnotch students, you could have five classes of ninth-grade

English filled to the gills with students like Lance Moffat."

"That wouldn't be ethical, Mr. Aneyh."

"We're not talking ethics here. We're talking football." The principal pushed a piece of paper lying on the coffee table toward her. "Help us out here, Karen. Just fill in this change-of-grade form and we'll all go home and enjoy Spring Break."

Karen shot a look at Rick Cook and then at her boss. She picked up the pen, scribbled on the form, signed her name, and handed it to Aneyh. "Here, this finishes our business," she said coldly.

"Yes, and I want to thank you for your coop..." The principal's jaw dropped as he stared at the "F" screaming at him from the change-of-grade form. "What's this supposed to mean?" he yelled.

"You wanted me to change the grade. I did. If I were you, I'd use the first one. It's accurate."

Aneyh tore up the form and jammed the pieces in the wastebasket. "Wait till you see next year's schedule."

Karen got up. "You can fill my classes with a thousand Lance Moffats, Mr. Aneyh. If they do the kind of work he did, they'll earn a thousand 'D's." She smiled at Rick Cook. "Enjoy your Spring Break."

"You're a real cunt, Merchant."

"And you are a wonderful leader of young men, Cook."

Karen stopped at the drinking fountain and gulped at the feeble stream produced by her trembling hand on the lever.

"One for the road?"

Karen straightened up. "Oh, hi, Alice. Not this. I need something much stronger."

"You may want the whole bottle when I tell you what I just heard."

"You know about Moffat?"

"Moffat? What about him?"

"Nothing." Karen waved her hand in the air. "What do you know that's going to drive me to drink?"

"DUTO's executive secretary just told me that every board member's for the seven-period day. We're going to teach six periods next year, Karen, whether we like it or not. How 'bout that."

"I can't," Karen said. "That's twenty percent more work for nothing."

Alice sighed. "There's nothing any of us can do."

"Maybe I'll just quit."

thirty-three

On Wednesday of Spring Break, Karen, dressed in jeans and sweatshirt, peered through her living room window. The lights of Nick's pickup truck stabbed through the predawn gloom. She grabbed her purse, turned off the lamp, and closed the door behind her. She was on her way to visit Nick's farm.

The door on the passenger side was open.

"Good morning," he said cheerfully. "Are you awake?"

"Of course I'm awake. Why are we going at this god-awful hour?"

"You asked for a typical farm day."

Karen stepped on the running board and hoisted herself in. Her feet raked through a pile of trash on the floorboard—pop cans, milk cartons, waxed paper, banana peels.

"Why is all this junk in here?" she wondered out loud.

"I eat breakfast on the way to school."

She kicked a space for her feet. "Any mice?"

"I've never seen any." If Nick felt any embarrassment about the miniature landfill on the floor of his truck, she couldn't detect it.

She held up a syringe. "What's this for?"

"Vaccinating cattle." He backed into the street.

"For what?"

"Clostridium chauvoie."

"Sounds like a mezzo soprano."

"I'd like to vaccinate for them."

"What is clodium-whatever?"

"Farmers call it black leg." Nick pumped the clutch. "Cattle get it orally from spores in the soil. Once infected, muscles deteriorate fast. A critter won't last long."

"How many cows do you have?"

"Eighty-five. Three bulls. I'll have eighty-five calves soon if they all live."

"What's the gestation period?"

"'Bout the same as yours, nine-and-a-half months. I turn out the bulls on the fourth of July. Calves show up in late April."

"Then you sell them?"

"When they weigh five or six hundred pounds."

"I couldn't do that. Calves are too cute."

"Wait a minute! You're not a mole for PETA, by any chance?"

"Are you kidding!" Karen licked her lips. "I'll bet I like steak better than you do."

"Great. I'll cook you one. Today. This afternoon."

"I'd love that," Karen told him. "What breed of cattle do you have?"

"Hereford. Grandpa bred this herd long before I showed up. He loved Hereford stock."

They turned onto a nearly deserted interstate. The sun, rising at their backs, cast the truck's moving shadow before them. And newly plowed fields, half in shadow half in light, took on an artistic pattern as if block-printed on the countryside. She watched silently as the gentle hills of western Iowa swept past the window.

Nick tapped her shoulder. "Penny for your thoughts."

"I envy you," she told him.

"Envy me? That wasn't worth a penny. Why?"

"Because you live out here. You just don't watch the seasons come and go; you're part of it. Just look at that black soil exuding fecundity." Karen smiled. "Ooh, 'fecundity.' I like that word."

"Me, too," Nick said.

"Throw down a seed, and—voila!—there's your crop!"

"More to it than that."

"Don't be so literal. I know about the sweat and worry that go into a crop. But you work through it. And there, at the end of your task, is the harvest in the glorious colors of an Iowa fall. You're instrumental in something important." She fiddled with the neck of her sweatshirt. "Does that sound corny?"

"You're in the right place to say corny things."

"Thanks a lot."

"I feel those things, too," he said. "I just don't say them as well as you do." He patted her thigh. "Tell me some more."

"No. I want to ask you something. If I'm prying, tell me so."

"OK."

"You talk about your grandpa all the time. Didn't you get along with your mother and father?"

Nick stared over the hood of the truck. "I really didn't know them, Karen."

"Why?"

"We all lived on the farm with Grandpa and Grandma. When I was in fourth grade, my parents and grandmother were killed in a car accident."

"Oh, Nick, that's awful."

He nodded.

"Who took care of you?"

"Grandpa."

"Just the two of you?"

"Yes. Things were not too good at first. Every time our eyes met, we reminded each other of our grief. He wouldn't talk about it. And I guess I felt the same way."

"What happened?"

"The summer after the accident I sneaked away to the pond. Grandpa wouldn't let me go there alone and never allowed me to use the boat, even when he was there. Water terrified him. But there I sat in the middle of the pond in that old boat when Grandpa popped over the hill on a tractor. I rowed as fast as I could. He was livid. I expected a thrashing, but he jerked me from the boat and said, 'Nick, you're all I got left. And I'll be damned if I'm going to let you end up food for the turtles on the bottom of that pond.'" A half-smile played on Nick's lips. "Right then I knew he loved me."

"Were you able to talk to one another?'

"About everything. He went to parent conferences, PTA meetings. Yelled his head off for me at football games. Too late to make a long story short, but whatever I am, Ivor Staal made me."

Karen stared over the hood of the truck, too. "You've had a lot of grief, Nick."

"Now don't go maudlin on me. Look, there's our exit."

A green and yellow sign just off the interstate proclaimed that this was Stuart, home of 1,600 good eggs and a few stinkers. Nick's hometown, like so many others across Iowa, was an island in a sea of grain whose fortunes rose and fell with rainfall and the price of corn and soybeans. Two-story buildings lined the two-block-long Main Street.

The truck creaked to a stop and parked diagonally in front of the Kozy Korner Kafe. Inside a grill sizzled and the café was alive with the aroma of coffee and the sounds of conversation and the clank of silver against china. A sign dangled from the cash register: "Special: eggs, bacon, hash browns, toast, 'n' beverage—just $2.50." Everyone knew Nick. He exchanged comments with a half dozen people, and Karen heard a bald-headed man in a bib overalls ask him where he'd found the good lookin' woman.

Finally, he led her to the rear of the café. In the center of the back wall, an 8-by-10 photograph served as the centerpiece for a montage of smaller snapshots of local dignitaries, many of whom were animals. A tall, gray-headed man stared at Karen from the photograph. A magnificent beast which seemed to be posing stood at his side. Karen moved closer to examine the handwritten inscription. "1943—Ivor Staal and his 2,400 pound Iowa State Fair Grand Champion Hereford bull, Nicholas."

"Nicholas?!" She straightened up. "The bull's name was Nicholas!" Karen looked from Nick to Nicholas the bull and back to Nick. "You were named after a bull!"

He nodded.

Karen's mind roared back to Bancroft's lounge where, months ago, she had characterized him as a bull amidst a pliant herd of giddy heifers. She placed a hand over her mouth, unable to stop laughing. By the time Nick steered her to a table, she was weeping. Karen continued to study the picture over a menu.

"I'm trying not to make a scene, but this is so funny!"

"Not working. Everyone's watching."

"I really am sorry," she gasped. "But, Nick, you were named after a bull!"

"Karen, he was a grand champion."

"And he spread his seed all over your farm."

"All over the Midwest," Nick said.

"Have you carried on the tradition?"

"I've never gotten a blue ribbon."

"Really?" She looked at him sideways. "You know the only way this could be better?"

"How?"

"If the bull were named after you!"

The Kozy Korner's elderly waitress and owner plunked two steaming platters before them.

"I'm all right," Karen giggled. "Is this the special?"

"Yes. I ordered for you."

"Hmm. Delicious." She stabbed a piece of bacon. "Your grandfather was a handsome, imposing man. He looks even more majestic than Nicholas."

"He was my best friend."

Karen ate all she could, then pushed her plate away. "Have I eaten enough to be a farmhand?"

"Let's find out!"

The old red truck headed south. The sun, filtered through dark clouds, cast a pinkish glow. Karen turned to look at him in the strange light. She suddenly realized that she had never seen him without coat and tie, other than the first day. His hair swirled in the wind blowing through the window vent. He wore a black short-sleeved shirt and jeans. Her eyes followed the white stitching down the inseams of his long legs toward a pair of pointed boots. Muscles rippled along his forearms when he turned the wheel. Karen remembered when Lydia Fletcher said Nick would look good in anything—she should see him now!

His hand reached across the seat and covered her eyes. "You're staring at me," Nick said. "Are you still dealing with that bull thing?"

"What am I doing here?"

"Pardon me?"

281

"Someone like you just doesn't ask someone like me…"

"Damn it, Karen! We've already been down that road." He fumbled for a cigarette and struck a wooden match on the dashboard. "I've explained this before."

Karen looked away.

"Haven't you noticed how well we get along?"

"Yes."

"What more do you need? I picked you up two hours ago. I've had fun from the moment you crawled in this truck. You've got a great sense of humor; you talk about things that interest me. That's enough for me."

"I'll quit talking about it."

"Good." He tossed the half-smoked butt through the window.

"Is it because I look like your wife?"

"You're talking about it!"

"Sorry."

"Who told you that?"

"Margaret Watkins." Karen raised her eyebrows. "Do I look like her?"

"Yes."

Wind whistled through the cab as they drove on silently.

"Karen," Nick said finally, "when I first saw you, I couldn't stop looking. But you're not here as a surrogate. Surely, you know that."

"What was her name?"

"Hannah."

"How'd you meet her?"

"She lived on a farm north of Stuart. We started high school together. Grandpa liked her even though her father raised Black Angus."

Karen smiled. "You married your childhood sweetheart."

"Yes."

"I promise," Karen said, "I won't talk about this any more."

"Deal."

She clasped her hands and laid them on her lap. "Does your house have indoor plumbing?"

He grabbed the base of her neck, pulled her across the seat, and kissed the bridge of her nose. "No," he whispered. "You can use the floorboard of this truck."

They turned off the county road into a gravel lane flanked by tall maple trees. The lane opened onto a wide lawn that ascended gently toward a red brick, two-story house. White window frames and green louvered shutters gave the façade a certain elegance. As they approached the house, Karen noticed that the Staal family home was perched on a knoll from which fields and farmsteads faded into the horizon. A white board fence separated the house and sloping lawn from a silo, a half dozen outbuildings, and a towering red barn, cut through at the gable by a massive hay door.

"See that window up there?" Nick pointed to the second story. "That's a bathroom. There's another off the kitchen next to the mud room."

"Where's the pond?"

"Over that slope behind the barn."

"How big is it?"

"Five acres."

"Let's go see it."

Nick stuck his head out of the cab. "There are some really heavy clouds in the southwest. Maybe we ought to wait."

"Let's go anyway."

Nick clutched and dragged the shift into low. They bumped along a dirt lane. From the crest of the hill, Karen saw a large farm pond framed by a string of weeping willows. Whitecaps danced across the water. He looked at the sky again, made a u-turn on the shore, and pointed the nose of the truck up the slope. They walked out on a rickety dock, where waves lashed at a wooden boat half-filled with water.

"Is that the one?" Karen asked.

"Yes."

"Your boat's in worse shape than the truck."

"A little pine tar," Nick said.

"Did you skate here, too?"

"After Grandpa tested the ice."

"How'd he do that?"

"Drove a tractor over it."

"That doesn't sound safe."

"He stayed on the shallow end. He could only break through up to the tires." Nick kicked a willow branch from the dock into the pond. "Do you like to skate."

"I can't. My ankle isn't strong enough." Karen

looked over the water. "In my next life, I'm going to be an Olympic champion and glide over the ice doing double axels and triple-toe loops."

"In one of those skimpy costumes?"

"Goes with the territory."

He pulled her close and kissed her forehead. "I'd love to see that."

Lightning sizzled on the western horizon, and a double clap of thunder echoed across the pond. The first drops of a spring storm splashed on their faces.

"Karen, we've got to get out of here." He took her hand and pulled her to the truck. They started up the grade in low gear. Suddenly, torrents of rain hammered the cab, obscuring their vision beyond the windshield, where the wipers ineffectively sloshed over the glass. Mud clinked in the fender wells as the dirt lane rapidly became a shallow stream moving the truck from side to side until finally it ground to a complete halt. They were stuck.

Nick winked at her, cracked the window, and lit a cigarette.

"Will this last long?" she asked.

"Could. You all right?"

"Yes." She used her sleeve to wipe steam from the windshield. "I can't see a thing."

"We're only a couple hundred yards from the house. When this lets up, we'll make a break for it."

"Any food in here?" Her feet flipped through the trash on the floor.

"Nothing you'd want to eat."

"I may get hungry if this lasts all day."

"I'm going to cook us steaks, remember?"

Just as suddenly as it had started, the rain stopped. "Let's go now." Nick jumped out and sloshed around the hood to Karen's door. He lifted her from the seat and carried her through the mud to the top of the hill where he gently set her down on the gravel. "You can make it from here," he told her and pointed toward the house where the gravel lane forked.

"Look at your pants and boots, Nick! They're all muddy. I'm not even wet."

"I think you spoke too soon." He grabbed her hand as the strong south wind blew in another band of showers. Rain sliced at their faces and clothes. They stumbled onto the concrete porch, where Karen saw her bedraggled reflection in the window.

Nick fished his keys from a wet pocket and opened the door to the mud room. They plopped onto a bench by the door where he tugged off his boots. Karen handed him her dripping shoes. He hung them on wooden wall pegs and grabbed a towel from the closet.

"Now my clothes are soaked," she said. "Do you have anything I can wear?"

"Sure." He draped the towel over her head. "Come on."

Karen followed him through a modern kitchen into a dining room filled with antique walnut furniture. After riding in Nick's truck, this room surprised her; every inch of it was clean and orderly. A long, rectangular table covered with an ivory damask tablecloth was set with china plates, crystal goblets, and sterling silver utensils for two. Strawflowers and silver candlesticks provided a touch that she never would have suspected.

Nick stopped at a curved staircase just beyond the dining room. "Upstairs," he said. "My robe's on the bathroom door. You can wear that until I get your clothes dry."

A robe on the bathroom door. The image momentarily stunned her. Karen slowly ascended the stairs, her mind flirting with the scene that still haunted her. A loft in Charleston, wet hair, wet clothes, an evil man. But this wasn't Lloyd Fraser's house. This place belonged to Nicholas Staal.

The carpeted stairs led to a landing the size of a small room. At the top she saw the open bathroom door, white wainscoting, green walls, tile floor. Nick's terry cloth robe hung from a brass hook on the back of the door. She brushed the sleeve across her cheek; the cloth felt soft and smelled of soap.

Karen blotted her hair in front of the mirror, peeled out of her sodden clothes, and wrapped them tightly in the towel. The long robe dragged behind her as she stepped into the hallway. There were five other doors, all closed. At the far end stood a small walnut table. She glanced down the staircase, then tiptoed toward the far end of the landing. A spotless white doily covered the tabletop, in the middle of which stood a silver frame.

Karen bent closer for a better look in the dim light. A young, dark-haired woman with almond eyes smiled at her, revealing a dimple under each cheekbone. "Hannah," she whispered. Karen could see what Margaret Watkins had noticed at the Grand View seminar. The resemblance was uncanny. She picked up the frame and ran her fingers lightly over the face as if by Braille she could learn more about this woman. Suddenly, Karen felt guilty. She carefully replaced the picture and straightened the doily.

"Here you are."

"Oh," Karen gasped. "You scared me."

Nick stood at the top of the stairs in clean jeans and bare to the waist. "I thought you might need something."

"I need to comb my hair." Her eyes swept the five doors. "Which one of these is yours?"

"This one." He took her hand and led her into a large corner room with windows on two sides. She sat on a cedar chest at the foot of the bed. The room seemed light and airy although it was filled with more dark antique furniture—washstand with bowl and pitcher, five-drawer chest, quilt rack, four-poster bed, platform rocker.

Karen walked to the windows. Bare, wet maple limbs jerked around by the storm looked like buggy whips. In the distance, cattle huddled in the rain with their backsides turned into the wind, and beyond them a blurry landscape disappeared into leaden skies. Over the slope up which Nick had just carried her, mist from the pond water curled in strange shapes. The rest of the world faded from reality as she felt Nick's chest against her back. His arms surrounded her, and his hands found her breasts. Blood raced to the pit of her stomach, her legs trembled. His touch aroused a need in her so exquisite she struggled not to cry out.

Suddenly Karen turned toward him and let the robe fall to the floor. Her eyes drifted toward her leg. "Look at me, Nick. This is what I am."

"No." He lifted her against his bare chest. "That leg is not what you are." He gave her forehead a head-butt. "In there, inside that pretty little head. That makes you what you are."

Nick placed her on the bed and clamped her face between his hands. He kissed her mouth hard, then deeply. She allowed his hands to explore. Each lingering touch was agonizingly delicious. His blue eyes, barely a millimeter away, left her lightheaded, and the smell of him filled her nostrils. Then, her nails dug into his flesh as she gave in to the gentle motion. Here in this room, above the sloping hills of an Iowa farm, a lifetime of fears faded into the mists of a rainy March morning.

thirty-four

Every Tuesday evening Karen Merchant's place served as a safe house for the staff of *The Emperor's New Clothes.* Crowded around her kitchen table, heaped with letters, clippings, and articles in progress, they breathed life into the project that had taken the Des Moines teachers by storm. On this night, the final strokes were being brushed onto a portrait of consultants, those itinerant gurus who traveled the nation hawking games, gimmicks, and canned lesson plans guaranteed to make education fun. The piece, authored by Karen, was on the table for suggestions and final approval, a process the staff used for every feature article and one that almost always generated an argument between Alice and David over words on the edge of good taste.

"Look, Brunhilde, why put our readers to sleep? We're not writing for *Family Circle.*" David looked at her as if he had said something important. "We've got to put some guts in these pieces or no one will read them."

"This isn't *The Harvard Lampoon,* either," Alice

told him. "If you were in a museum, I suppose you'd try to pry fig leaves off statues."

"Not your statue, Big Mama."

"I'd break your arm if you did."

David opened the refrigerator and pulled out a Diet Coke, which he slammed on the table. "Look, a few colorful words would drive Aneyh up the wall. He loves consultants. He loves anyone with a title. He's in bed with them."

"That's more true than you think," blurted George Moore.

"Yeah, what does that mean?" David licked Coke from his lips.

"Nothing." George reddened.

"Then why are you blushing?" David asked.

"Do you know something we don't?" Alice asked.

"Out with it, Moore!"

"Maybe I shouldn't."

"Then don't tease us, George," Alice said.

George Moore pushed his glasses to the bridge of his nose and examined the spine of a legal pad. Suddenly he sat straight up. "Minneapolis. The Mall of America," he said quickly.

"Yes, the Mall of America," David said. "That was certainly interesting."

"My wife and I went on a weekend bus trip to the Mall of America. I didn't want to drive in a strange city."

"Who cares." David plinked the tab on his Coke can. "Get to the point."

"They have so many stores. Three levels."

"So?" David said.

"Well, my feet got tired. While my wife shopped, I went into this bar place. I didn't want a drink, just a place to rest. The bar was so dark. But when my eyes got used to the light, I saw him."

"Who?" David demanded. "Moore, did you experience an Elvis sighting?"

"No. I sighted Mr. Aneyh."

David shrugged. "That's it? You ran into Aneyh at the Mall of America?"

George squirmed in his chair. "With a woman."

"Mrs. Aneyh?"

"No."

"What were they doing?"

"Kissing."

"No way!" Alice said. "George, this is important. Are you sure the man was Mr. Aneyh?"

"Yes."

"Did he see you?"

"No. They were in a corner booth. The place was full of people telling jokes and laughing. And the air was full of smoke. Anyway," George sighed, "Mr. Aneyh wasn't noticing anybody else because he had his hand inside the lady's blouse."

"Rubbing her tits!" David yelled.

"If you insist on putting it that way, I suppose he was."

"Are you absolutely sure, George?" Alice asked.

"Well, I couldn't see inside her blouse. But that's where his hand was."

She patted his shoulder. "Go on. Just tell us what you saw."

"Karen, could I please have a glass of water."

"Come on, Moore," David demanded.

Karen set a glass of ice water in front of him. George took one long drink and then another.

"Well," George said finally. "I had trouble seeing from then on because Mr. Aneyh's arm disappeared."

"Where?"

"Under the table. I couldn't testify to this in court. I want to make that clear. But I believe he was rubbing her down there."

"Rubbing her!" David erupted.

"Well, remember, I couldn't see. But I believe his hand may have been—ah—inside—her panties."

"For God's sakes, Moore," David squealed, "you mean he was giving her a hand job!"

Alice moved closer. "Could you be mistaken, George? After all, you said the place was dark."

George sighed again. "Her mouth moved, Alice. I saw her wiggle."

"Wait a minute," David said. "Have you ever seen Mrs. Aneyh?"

"No."

"Then how do you know the woman wasn't Aneyh's old lady?"

"Because it was Dr. MacIntosh."

Alice clapped a hand over her mouth and turned a face covered with amused disgust toward the others. David exploded from his chair and stomped around the kitchen in a state of euphoria, congratulating himself on his prescience. "I called this! The very first time that woman appeared at Bancroft. I called this! No one here is equipped to write an expose on the hyena like I am. I've watched that fiend hammer innocent people for ten years." David leaned over the table. "This article is mine! I'll stoke the fire, stick the spit through him, and watch him slowly turn over the coals."

"We can't print this," Karen said quietly.

Alice nodded.

"But this is perfect." David's eyes gleamed. "That jerk would cut his mother's throat or sell his kids into bondage to advance his career. Now it's my turn to cut!"

"We can't do this," Karen said.

David stood in front of her. "Why are you defending this guy?"

"She didn't defend him," Nick said. "She just said we can't print this."

"Look, Moore caught this guy red-handed buggering a woman who isn't his wife. We owe this to our readers."

"We agreed this paper wouldn't trash people," Nick said.

"This is different, Staal."

"No, this isn't. Aneyh's sex life has no bearing on our mission. Our quarrel is with what he thinks. Why squander the credibility we've earned just to paint Robert Aneyh as an unfaithful slob? You want to get off on Aneyh's getting off, David? Go write a signed article. Send it to a tabloid."

thirty-five

Since Karen had moved from her mother's home, she had never spent a night there and ate with her only when invited. Leaving home, even if only across town, marked the start of her rite of passage. Each had her independence, but the strong bond forged between mother and daughter had been stretched a little by Karen's move. Their relationship resembled a long rubber band that snapped them together again when one of them pulled. Grace, always on guard against obstacles that might inflict pain on her vulnerable daughter, did most of the pulling.

Grace's appearance at Karen's door at 3:00 on Saturday afternoon, just one half-hour before Nick was due, broke one of their unwritten rules: each would call first before dropping in.

"Mother!" Karen blurted.

"I'm sorry I didn't call, Honey Bunny. Well, I did try to call, but your line was busy. As a matter of fact, it's been busy a lot lately." Grace charged into the living room. "You never used to talk that much."

"I don't talk that much, Mother." Karen wondered how she could get rid of her before Nick came.

"Well, never mind. I just came to drop off these pictures." Grace opened her bag and spread photographs on the coffee table. "I got these yesterday. They're wearing the outfits you gave them for Christmas."

"Oh, aren't these cute!" Karen's niece and nephew grinned at her from a Kmart photo package winter scene. "Jenny looks so ladylike in that sweater."

Grace scooped up the pictures. "Doesn't she, though. I'm going to pin them on the bulletin board in the den."

"No!" Karen said quickly. "I mean, you probably have other things to do."

"Nonsense. I have all afternoon. We haven't had a good talk for ages." Grace headed for the den. "Do you have any pins in there?"

"Top desk drawer." Karen glanced through the window just in time to see Nick on the front stoop. She tried to get to the door before the bell rang.

"Someone's at the front door," Grace announced from the den.

"I know, Mother. You stay there. I'll get it."

On her way, Karen glanced behind her as though she expected her mother to be right on her heels. She had not discussed her relationship with Nick with her mother, nor anyone, for that matter. She had often considered what to say if Alice or Darlene should back her into a corner. Karen wanted what she had with Nick—the paper, the long phone conversations, the double meanings they shared in front of others, the nights they spent together on the farm—to remain a private matter. That not one person knew only heightened her thrill. She felt different and apparently looked different. Just last week Michelle Valder had told her she looked "magnifique, positively glowing" and asked if she were on something. Karen had only smiled. She had an inexplicable unwillingness to share her secret as if that revelation would make it all go away.

"Nick!" She glanced at a large envelope in his hand. "I see you got the stuff."

"I sure did. I can hardly wait to read what you do with this material."

Karen stood in the doorway. "Well, thanks."

"Thanks? Aren't you going to invite me in?"

"My mother's here," she whispered.

"Good. I'd like to meet her."

"Who's at the door?" Grace yelled.

Nick stepped by Karen into the living room. "Nicholas Staal," he said.

"Oh?" Grace emerged from the den. "I'm Grace Merchant."

"This is a colleague of mine from Bancroft," Karen said. "I mentioned Nick to you. Remember?"

Grace frowned. "I'm not sure. Well, how do you do, Mr. Staal?"

"Karen talks about you all the time." Nick extended his hand.

"She does?"

"Yes, and I think you've raised a lovely daughter."

"Well." Grace tugged at her skirt and patted her hair. She nodded at the sofa. "Won't you sit down, Mr. Staal."

"Yes, of course."

"So you work with Karen?" Grace asked.

"Yes, I teach right down the hall."

In a matter of moments Karen was out of the loop. They were calling each other Nick and Grace. Her mother, animated and giggly, sat chatting like an old aunt who had not seen her nephew since he'd left for college. At any time she expected her mother to tell Nick how much he'd grown since she'd seen him last. By the time Karen retreated to the kitchen to make coffee, they'd discussed cattle breeds, Social Security, craft shows, several of Grace's ailments, Nick's tie, and, of course, the weather.

When she returned, Grace spoke to Karen as she would to a child. "Where are your manners, Karen? You only have two cups."

"She knows I don't drink coffee, Grace."

"But surely you have some cranberry juice or something, don't you, Karen?"

Nick rose. "Thank you, Grace, but no. I have another appointment at 4:15." He took her offered hand in both of his. "I really enjoyed talking with you."

"Yes, I did, too. Perhaps I'll see you again."

While Nick let himself out, Karen headed for the kitchen with the coffee tray. Her mother followed and sat at the table, from which she launched an interrogation.

"Why didn't you tell me about him?"

"I did."

"No, you didn't, Karen. I wouldn't forget someone like him. Goodness, that man could charm Aunt Minnie right out of her bloomers. And you know what a sour puss she is."

"You thought his name was Mick."

"Oh, that. You certainly told me a lot about him that night, didn't you?"

"Don't be sarcastic, Mother. More coffee?"

"Half a cup. By any chance did he go to a country school?"

"Yes."

"I see."

"No, you don't see, Mother." Karen sat down across from her. "I work with him. That's all."

"Oh, for heaven's sakes, you've been to his farm. He told me that when you were in the kitchen." Grace added sugar to her coffee. "How serious is this? You can tell me the truth."

"All right, then, Mother." Karen leaned forward and took a deep breath. "I guess I love him."

"Then you must be careful," Grace said barely above a whisper.

"You can't possibly know that from meeting him just once. You don't know how good he is to me. You don't know how much fun we have together. Mother, he's the only man I've ever known who's treated me like a woman."

"He is delightful. He makes all the right moves, says all the right things," Grace paused, "but, Karen, you don't know men. Oh, he'll keep coming back all right. But he'll stop when he's gotten what he wanted."

"Mother, I don't need to hear this." Karen began to clear the table. She placed her cup in the sink and dumped coffee grounds down the disposal.

Grace Merchant pressed the coffee cup to her lips. "You're different, Karen," she said finally. "You've had so much pain. You don't deserve to be hurt."

Karen moved to the kitchen window and stared into the backyard with tears in her eyes. "Mother, I will not be your helpless little girl any more."

thirty-six

Hal Delaney missed the interaction he watched going on through Karen's open door: those inexplicable moments between teacher and class when their minds really came together, the impulsive nod of a student who had just gotten it, those little smiles of gratitude. For him, all of that died fifteen years ago when he exchanged his classroom for a desk. As vice principal, Hal had become the enforcer, and his office, populated by loafers, truants, swearers, fighters, smokers, and users, too often resembled a combat zone. Year after year the ranks of these rebels swelled as his authority to deal with inappropriate behavior was emasculated by board policies tailored to fit court decisions.

As students filed out, Delaney walked up to Karen, who banded papers at the window ledge.

"I saw you out there, Hal," Karen said. "You're my favorite eavesdropper.

"Sorry."

"Nonsense. Nice for someone to show some interest."

"I'll tell you how interested I am." Hal absentmindedly cranked the pencil sharpener. "Alice Cain dropped by my office yesterday. She told me, confidentially, of course, that you were thinking…"

"About quitting."

"Right." He folded his arms over his chest. "I don't want that to happen, Karen. Why don't you stop by my office after school. We can't talk with these kids around."

"Hi, Mr. Delaney."

"Hi." The vice principal patted the shoulder of a bespectacled redhead. "How's it going, Will?"

"Great!"

"That's what I like to hear." He winked at Karen. "See you after school."

Karen waited in the outer office while the vice principal held a student conference. Bits and pieces of a heated conversation seeped under the door. Finally, two students, subdued and thoughtful, emerged, followed by a third, a tough-looking girl, her left eyebrow pierced by a silver ring. She stomped and tossed her peroxided tresses defiantly while indecipherable noises gurgled in her throat.

Delaney smiled from the doorway. "Welcome to Shangri-la, Karen. Come in and have a seat."

Family pictures on his desk, a gigantic painting of Pebble Beach's eighteenth green behind his chair, and the curtained windows that actually matched the walls gave this office more character than Aneyh's. He plopped into his chair and immediately got serious.

"Karen, you probably don't know that Aneyh delegates all the scheduling to me."

"No, I didn't," Karen said.

"So I know the problem you're wrestling with. He came in last week madder than a hornet, bellowing about your schedule. He wanted me to load you up with ninth grade general English. He wouldn't tell me why."

"He wanted me to change Lance Moffat's grade," Karen told him. "I wouldn't do it."

"Oh, for Christ's sake." An array of emotions crossed Delaney's face faster than Karen could catalogue them: disbelief, disgust, disdain. His expression, the way his eyes smoldered, looked incongruous above his precise tan suit. "Don't worry, Karen," he said. "This isn't going to happen. I told Aneyh last week I wouldn't treat you that way. Now that I know what he's up to, I guarantee your schedule won't change." He leaned forward. "I still have a little capital left in this system, and there's always the *Des Moines Register*. If Aneyh persists, I'll bring him down."

"Hal, don't waste your chits on me."

"Waste? Are you kidding? What he's doing is dreadful."

"But, Hal, that's not the only thing."

"Oh?"

"I can teach ninth grade English or anything else Aneyh throws at me."

"Believe me, you won't have to do that."

"Doesn't matter." Karen rested her arms on his

desk. "The seven-period day's driving my decision. Grading papers already eats up most of my spare time. Next year they'll dump 30 more kids on me and expect me to teach them for nothing. I've been here seventeen years. Never once have I ever been asked to do less, only more. This time twenty per cent more. In my book, that's piling on."

Delaney nodded. "I can't do anything about that one. I'd like to tell you things will get better." He looked at her sympathetically. "I'm being selfish here—but Bancroft can't afford to lose a teacher like you." He knitted his fingers together on his lap. "Promise me you'll think this through before you make a decision."

"I will," Karen said. She stopped at the door. "I like you, too, Hal."

thirty-seven

Hattie Reins chiseled her deadlines in stone. The counselors' reports for next fall's course enrollments were due on her desk at 3:10. Hattie called George Moore's office at that precise time in order to chew him out for being late, only to hear a student helper say sweetly that she didn't know where Mr. Moore was.

"Oh, really," the secretary muttered. "Well, I'll take care of that."

She pushed away from her desk and plowed through the office and across the hall toward the counseling center. Inside George's office, she rifled his desk drawers with ferretlike strokes until her nails rested on a sheaf of papers bound with a heavy metal clip. "Layout: *Emperor's New Clothes*" read the cover sheet. Her lips wrinkled as if she were staring at an infected sore. Only for a moment did a teacher's right to privacy deter her from ripping the layout from the drawer. She folded the pages and pressed them against her side and upper arm. She knew exactly what to do.

Hattie ignored the phone jangling on her desk

and several students waiting in the outer office and headed straight to Aneyh.

"Hattie, something wrong?"

"I've caught him, Mr. Aneyh! I've caught him red-handed!"

"Who? What happened?"

"The teacher behind *The Emperor's New Clothes.*" She placed the pages before the principal triumphantly.

For the briefest moment, the realization that this paper had flourished at Bancroft, on his watch, overwhelmed him. The negative implications were obvious. But yet, if he unmasked the authors, surely his name would be on the lips of those who could advance his career. Aneyh poked through the layout like an ancient priest divining the entrails of a goat. This was something he could turn to his advantage.

"Where'd you get this?"

"George Moore's desk," Hattie told him.

"Hmmm. Good job, Hattie." The principal stroked his chin. "You get that little twerp in here immediately."

Hattie turned on the school all-call and barked out a terse message for Mr. Moore to report to the main office. Moments later, George blithely entered the outer office, where he was greeted by Aneyh's magnificent scowl.

George stood in front of the principal's desk, as he had ten years ago, without a hint of what was coming.

"Moore, how did you think you could get away with this?"

"Get away with what?" George asked.

"You don't know what I'm talking about?"

"No."

"No? How 'bout this?" He tossed the purloined pages on the desktop. "You know where I got these?"

"No."

"Your desk drawer."

George's lip quivered briefly. He knew Aneyh would savage the paper and anyone involved. The fear that sickened him was not for himself, but rather for Nick and the rest, who had the talent to expose tyrants like the one on the other side of the desk. The necessity to protect them reined in his jangled nerves.

"All right, Moore, let's have it. What do you know about this paper?"

"Nothing."

"Nothing! You deny your involvement?" Aneyh's words bounced off the office walls.

"I don't know what you're talking about," George said.

"Look, Moore, get this through your head. You have one chance to stay in this system, and that's by naming names. You don't have the brains to pull this off alone. Now," the principal snorted, "you come clean. Who's in this with you?"

"Even if I knew," George said calmly, "I would never tell you."

"Listen, you little squirrel. You don't get it. Your job is on the line here. I'm going to give you one more chance."

"There are some things more important than a job, Mr. Aneyh."

Aneyh grabbed the phone. "Get the hell out of here. We'll see what kind of stud you are when I get through with you."

"You can't do any more to me than you've already done." George paused. "Mr. Hyena."

The little counselor left Aneyh's office and made his way to the counseling center in a fog. He collapsed in a chair and grabbed the arms to steady his trembling hands. His mind was mush. What he had to do now was collect himself and then let the others know that Aneyh had fingered him, that he had compromised no one's identity. George pulled off his glasses and rested his head on the chair back.

"Siesta time, Moore?" David's head popped through the doorway.

George took several deep breaths. "Shut the door, David."

"Why?" David's tone changed. "There's something wrong."

"I swear I don't know how this happened."

"What, what?" David stared down at George. "Out with it, man."

"Go tell Nick the hyena found the paper."

"What do you mean he found the paper? Did you give it to him?"

"Of course not. Nick gave me the layout pages this morning to take to the printer. They were in my bottom desk drawer. I don't know how Aneyh got them. He wanted me to name names, but I didn't tell him anything. Nothing!"

David bolted. He wasn't listening any more.

Karen heard footsteps pound down the empty upper hall. She looked up in time to see David carom off the door jamb into her room. His tie gaped at the neck, and beads of sweat tattooed his forehead.

"We need to talk," he hissed.

"OK."

"I'm through. George Moore sold us down the river."

"What?"

"Aneyh's got the layout of the paper."

"How?"

"Who knows. It was in George's desk. Aneyh grilled Moore. He claims he didn't out anyone, but I don't trust him."

"Believe me, you can trust George Moore." Karen stood. "Does Nick know?"

"I just came from his room. He told me not to worry, that he'd take care of everything. I think he's on his way to Aneyh's office right now."

"Calm down, David."

"Bullshit!" David kicked the wastebasket. "I need this job. We can't live without that insurance. Don't you forget, Karen, I didn't want Moore in this from the beginning."

"George Moore would never betray us." Karen grabbed her bag and keys and walked toward the door. "We don't know what's going on here. Let's just go home. Give Nick a chance to work this out. He'll call us."

"What in the hell can he do?"

"Maybe nothing," Karen told him. "But we're not doing any good here."

"Moore's going to rat on us, Karen. You can make

book on that. Aneyh just looks at him and he pees his pants."

"Well, Aneyh hasn't even looked at you and you're not doing very well." Karen pushed him through the door. "Let's get out of here. This is depressing."

Nicholas Staal breezed past Hattie Reins, who stood behind the counter, hands on hips. "I'm going to see Aneyh," he said out of the side of his mouth.

"Just one moment," Hattie said. "I'll announce you."

"I'll announce myself."

Aneyh looked up at Nick towering over his desk. "What do you want, Staal?"

"I came to talk about George Moore."

"There's nothing to say about that worthless creep. You can't save him." Aneyh reclined in his swivel chair until his head rested against the wall. "Now I want you out of here."

The grin that so infuriated Aneyh played on Nick's lips. "George told me about your conversation. You've accused an innocent man."

"Staal, you're an idiot. I have the goods." He opened a drawer and spread the layout pages on the desk like a poker hand. "Do you know what these are?"

"Of course I know what they are," Nick said. "I should. They're mine."

Aneyh pushed himself to the front of his chair. "What are you talking about?"

"When you go after someone, you usually get the right man."

"God damn it, Staal."

Nick stepped back and closed the door. "There are students out there. They don't need to hear this."

Aneyh's beefy neck turned red. Something about Nicholas Staal's demeanor, his condescension to someone of a principal's importance, invariably pushed him into a snit of cognitive dysfunction.

"I lost the layout two days ago. George Moore must have found it. George has been a loyal member of this staff for 30 years, a team player. If Hattie Reins hadn't torn his desk apart, he would have turned that layout over to you on his own."

"How'd you know she found it?"

"I didn't. Trial balloon."

"Why, you bas…" Aneyh stopped short. "My God! I should have known you were behind this." His fingers drummed the desk. "Oh, I know all about you, smart ass. Every principal does. And you've just handed us your head on a silver platter. You've rescued me, Staal. I was worried about this pimp sheet being published under my nose. Not now. When the board finds out you're behind this, they'll pin a medal on me." He swiveled toward the window and smiled. "We can finally get rid of you."

"Maybe you'll be principal of the year."

"Maybe." Aneyh chuckled. "Anybody help you with your dirty rag?"

"No one in this building," Nick told him.

"Doesn't surprise me. This is a committed staff. They wouldn't step in the gutter with you."

Nick folded his arms across his chest. "You don't

have a clue, do you? You know less about this staff than anyone in the building. The janitors have a better sense of what's wrong around here than you do. You've glommed on to all the wrong people. Every weak sister who'll kiss your ass to crawl up the career ladder."

"You can't talk to me that way! Get out of my office!"

"You and your ilk have stitched together a Frankenstein that's ripping public education to shreds. Teachers know it, students know it, and their test scores show it. But not you; you don't know it. You're too busy wallowing in platitudinous crap like shared decision-making and teacher empowerment; then you pounce on a defenseless little man with a few sheets of paper in his desk as if he were a vicious felon. For Christ's sakes, Aneyh, this isn't Tiananmen Square, and you're not the grand poobah of the universe."

The principal leapt to his feet and leaned forward as far as his stocky frame would let him. "You think your size and glib tongue give you an edge, Staal. Let—me—tell—you—something." A white-knuckled fist punched out each word on the desktop. "I wield the ax around here. Any teacher, and that includes you, who doesn't like that can be damned."

"We work for you, Mr. Aneyh. We're already damned."

The principal stormed from behind the desk and stood directly in front of Nicholas Staal. His cheek twitched, and his eyes, pinched into slits, betrayed the uncertainty of a man forced by rage into an aggressive posture without knowing where to go with it. He held a clenched fist under Nick's nose.

"What are you going to do with that?" Nick pointed at Aneyh's fist.

"Here's what I'm going to do." His fist turned into a pointing finger. "My friends downtown will kick your ass back to that farm. That's where you belong, not in a public school. Now! Are you going to get out of here, or do I throw you out?"

"Don't bother. You've had enough exertion for one day." Nick stopped at the door. "Before you leave tonight, Mr. Aneyh," he nodded at the layout, "why don't you read *The Emperor's New Clothes*. Might elevate your sensitivity."

Karen's kitchen became a situation-room. Calls poured through her phone from every member of the paper. She talked nonstop for nearly three hours.

Several things became clear as the evening waned. *The Emperor's New Clothes* was now defunct. Alice wanted Aneyh dead. George Moore, heartbroken at being caught, languished in remorseful culpability. Nick reassured everyone that Aneyh believed the paper involved no one but him.

Paranoia oozed from David's eight phone calls. He refused participation in a plan where they would all step forward in support of Nick. His last call, during which Karen decided he'd forsake both his wife and mother to save his job, left no doubt he intended to disavow them all if the crunch came.

Karen first considered martyrdom, stepping

forward on her own, as a way to absolve the nagging guilt that they had allowed Nick to fall on his sword. Nick convinced her that while martyrdom might feel good, it would help no one. Fighting tears, she sorted through a pile of editorials, poetry, and articles from teachers who wanted to be heard. But now, instead of a voice, there was a void. A window had slammed shut, and something important slipped away.

She now needed to send a refund and an explanation of the paper's demise to subscribers in Minneapolis, Fort Worth, Omaha, Baltimore, and many other cities. How the paper found such faraway readers amazed her. Alice Cain had stuck a dollar bill on the kitchen bulletin board that came from a teacher in Hungry Horse, Montana, as an emblem of their far-reaching success, and beside that dollar, a letter from a Jane Rich, from Lost Nation, Iowa, a town in which David claimed all teachers should live.

Ringing again.

"Hello."

"I thought you might still be up."

"Nick, I'm so glad this isn't David."

"Go to bed. Get some sleep. This mess is over."

"Nick, what's going to happen to us?"

"I'm going to lick your neck the next chance I get. Good night."

thirty-eight

Thunder above the school administration building in downtown Des Moines rattled windows in the office of Burton Ramsey, Director of Human Resources. He sat across a Formica-topped table from Robert Aneyh and Antonio Pagano, haggling over the fate of Nicholas Staal. Ramsey, a studious man with a full head of gray hair, pushed a single personnel folder to the middle of the table and refilled three Styrofoam coffee cups. He listened as Bancroft's principal painted a dastardly portrait of Nicholas Staal: a renegade; poison; a thorn in his side specifically, the system's generally; the leader of a rat pack of troublemakers whose libelous publication undermined the administrative goal of excellence.

"I agree with what Bob says," Tony Pagano added. Pagano's ascent up the career ladder had been breathtaking. Barely 30, he arrived in Des Moines with a Ph.D. from Minnesota and a wagonload of ideas for attracting federal dollars. He knew his way around the federal bureaucracy, a talent that made him the board's darling. Pagano, a tall, austere man, prided himself in rallying others to his point of view. "We can nail Staal for undermining morale," he told Ramsey. "That contract clause on moral turpitude is so vague we can make it mean whatever we say, like inciting others to rebel, for example."

Ramsey sipped his coffee slowly and studied the fluorescent lights, which flickered in concert with another thunderclap.

"Excellent!" Aneyh agreed. "Principals who refused to put that paper in teachers' mailboxes had a riot on their hands."

"Did they call out the police?" Ramsey asked.

"Get off it, Burt," Aneyh shouted. "You know what I mean."

"Bob, why don't you calm down."

"Call Jean Forbes over at Mark Twain. She had two teachers threaten her with legal action for not distributing the paper. Legal action! That's what that bastard did—turned teachers against administrators."

"They should have named the paper Horace Mann Insurance," Ramsey said. "Those brochures always find teachers' mailboxes."

"Are you with us here, Burt?" Pagano asked.

"Am I with you? Moral turpitude?" Ramsey put down his coffee. "Why don't you guys get serious. You're in over your heads. No court would characterize the publication of a newsletter as moral turpitude. The only riot *The Emperor's New Clothes* incited was riotous laughter. Staal didn't name names or finger anyone specifically. He just gave another slant on what goes on in this district."

Aneyh persisted. "You don't know what happened in the schools when that paper hit the fan."

"Yes, I do. *The Emperor's New Clothes* was like a breath of fresh air. You guys are too damn jaded to remember what it's like to be a teacher in mid-winter. Staal exposed some of the idiocy that passes as educational philosophy around here. The teachers liked that—I liked that. But you feel threatened, don't you, Bob?"

"Come on, Burt," he grunted. "Staal's caused trouble in every building he's been in. Let me remind you, there've been seven of them. On top of that, he can't teach worth shit."

"Wait a minute," Ramsey said. "I live in the Bancroft area and know a lot of parents who have kids in his classes. They're not only pleased with his teaching, their kids love him. If you don't know that, you don't know what's going on in your own building."

Aneyh picked his fingernails.

"He's a gadfly, and you can't swat him. That's what galls you."

Aneyh came to the edge of his seat. "He attacks leadership. That's what galls me."

Ramsey stared at them, a couple of pit bulls who felt they had treed Nicholas Staal, smelled blood, and would be silenced by nothing less than Staal's hide nailed to the wall. He regretted a system that enabled guys like these to advance to positions of power. He pushed back his chair, walked to the window, and watched rush hour traffic creep through a rain-soaked intersection.

"I served in Vietnam," he said with his back toward them. "Nick was there, too. I found that in his folder. I don't know what he was doing there. I don't know what I was doing there." He turned and faced them. "They laid a lot of reasons on us—saving democracy, for example. Can you imagine anything more ludicrous? You slop around a jungle for a year and a half fighting for someone else's freedom, only to be canned in the bastion of democracy because you expressed your views." Ramsey shook his head. "Why don't you guys just go home."

"I understand your compassion, Burt," Pagano said, "but you can't characterize Staal's insubordination as 'expressing his views.'"

"Listen, Burt." Aneyh's eyes stiffened. "Staal's dead meat. I don't give a damn how many years he spent in Vietnam. There isn't a secondary principal who doesn't want that son of a bitch gone."

"No secondary principal can make that decision, Bob, and that includes you."

"Fine! If you won't get rid of him, I'm going straight to the board."

"Go ahead. They'd be with you. Because they don't understand legal matters, either." Ramsey pulled some letters from Nicholas Staal's folder and tossed them among the coffee cups. "Read these. From Des Moines parents who either heard that speech Nick made to the board or read about it in the paper. Laudatory, every one. A couple of them even suggest we make him superintendent of schools. I also got 30 or 40 phone calls from people wondering why we can't run this system the way that guy said in his speech."

"What's the point?" Pagano asked.

"What's the point? Nicholas Staal's got a following in this town, and he doesn't even know it. Do you know Gordon Foster, Tony?"

"Sure. The board's attorney."

"Let me set this up for you," Ramsey said. "You go to the board, hit them with moral turpitude, and Foster will make you two look like jailhouse lawyers. He'll tell them that as a board they'd be laughed out of the state. Foster will quote the *Des Moines Register*'s banner headline: 'Teacher-editor of Paper Criticizing System Fired.' You know this will hit local talk shows. Hell, it might even make the network news on a slow night. Civil libertarians will swarm like bees on a honey pot. And teachers. Fifteen hundred of them yelling, 'Foul. Censorship.' The board will never jump into that dung heap."

Aneyh, fingers interlocked, rested his elbows on the table. For the first time since this conversation began, he looked unsure of himself. Pagano paged through Nicholas Staal's personnel folder. "Look at this, Burt." He shoved a paper in front of Ramsey. "Social Science 7-14. PE K-14. Staal's certified to teach physical education in elementary!"

"That's what it says."

"Why, hell, we've got him. Make Staal an elementary PE teacher. Put him in two or three buildings. Run his ass all over town."

Aneyh revived. "Burt, will you help us with this?"

"Not a chance," Ramsey said.

"The board will." Pagano picked up his briefcase. "There will be absolutely no publicity. He won't be fired. His contract isn't for a school or a position; his contract is for whatever the district says it's for."

Aneyh's head slowly nodded and a smirk crawled over his lips. "I know a couple of board members that would love to make Staal's life miserable." Aneyh got to his feet. "And I'll be rid of him."

Ramsey shook his head. "Would it do any good to say you ought to be ashamed of yourselves?"

"Listen, Burt," Aneyh said, "we look at this differently. That's all. Nothing personal. We're going to do a lot of business together in the future." He grabbed Ramsey's hand. "Thanks for your time."

Footsteps echoed in the hall. Burton Ramsey knew Pagano, the board's pet, could convince them to stick Nicholas Staal in three different elementary buildings. He had heard several of them vilify *The Emperor's New Clothes* and knew the board president felt embarrassed by Nick's speech. The board should move heaven and hell to keep teachers like Nicholas Staal in front of a class, but he knew they wouldn't. Ramsey caromed coffee cups off the inside of the wastebasket as if he could eliminate the hypocrisy of his visitors by destroying their trappings.

He closed his office door and wandered through the maze of offices and cubicles that honeycombed the administrative fortress. The number of these offices and the apparatchiks who staffed them grew exponentially with the arrival of each new federal grant, state mandate, or special interest agenda. From these desks, floods of paperwork swamped beleaguered teachers with committees and reports in triplicate that had little to do with educating children and everything to do with legitimizing the existence of these offices.

Ramsey paused at the main door. He'd grown weary of Ivory Tower games: knowing which buttons to push, which board members to stroke, who had clout and who had lost it, who was screwing whom (literally, sometimes). "Lard," he muttered looking back at the bloated corridors. "Mostly lard."

thirty-nine

They stood on a bridge spanning a lazy brook that gurgled beneath them. Karen stared into the clear water below; Nick rested against the rail, facing the opposite direction. She had called him to meet her at this quaint park in DeSoto, halfway between Des Moines and his farm.

Nick turned and rested his arms on the rail as the sun dropped behind the trees lining the little stream. The picnic tables around the park were all deserted except one, where a gray-headed woman waited with two small boys while an old man tended hamburgers on a park grill amidst a cloud of billowing smoke.

"So. What did you want to tell me?" Nick asked. "Or are we just here to listen to the frogs croak?"

"Aren't you glad to see me?"

"I saw you at school today. What's wrong?"

Karen's eyes went flat and she talked mechanically. "I don't want to do this anymore, Nick."

"You mean you want to dump me?"

"No, no. My job. I'm going to resign."

"Resign?"

When she made this decision two days ago, she thought the crying was over, but tears flooded her eyes.

"Why?" he whispered.

Karen watched a small branch float under the bridge. She crossed to the other rail and watched it bob and lurch downstream. "I just can't do this job any longer," she said finally.

"Who else knows?"

"Only you. I had to tell someone. I couldn't hold it any longer. The school board will get my letter of resignation after school's out."

Nick crossed the bridge and put his arms on her shoulders. "Did the paper have anything to do with your decision?"

"Partly. And that fool who expected me to change a grade. But mostly the seven-period day. The board's spinning this already—more choices for students and all that crap. The same way they beguiled middle school teachers. Why are they so dishonest, Nick? Every teacher knows he'll have another class to teach."

"I believe that," Nick said.

"They intend to save money. Period. Money extracted from my hide and yours. I'm not going to teach 30 more kids for nothing."

"I believe you." He put his arm around her, and they walked off the bridge down a gravel path that led toward the parking lot.

Karen stopped. She took his fingers and traced

them over a lump on the inside joint of her middle finger. "Do you know how I got that?"

Nick shook his head.

"Grading papers. On Fridays after school I lock my door behind me and assume the persona of a medieval monk. The floor is strewn with student papers, ten in each stack. Takes an hour and a half to do one pile. I invent games to make them go away, Nick, offer myself a reward or a treat. 'Do one stack, Karen, and you may have a pop or go to the bathroom.' I've spent most of my adult life guzzling Coke and going to the can."

He laughed and squeezed her arm.

"Not funny, Nick. The board's decision means three more piles on my living room floor every weekend."

"I'm not laughing about the extra work," he said.

Karen walked ahead. "If I died tonight," she said over her shoulder, "the board would never send flowers. They'd toss a couple hundred ungraded themes in my coffin and dispatch a somber-faced kid fresh out of seminary to eulogize me. 'This remarkable woman, during her career as a public schoolteacher, has read 2,856,203 student papers.'" She stopped and waited for him. "You certainly don't have much to say about this."

"I haven't had a chance."

"Oh, Nick, am I doing the right thing?"

"You're doing exactly what most of the people in this system would like to do. They just don't have the guts. They're afraid to lose their pensions, afraid to lose medical insurance. And they're afraid to look for another job. You not only have the guts—you have the talent. If I were an entrepreneur looking for an associate who could write, someone with creative ideas and a great work ethic, I'd snap you up in a minute."

"Really?"

"Really. The job market out there cries for people like you." He pulled her closer. "You've made a decision, Karen. Never look back."

They left the path and sat on a bench. Trees faded into the dim light. The old man's silhouette across the park hobbled toward his table with a plate of hamburgers. Nick wrapped his arm around her as Karen shivered in the descending chill.

"This won't make any difference in us, will it?" Karen asked. "I mean, will you still want to see me if I'm not a teacher?"

"I don't see you now because you're a teacher."

"I'm so glad I told you." She laid her head against his shoulder. "You always make me feel better."

"What doesn't make me feel better is that a school system gone crazy has won again. We're losing good teachers like you all over this country. But what else could you expect when a bunch of troglodytes call the shots?"

"Nick, don't tell Alice or anyone else."

"I won't."

"I need to tell my mother first. And I don't know how to do that."

"Straight out like you told me."

forty

"Hello," she said breathily into the phone.

"Have you been jogging or something?"

"Oh, Darlene. No, I was outside."

"You'll hear this tomorrow, Karen," Darlene said. "But I wanted to give you a heads up."

"OK."

"Do you know Marlyce Garvey?" Darlene asked.

"No."

"She's in the LD self-contained program."

"Senior?"

"Yes. And her mother wants her included in the class ranking."

"Class ranking? That's a no-no, isn't it? LD guidelines and all that stuff you fought for?"

"Right. No one in self-contained has ever been included in the class ranking. Self-esteem, feelings, and all that crap."

"That's what I thought."

"Special Ed kids don't compete in the real world, Karen. Most of them watch a movie for a final test."

"Then what's the deal here?"

"Well, this girl's mother, a Mrs. Wormser, thinks excluding her daughter's like affirmative action in reverse. Discrimination, she told me on the phone. This will mess up her head. Mess up her head! She must have said that a half dozen times."

"So where does this girl stand?"

"You sitting down?"

"No."

"Marlyce Garvey's number two."

Karen pulled the receiver away to avoid her old friend's stream of expletives. "How could that be? You mean she has all 'A's?"

"She's gotten an 'A' in every LD class. You know we grade those kids against their ability. She did everything that was expected of her, which wasn't much."

"Didn't she have any academic classes?"

"Drivers Ed. Pass or fail. The resource teacher read her the tests. She took art classes for electives. Had those tests read to her, too. And she had Family Living. You know what the major project in that course was?"

"Tell me."

"Students had to pack an egg around with them for a month every place they went in order to get a feel for parenthood. Marlyce must have cracked hers. She got a 'B' in that one. On graduation night, she'll have exactly 20 credits and a 3.95 grade point."

Karen sat in the kitchen considering the implications of what she'd just heard. Here was a school system caught in its own trap. A pleasant Special Ed student shielded from the rigors of academic competition out of concern for her self-esteem and lack of academic ability was about to be anointed salutatorian of Bancroft Senior High School.

"Well," Karen said. "What's going to happen?"

"Aneyh's going to throw this at us after school tomorrow—department chair meeting."

"He wants our approval?"

"Right."

"Has Mrs.—ah…"

"Wormser."

"Has she mentioned a lawsuit?"

"Oh, yes."

"Then this is over, Darlene."

"Do you have any idea how I feel, Karen?"

"What do you mean?"

"Half the staff hates Special Ed now. I can understand that. I have ten kids a day; they have 150. When this gets out, arrows will fly, all of them dipped in sarcasm."

"No one will blame you, Darlene."

"Stuff like this makes it impossible to run an honest program."

Karen didn't know what to say.

"Well, kid, you've been warned," Darlene said. "See you tomorrow."

Karen returned to the patio. She pulled a chair close to the table and parked her feet on the glass top. Darlene was right. Special Education had become a contentious program. When Karen hired on at Bancroft, Darlene was the only Special Ed teacher, but she had been good seed. Fertilized by federal bucks, the school had harvested one or two new teachers each year until Special Ed became Bancroft's largest department with 22 teachers.

What began in 1969 with PL-91-230, the Federal Children with Specific Learning Disabilities Act, grew into the 1975 Education for All Handicapped Children Act, PL-94-142. The cross-pollination of guidelines in these two acts produced a definitional hybrid that lumped together such disparate disabilities as Attention Deficit Disorder, hearing loss, and profound retardation. Federal dollars became a mother lode mined by administrators, who panned the student body for nuggets—prospects for the Special Ed program. They tailored student profiles to fit the program's fuzzy guidelines and bragged to constituents about the federal gold brought into the district's coffers. Along with the money came a tier of bureaucracy unmatched by any other educational program: supervisors, directors, consultants, itinerant teachers, cooperative teachers, therapists, aides, and other assorted barnacles, all marshaled to service what was supposed to be by law no more than ten percent of a district's enrollment.

Karen and Alice sat across the table from Darlene, who stared at the blue-carpeted floor. No one made small talk. John Overton, the math chair, graded papers at the end of the table. Several students checked out books at the counter; others chatted and giggled as they worked together on assignments.

At 3:00 Aneyh led an entourage through the library's double doors—a tall, thin man, a middle-aged woman with tight curly hair, and a somber man in a three-piece suit. Aneyh steered them toward the tables where the department chairs sat.

"Let's get started," the principal began. "Are we all here?"

Karen figured Aneyh was nervous; he'd forgotten to introduce his guests. Marcie Reynolds, the librarian, told him that Rick Cook sent a message about a track meet. "Yes, yes, that's fine," he muttered. "Now, will you get these kids out of here, Mrs. Reynolds. And lock the door. We don't want to be interrupted."

Alice scribbled on her notepad, "Who's the suit?" and shoved it toward Karen.

"? ? ?" Karen wrote back. "The tall guy's an assistant sup. The Brillo pad's Judy Kraft, an LD consultant."

"All right, people," Aneyh said, "we're here for a very important decision that needs your endorsement. Marlyce Wormser…"

"Marlyce Garvey," Darlene said without looking up. "Her mother's the Wormser."

"All right. Yes. Of course." The principal cast his scowl at Darlene, who still looked at the floor. "Mrs. Wormser has requested that we include her daughter in the class ranking. We will honor that request. Furthermore, any other student in a self-contained program who wants it can be included in the ranking, too. The district's legal counsel," he nodded toward the three-piece suit, "has advised us that we must do so in order to avoid possible litigation. But most importantly, Bancroft can be a leader in promoting equity in educational opportunities."

"Wait a second." John Overton placed his pencil on the papers he was grading. "You mean this only applies to Bancroft?"

"Of course not, John. The point I'm making here is that the atmosphere at Bancroft, the way we treat all students equally, has led to this girl's request. We should feel pride in our leadership."

"A purse out of a sow's ear," Alice scribbled on her pad.

"He's amazing, just amazing," Karen wrote back.

"Mr. Aneyh." Darlene clasped her hands tightly in front of her until the knuckles turned white. "If Marlyce Garvey were in a regular section, she'd finish in the bottom half of the graduates. You and the apostles of self-esteem have just moved her to the head of the class. Let's talk achievement, real achievement, and forget about this egalitarian crap. Do you know Averil Dorsey?"

"No, I don't, Mrs. McGimpsey." Aneyh was hot. Darlene had never been married.

"She's the student being bumped by this decision. Averil took advanced placement courses—five years of math, six years of French. She has 26 credits and a 3.94 grade point. Tell me, how do you explain to Averil and her parents that a Special Ed student with

331

no academic potential is taking her place as salutatorian?"

"You surprise me, Mrs. McGimpsey," Aneyh said. "I would think you, of all people, would understand the trail we're blazing here."

"Oh," Darlene struggled for a word, "poop! We're on this trail because a parent threatened a lawsuit. No one has the guts to tell her no. We should either stand for something or just admit the inmates are in charge."

Karen rolled her eyes at Alice. Although brash and outgoing, Darlene never had much to say at department chair meetings. Considering Darlene's mood on the phone yesterday, Karen was certain that Darlene had lain awake all night planning this assault.

"Look, Mr. Aneyh," Darlene went on without drawing a breath. "Special Ed students, for the most part, are good kids. But some of them can barely read. What you propose we do is not only ludicrous, it makes a farce out of the program. That concerns me since I've spent 20 years of my life working with these kids."

"But, Darlene," Judy Kraft said with a weak smile, "I think you might be overreacting just a tad."

"How?"

"Perhaps you're coming at this from the wrong perspective." Judy fiddled with her glasses and broadened her smile. "Let's look at this as a reward for a hardworking Special Ed student."

"Oh, come on, Judy," Darlene said. "Class rank is not a reward. You have to earn that. Marlyce Garvey hasn't. She's just a nice, pleasant girl who works hard with what she's got." Darlene got up and leaned on the table with her fingertips. "I sat in on the staffing with you and Mrs. Wormser when Marlyce entered Bancroft. You couldn't come up with a three-syllable word Marlyce could spell or pronounce. If you want her to have a reward, go buy her a trophy, but don't politicize this program." Darlene wrenched her purse from the back of the chair. "I'd like to know something else, Mr. Aneyh. If you've already made this decision," Darlene moved toward the exit, "what are we doing here?" Without waiting for an answer, she charged through the library doors.

The principal looked at his watch and cleared his throat. "What just happened here," he smiled at Judy Kraft, "was incredibly childish. Mrs. McGimpsey is a good teacher, but this has been a long year. She's tired. I'm sure she'll look at this differently tomorrow. Anyway, we have made a decision, which I know most of you agree with."

John Overton looked up again from his papers. "We, Mr. Aneyh? We had nothing to do with your decision." He glanced at his colleagues, who nodded in agreement. "Let the record show, if there is one, that this faculty committee does not agree."

Aneyh looked at the board's lawyer. "Do you want to say anything about this, Gordon?"

The attorney stopped playing with his moustache, rose, and tugged at his vest. "Look, folks," he said, "what you think about this really doesn't matter. What that brash woman who just stomped out of here thinks doesn't matter. This decision was made downtown. That girl will be ranked number two. Period." He picked up his briefcase. "Now, if you want to argue this with the board and the rest of the legal staff, go ahead. But I would suggest that this committee should put the best face on it by giving your approval. Thank you for your attention." His curt summation ended the meeting.

"Darlene was magnificent," Alice said as Aneyh and his group left.

Karen nodded.

"But no one is going to win an argument with these people."

"Mrs. Wormser did," Karen said.

"I mean no one on our side. Daniel Webster couldn't help us."

"Oh, I don't know, Alice. He won his case against the devil."

forty-one

The sun blazed overhead. Bancroft's clammy corridors fell silent at high noon on the last day of school. Students left and teachers stood in the checkout line winding around the office like a disjointed snake slinking toward Hattie Reins who sat at her desk behind a pile of checks. She viewed this task—collecting keys and grade sheets in exchange for paychecks—as her last power trip of the year.

Karen looked down the line for Nick. For two weeks she had seen him only in passing. No conversation. No phone calls. Nothing.

"Have a good summer, Karen." That was Hattie's ritual good-bye. "And don't spend this all in one place."

"I won't. Take care of yourself, Hattie."

"See you in August."

"Sure," Karen lied. Nick knew about her decision, no one else. A letter of resignation next week would avoid painful explanations.

She spotted Nick across from the office and

waited for him. He leaned against the trophy case with his suit coat over one shoulder, his tie over the other, in solemn talk with Alice Cain. Nick grabbed Alice's hand with both of his and gave her a pat on the shoulder, but suddenly Alice's beefy arms enveloped him in a mighty hug. Karen was certain she saw the glint of tears in Alice's eyes.

"What was that all about?" She nodded at Alice, who was now engaging George Moore in conversation.

"Alice gets emotional," Nick told her as he stepped up beside her.

"Nick, something is wrong. You've ignored me for two weeks."

"Something *is* wrong, Karen," he said.

She felt a surge of vertigo. "Tell me."

"Not here. Not in this blasted hall. I need to pick up my check and go to Frank Nolden's stag. I'll stop by your place around 5:00. We'll talk then."

"You sound so impersonal. Can't you give me a hint?"

"I'll see you at 5:00."

Nick fell into the check line, which had dwindled to half a dozen or so, behind George Moore. He tapped George's shoulder.

"Nick," George whispered, "Alice just told me. We can't let Aneyh force you out. We're going to fight this transfer. Middle school kids have heard of you. During enrollment they ask to be in your classes. Now, I have a plan. I'm going to start a petition drive. We'll get the parents involved. We'll beat this."

"George, slow down." Nick pulled him aside. "Nothing you do can change Aneyh's mind. The board's behind him."

"But you have tenure."

"They didn't fire me, George. They're only required to give me a job. They gave me one. I can either take it or quit."

"Mr. Moore," Hattie barked. "Do you want your check? You two are the only ones left."

George placed his keys on the desk, took his check, and waited at the office door.

"Mr. Staal," Hattie oozed. "I do hope you have a particularly pleasant summer." She handed him his check.

"You know something, Hattie," Nick said. "You've educated me. I didn't know what a secretary was capable of before I met you."

"Well," she said smugly, "he who laughs last laughs best."

"I never suspected that you ever laughed."

"Aren't you hot in that suit and tie?" Nick asked as they walked down the steamy hallway.

"Listen, Nick," George said doggedly, "we've got the goods on Aneyh and MacIntosh. You know what they've been doing."

"Sure."

"That's what I'm saying here. We go back, march straight into his office right now. We confront him— lay our filthy cards on the table." George pushed his glasses to the bridge of his nose. "I suppose the ethics of this would bother you, so I'll do all the talking. I'll tell him straight off, either you pick up the phone and get Nick's transfer stopped or—I'll tell Mrs. Aneyh that you are—ah—fooling around with Dr. MacIntosh."

Nick stopped at the corridor leading to the back hall. "George, are you going to give up shaving?"

"What do you mean?"

"How can you crawl in the slime with Robert Aneyh and look at yourself in the mirror every day? Aneyh does stuff like that, not George Moore."

"But, Nick," George pleaded, "when has Aneyh been ethical about anything?"

"Not often. But you are an ethical man, George. You stand for something. You should be the principal of this building."

"If I were, you wouldn't be leaving. This building," George's eyes filled, "will mean nothing to me if you're not here."

Nick grabbed his shoulders. "George, you've been a good friend to me. I've heard you talk about fishing. I have a farm pond that hasn't been fished right for years. What do you say? Come out this summer and we'll change that."

"Do you mean that?"

"Of course I mean it. I'll call you."

George studied his shoes as Nick made his last trip down the back corridor. Nick stopped at the door and waved. "Give 'em hell next year, little buddy."

Karen fled to her patio at 7:00. She had run out of things to do. The deep, earthy smell promised a storm. Leaves dangled lifelessly. Dead, humid air amplified the sound of yapping dogs and lawn mowers. A door slammed in the driveway like a rifle shot. He came around the house and greeted her with "sorry." Karen thought he looked troubled as he stepped onto the patio and dropped into a chair.

"Nick, I'm concerned. What's wrong?"

"Nothing you need to worry about, Karen."

"Well, why all the mystery? Why don't you just tell me?"

Nick moved to the front of his chair. "A couple weeks ago I got a call from the downtown office. I'm being transferred."

"Where?"

"Three elementary buildings. PE. First two periods at Osage. Then I drive to Hancock for periods 3 and 4 and lunch. I finish off the day at Decatur."

"That isn't fair," Karen said. "That's got to be retribution."

"Sure."

"What are you going to do?"

"Resign."

"That doesn't matter." She moved toward him. "We don't need Bancroft. We can do more things together."

"Karen," Nick hesitated. "I need some time by myself." He got up and wandered aimlessly around the patio. "You'll be in Des Moines and I'll be at home. We won't see each other every day."

"We both have telephones."

"Yes, but I need to get away from this for awhile."

"From me?"

"No, not from you."

"That's the way it sounds."

"I'm confused about several things right now, Karen. I want some time to think. Can't you understand that?"

"No, I can't." He blurred through her tears. "This makes no sense at all. Why don't you let me help you?"

"Karen, I didn't come over here to upset you."

"Of course not! You came over here to dump me!"

"No, that's not what I said. I mean, I want to back off for a while, that's all." He stood in front of her. "Would you prefer a clean break?"

"Oh, I already know how that feels. You haven't spoken to me for two weeks. And then you waltz in here two hours late and announce a unilateral pause. How long did you want? The summer? A year? Ah, forever. You intend to get in that crappy truck and drive out of my life."

"I didn't say that."

"You don't understand what I feel. I don't want to back off. I want to be where you are. I want to know what you're thinking. Don't you see, Nick, I love you."

"You haven't known me long enough."

"How can you say that to me?" She began to sob. "Oh, Nick, I'm sorry I called your truck crappy."

"My truck is crappy. And you're making me feel crappy."

Karen buried her face in her hands. "I just can't explain, Nick. I need you." She looked at him. "You've helped me so much. You've straightened out my thinking. Why, I wouldn't have had the courage to do anything I've done this year without you. Because of you I can stand straight up."

"You've never needed anyone but yourself to stand straight up. Give yourself some credit. You only have one flaw—using your leg as an excuse."

Her face turned ashen. She had been a fool! Her leg! He didn't need time to think. He wanted out. Karen bolted from her chair. "You used me!" she screamed.

"That's not true at all."

"You felt sorry for me. Yes, that's what you did. You felt sorry for me. The poor little cripple. That's what this has been all along. I thought you cared, Nick. You kept coming back. But you're no different from other men I've known. This is exactly what my mother warned me about you." She slapped the picnic table with her fist. "I'm nothing to you but a mercy fuck."

Nick raised his hands as if someone had a gun in his back and shook his head. "You're being cruel, Karen."

"Go on home," she sobbed.

"Karen, I just want some time to think. I'll call you in a week or so."

"No. I don't want to spend my life sitting by the phone. That *would be* cruel. Go back to your damn farm, Nick. Have a good life."

forty-two

The old pickup lumbered along I-80. Nicholas Staal had driven this stretch twice a day for 19 years. This was his last commute. Burton Ramsey, director of human services, had called Nick two weeks ago about his punitive transfer, mainly to disassociate himself from that decision. The moment "elementary" passed Ramsey's lips, Nick knew he would resign.

Dark clouds laden with moisture swallowed the sun, and light rain obscured his vision. Nick twisted the wiper knob and listened to the blades slup-slopping across the windshield, a monotonous cadence that beat in his head like a drum. Huge drops now battered the truck and turned the road ahead into a misty thread. Jagged streaks tearing through the black sky framed his gloomy mood.

For two weeks Nick had thought of little else but her. Whenever he reached a crisis, a fork in the road, Hannah appeared as if his need released her from the recesses of his mind. He knew all about grief. Grief was cyclical; it came in waves. But right now, he could not shake those painful memories—the long, cancer-ridden year; eyes that pled, beseeched, and closed forever; his pitiful helplessness. Why? Why Hannah? Why not a ruthless bastard like Robert Aneyh? Hannah was clean, wholesome, and fair. Aneyh was the one who deserved to die. Nick hated this kind of ghoulishness, but no one distorted reality like the dead.

Nine months ago Karen Merchant helped him push back the emptiness. The first time he noticed her in Bancroft's lower hall, she appeared as an apparition, a ghost. The resemblance was uncanny. The two women looked alike; they had the same voice and the same mannerisms. In spite of her skitterish reaction to him in the beginning, he pursued his obsession to know if his attraction to her was more than cosmetic. Unlike Hannah, with whom he shared a love of nature and the land, Karen was deep, an intellectual. She made him think. He realized, even though he had denied it, that Karen helped him seal off the pain he felt for the woman who was gone. But this juxtaposition of Karen against a ghost had to stop.

Why couldn't he open up to Karen as fully as she had to him? Was this reluctance born of fear, a fear that an interest in Karen betrayed his loyalty to Hannah? Or did he simply lack the courage to commit again? He wanted the summer to sort this out, but he had not presented his case very well. No wonder Karen became upset, dreadfully hurt to the point where she put her own spin on something she didn't fully understand. He had allowed her insecurity to grow for two weeks while he wallowed in self-pity. He had just called Aneyh a bastard, but he was no better. Karen waded through her emotions, exposed every nerve, while he sat in the audience like a patron of the arts watching a dramatic scene unfold.

He could have prevented that. Not once had he ever told her what she had done for him. Was she supposed to sense what he felt or absorb it through osmosis? Three little words would have helped, but he had not said them. He didn't know if he could. He didn't know if he did. No matter. What they had was over now. He would recover. She would, too. Time healed wounds. Most of them.

Blurry lights shimmered in the distance. Nick left the interstate and headed south toward home. He felt crummy and disappointed in himself. He'd given education a big piece of his life. And despite the pestering administrative interference that dogged his career, he knew he could do the job. As Des Moines and Bancroft sank in the distance, Nick thought about the Brave New World he left behind. How surreal this phantasmagoria of social agendas driving education had become, when all he ever wanted to do was teach.

Wet maple leaves glistened in the headlights as he entered the lane and stopped before the old family home. He sat quietly in the cab for a few moments. "I'll give this place all my attention now," he whispered. Lightning cracked overhead illuminating the brick façade, followed by a rumble of thunder. "Grandpa, I wonder what you'd think of me now."

forty-three

Karen hired Eddie Barnes, a reliable teenager from across the street, to haul the tools of her trade home from Bancroft. Eddie filled the trunk and backseat of his car three times. Karen stared at the remains of her teaching career—books, journals, full file folders, and other paraphernalia in piles across the living room floor. By the time she had catalogued and stored these materials away memory by memory, a form letter arrived signed by the president of the board accepting her resignation. The board thanked her perfunctorily for 17 years of service but expressed no interest in her motives for packing it in. The process, just a paper transaction, was as impersonal as a cremation.

Karen Merchant was now a statistic, part of that seven percent who flee the teaching profession each year. Her income, remitted on a 12-month calendar, wouldn't dry up until September. That gave her ten weeks to re-order her life before she looked for a new job.

One evening she sat on the patio with a legal pad.

"PLAN OF ACTION" appeared at the top of the page in bold letters. Below, with officious strokes, she wrote "I. Gardening." Karen clutched the pencil between her teeth and glanced toward her garden in the back yard. She could spot a weed at 50 paces. A diagram on the refrigerator marked the spot where each seed lay. That plot of dirt would take time and offer her solace. "II. New Curtains—Bathroom and Kitchen. III. Books to Read." The pencil moved slowly across the pad tracing two double lines through "PLAN OF ACTION," above which she printed "MY FORGET-HIM LIST." After all, that's what this was. His name appeared as if an unseen force moved her hand. Nicholas Staal. She carved a circle around the name again and again until tears dampened the page.

In spite of mind-control games and elaborate dodges to erase him from her memory, Karen could not let go. She knew what made her toss and turn at night. Sometimes his ethereal presence during half-sleep made her wonder whether he had been real or merely a fantasy cooked up by a tormented brain. Had she really touched him? Kissed him? She awoke in a panic sometimes with eyes as wide as saucers unable to remember how his voice sounded or what he looked like.

Karen shifted in the chair. *I can't believe how cold, how indifferent he was that last day. We had been so close. He may think I overreacted, but I saved myself from another rejection. He didn't have the guts to come right out with it. He might as well have said his plans didn't include a woman with a gimpy leg. I didn't have a claim on him; I know that. But when I'm a 90-year-old pensioner pulling weeds out there in the garden with my butt in the air, I can smile and remember that I sent him packing.*

She dropped the pad and went inside.

Grace Merchant knew instinctively that something other than the loss of a job devastated her daughter. She posed no questions and never once said "I told you so." Begrudgingly, Karen remembered when Nick had said that her mother would be a cheerleader if she ever quit her job. In fact, her mother's support for Karen's decision to resign had been nothing short of magnificent.

Grace noticed a letter from the DMPS spelling out health insurance options on the kitchen counter one afternoon while Karen worked in the garden. She could sign on to her new employer's plan or stay with the DMPS group for 18 months at her own expense. Her mother feared that with Karen's preexisting medical condition, insurance would be difficult to change and expensive.

"Pour us some ice tea," Grace told Karen from the kitchen table when she carried in a colander of green beans. "When do you…"

"I haven't got a job yet, Mother."

"No, that isn't it."

Karen poured. "What then?"

"That insurance. How much will it cost?" She reached for the sugar bowl.

"Did you read my letter?"

"It lay there begging to be read." Grace patted Karen's hand. "How much?"

"I don't know. Four or five hundred dollars a month, maybe. I haven't checked yet." She put her cup down. "Don't worry. I'll take care of this. Anyway, the school pays through August."

"I'm not worried." Grace turned her spoon over and watched sugar sift into her tea. "I'm going to pay your insurance until you get a new job."

"Why would you do that? Insurance is my responsibility."

"That's not the point."

"What is the point?"

Grace tugged at the collar of her dress. "Well, you see, you remember I paid for your sister's wedding and…"

"You think I'm doomed to spinsterhood, and you want to make everything even."

"That's not it at all. I don't think you're doomed to anything. I just want to help you right now while you need help. That's what mothers do, Karen."

They watched each other across the table for a few moments. Mother and daughter had no history of ritual emotion, but over glasses of ice tea on this warm summer afternoon the two rekindled the bond that had been forged years ago in the crucible of poliomyelitis.

Karen walked around the table with tears in her eyes and wrapped her arms around Grace Merchant. "Oh, Mother, I love you."

"I love you, too, Honey Bunny."

"Part-time Help Wanted." Karen glanced at the sign as she entered her favorite bookstore. Marilee Gorman, proprietor, stood behind the counter chatting with customers. Short, slender, and studious in half-glasses, Marilee looked like she'd been pulled from a mold for this job. Karen had become friends with her through literature discussion groups. People in the neighborhood joked that Gorman was standing on the corner one afternoon and a gang of workmen showed up and built a bookstore around her.

When Karen expressed an interest in the job, Marilee thought she was kidding.

"This job doesn't pay much, Karen. Mostly fill-in work, you know. Anyway, you won't have time after August to teach and do this, too."

"I've got time for everything," Karen said. "I've resigned."

"You resigned?" Marilee Gorman looked over her half-glasses.

"What about the job?"

"No. I mean, we'll talk about the job, but why did you resign?"

Karen sighed and rested her forearms on the counter. "Mostly because of the seven-period day. I would have to teach six classes instead of five."

"Did they offer you more money?"

"Now you've got to be kidding," Karen told her. "That's not the way the system works."

"Surely, they tried to talk you out of it."

"They might stroke a winning coach, Marilee,

but not an English teacher. Anyway, the board can hire two beginning teachers for what they pay me. Two for one. The board thinks that's good business." Karen straightened up. "What's this job pay?"

"Well, I think that's just awful," Marilee said. "The DMPS is the loser. I remember reading the speech that teacher made before the board last fall. What ever happened to all his good ideas?"

"What about this job?"

"Well, yes. Yes, of course. You can start Monday."

The store, sandwiched between a dry cleaner and a mom-and-pop grocery, was located near a busy intersection. But inside, Karen loved the scholarly environment, the book-lined shelves, and in time learned to block out the world.

One July afternoon Karen stood by the window reading. Suddenly she felt uncomfortable, as if someone stared at her or beckoned. She glanced down the aisle behind her, then through the window. Her eyes riveted on a rusty red pickup waiting for a green light at the corner. Karen hurried down the aisle and onto the walk in time to see the truck swallowed by traffic in the distance. The glare of the sun obscured the driver's head, but she knew who he was.

After another restless night, the digital alarm set for 7 a.m. aroused her weary body. Karen wrapped the pillow around her ears. Suddenly she sat upright, her eyes wide open. This was August 13, Nicholas Staal's birthday. In happier times she had planned a party—a picnic at the farm—for this day that he would never forget. Now, all she wanted to do was forget the party, his birthday, and him.

A bushel of tomatoes waited in the kitchen to be made into spaghetti sauce, a task that would fill most of the day and at the same time steam him out of her mind. She cored and cut away cracks, dropped the tomatoes into a large kettle, and turned up the burner. Her sauce, which she gave as Christmas gifts, had a reputation. The secret ingredient, a little brown sugar stirred into the first boiling, made her sauce special. Last year she had canned 24 quarts of sauce and 18 pints of salsa; this year she'd probably make even more. But nothing would be special about this day.

Steam clouded the windows and turned the kitchen into a sauna. Karen crumpled into a chair and stared at the phone. *Maybe a friendly call would be appropriate. Birthday greetings. No more. Bad time, though. Farmers sweat in the field all day. Perhaps tonight. No! He might be locked in the arms of another woman.*

Karen left the kitchen to sniff fresh air on the patio. She leafed through a magazine and walked in her garden, peeked through the back door at the stove, and came to rest with folded arms leaning against the back of the house.

She knew exactly when this started—the very first time she laid eyes on him. Her heart had stuck in her throat, a palpable surge of pathos, when Aneyh climbed all over him for being late. And she remembered the thrill that swept over her when

Nicholas Staal so effortlessly painted the principal as the schoolyard bully.

Karen slid down the back of the house until she sat on the patio with her chin on her knees.

He had been forbidden fruit, of course, but she never intended to be a player. His constant ogling changed that. In a short space of time, laced with her feelings of both distrust and love, he had become the most powerful force ever to enter her life. He had plucked her from the sidelines and put her in the game, taught her how to live. *So what happened? Why am I sitting here on this piece of cement feeling sorry for myself?* Her jaw dropped. Nick's words "back off for awhile" and "time to think" flashed before her like neon signs. Her body stiffened in the throes of an epiphany. *Why am I sitting here? Because I couldn't keep my big mouth shut, that's why.*

Until this precise moment, she had viewed their last conversation only as boy-dumps-girl. *Maybe he would have called. Maybe he did need time to think. But I wouldn't give him any. I always think about myself. He was always so sure, so confident. Why would I assume that he had a problem? So I sent him packing. When he needed me to understand, I shut him out. He won't come back. I'm the one who slammed the door.*

Karen heard tomatoes bursting from their skins in the large kettle. She struggled to her feet.

Back-to-school ads evoked a twinge of nostaglia, but even though she had gone to school most of her life, Karen felt no remorse. She pulled down minimum wage four days a week now at the bookstore and had two interviews scheduled for full-time jobs: one as an assistant at the main library and another as a technical writer for a local manufacturer.

This week, teacher-preparation week at Bancroft, did pique her curiosity about Alice, David, and George. *The Des Moines Register* had delivered the school year's first broadside a week ago; a terse paragraph in the Metro section announced that Robert D. Aneyh had been elevated to a downtown administrative post, Assistant Superintendent for Secondary Programs, under Dr. Anthony Pagano. Karen knew that from his new position he would now inflict the entire system with the inanities previously reserved for Bancroft. The second broadside struck the good ship Bancroft in the captain's cabin. The Board of Education elected Dr. (E.D.) Edwina MacIntosh as Bancroft's new principal, only the second female in the city ever to hold that position. Karen was in the den when she read this information. Her eyes wandered slowly to Martha Y. Bancroft. "I am so sorry, Martha," she said out loud. "This is an insult to your memory."

Karen unlocked the door Friday on the last day of preparation week and raced to the ringing phone. Old habits die hard. She wrenched the phone from the cradle, still hoping to hear that deep voice.

"Karen, this is Alice. I'm calling from the medieval fiefdom of Dr. Edwina MacIntosh."

"Hi, Alice. I've been wondering about you."

"I've only got a minute. We've got another

meeting *tout de suite.*" Alice sighed. "You should see Hattie, Karen. She follows Edwina around like a lap dog. Hattie came up to George Moore and me in the office yesterday and told us that Edwina prefers to be called 'Doctor.' " Alice laughed. "George asked her if just 'Doc' would do or maybe 'Mac.' "

"I love it. Isn't George something! The only thing I miss is you guys."

"Well, you were right, Karen," Alice went on. "Almost all of us have six classes." Karen heard a muffled PA announcement in the background. "Oh, lordy. I've got to go, kid. It's 2:45. We should be out of here by 3:15. Will you be home?"

"Yes."

"I'll drop by and give you the dirt."

"I can't wait."

Karen quickly kicked off her shoes and walked through the garden, muddy from last night's rain, snapping off a sack of tomatoes for Alice who was simply nuts over fresh garden produce. She hosed off her muddy feet and headed for the shower. Tepid water splashed over her neck and shoulders as she thought about her friends sweltering in Bancroft's steamy rooms. Alice's quick update on the school's current ills and the tinny PA mustering the troops to another meeting removed the last doubt about her decision: she didn't want to be there. A new job and new people would be the elixir she needed.

Karen stepped from the shower into a heavy towel. Two loud thumps rattled the door. She glanced at her watch on the vanity. Alice was fifteen minutes early. She wriggled into shorts and a clean t-shirt, quickly ran a comb through her wet hair, and hurried to the front door. Two flies buzzed lazily on the screen. She stepped out and looked both directions. Across the street, Eddie Barnes' feet protruding from beneath his parked car moved in time to the bass line from the car stereo. Karen cuffed the side of her head and decided she must be hearing things.

Then she heard two more thumps. Karen smiled and headed for the kitchen. Alice must have been inspecting her garden.

She opened the back door and froze. He looked down at her through the screen door with eyes bluer than the August sky.

"Hi," Nick said quietly.

Her mouth wouldn't work.

"I want to come in, Karen. I didn't think you'd allow me to walk through the front door."

The sound of that voice again made her lightheaded. Joy and longing rushed along her veins like a tidal wave. Her hand shook as she fumbled for the latch.

About the Authors

Charles Newton

Charles Newton was born at Stuart, a small agricultural community in west central Iowa, where he spent his boyhood. After graduating from the local school system, he pursued a degree in education at Northwest Missouri State University. Newton received his diploma in 1950 and was immediately drafted into the United States Army for a two-year hitch, part of which was spent in the Korean Theater of Operations.

He earned a master's degree in history at the University of New Hampshire after the military and began a teaching career that spanned a period of 36 years, 34 of which were spent in Des Moines, Iowa. During his teaching career he taught world history and English in grades 7-12.

In retirement, Newton was an occasional guest columnist for *The Des Moines Register*, where he commented on the educational and political scene. His interests include golf, woodworking, and reading. He has maintained a keen interest in public education and became involved in this book in an effort to unmask some of the flaws gnawing at the vitality of the American education system.

Gretchen Kauffman

Gretchen Kauffman grew up in Des Moines, Iowa, and received BA and MA degrees in English from the University of Iowa. She taught Advanced Placement English at Lincoln High School in Des Moines where she also chaired the English department until her career was interrupted by a runaway cement mixer. During a year off to recuperate from ankle reconstruction surgery, she began work as a freelance editor and writer for Perfection Learning Corporation, the *Iowan* and *Welcome Hone* magazines, Meredith Corporation, and other publishers across the country. After her recovery, she returned to the Des Moines schools as Librarian/Media Specialist in a middle school. She retired from this position in June of 2002 to pursue her freelance career fulltime.

Kauffman has presented programs at national, regional, state, and local conferences as well as serving on countless curriculum committees. She enjoys traveling, reading, and gardening. Walking is her favorite exercise.

In writing this story, Kauffman was able to explore an issue that frustrates many adults: How to be passionate about your work without letting it define you as a person.

For further information about the authors or to book them for speaking engagements, contact Kathleen Myers at myershousemail@aol.com.

Please write your thoughts on this novel on the following pages, then pass this book on to another reader. When the pages are full, please mail to Myers House, P.O. Box 23068, Des Moines, IA 50325-6468. Or email your review to myershousemail@aol.com.